ROOM 732

MERLE R. SAFERSTEIN

ISBN: 1479268887

ISBN 13: 9781479268887

Library of Congress Control Number: 2012907014
CreateSpace Independent Publishing Platform
North Charleston, South Carolina

With love and gratitude to my mother,
Ruth Rothenberg, of blessed memory

CONTENTS

HOLLYWOOD BEACH HOTEL

The seasons come and go.
The grand hotel survives the hurricane.
The Navy arrives.
The war ends.
The hotel revives.
The bible college moves in.
The bridge connects.
The gardens disappear.
The vacationers come back.
The years pass by.
The ocean beckons.
Room 732 remains with its secrets and its stories.

INTRODUCTION

Each time I approach the beach driving east on Hollywood Boulevard, I am struck by the magnificent entrance – the imposing and exquisite Hollywood Beach Hotel. This landmark structure, which sits on an entire city block with its back to the Atlantic Ocean, was the vision of Joseph W. Young, Jr., who developed it in 1926 as part of his vision for the city of Hollywood-by-the-Sea, Florida.

In its earliest years, the hotel served as a destination for wealthy Midwesterners, famous entertainers, and gangsters like Al Capone. During World War II, the United States military took over many South Florida hotels including the Hollywood Beach Hotel. It became home to the United States Navy, which used the facility as a training and indoctrination center for officers.

Shortly after the war ended in 1945, hotelier Ben Tobin purchased the hotel and restored it back to an elegant, five-star status vacation spot with a beautiful pool, an off-site golf course, tennis courts, and many other splendid features. At some point toward the end of the '60s, the hotel began to lose its charm, and in time, it was abandoned. In 1971, Florida Bible College bought the building, moved in immediately, cleaned it up, and began classes within days.

The college left at the end of the '70s, and in the '80s, the hotel transitioned into a timeshare followed by condos. In 1988, Oceanwalk, a mall with shops, restaurants, a movie theatre, and artist studios, was opened on the first and second floors with the intention of completely revitalizing the hotel and attracting people from all over the country to Hollywood Beach. Its popularity didn't last long, and once again, the building saw a decline as many of the stores and restaurants emptied out.

As the hotel underwent steady changes in ownership, the neon letters across the front of the building reflected its new names. Today in 2012, it reads *Hollywood Beach Resort* and is a combination of timeshare units, condos, and hotel rentals.

As I began to do in-depth research on the history of the hotel, I considered what was happening in the country during each of the decades. The characters and much of the content within this book reflect the attitudes, social values, and political issues that define the various time periods in American culture. Thus, the fictionalized characters and stories are based on a foundation of historical fact.

BROKEN SILENCE
HOLLYWOOD BEACH HOTEL
1934

As soon as the nurse places him in my arms, I feel his tiny body through the blankets that swaddle him. Glancing at his delicate features, I instantly see a younger version of Raymond's face looking up into my own. Nine months of waiting is over. The miracle of life surrounds us.

Seconds later, joy sweeps over me. The nurse finally has left me alone with my baby. When I uncover him to gaze into his deep blue eyes and to count his fingers and toes, I notice that his serene, beautiful face is aglow like a shining, bright, almost ethereal light.

In the next moment, he is once again wrapped in a powder blue, soft cotton blanket, and I am slowly walking down a long corridor with my baby cradled in my arms. I look up and see a dark, looming shadow from behind making its way toward us. Something deep within tells me to run, and I'm frantically stepping up my pace as I dash down the hall. The shadow grows larger and more ominous as it fills my view ahead.

I rush forward, tightly embracing my newborn in my arms. Heading toward the exit, I don't take the time to look back. I continue to feel the presence of someone following me – covering my entire being in darkness. I hurry down three flights of stairs in a desperate attempt to escape from whatever is moving just steps behind.

Once I arrive at the landing, I look down and see that my hands hold an empty blanket. My baby is gone. Horror rages through my body. I begin to scream – yelling to anyone who can hear me, pleading not to let the shadow take away my son. My shouts *grow louder as I cry out for help. The silence around me becomes deafening.*

❧

I can feel someone softly touching my shoulder, but for the life of me, I am unable to figure out who it is or where I am. I only want to find my way back into my dream and craft a different ending.

Slowly, I begin to stir and then remember that my sister Marie is next to me in bed. My reality surfaces within seconds.

Our parents had insisted that the two of us come to Florida for a vacation. While I probably will never know the real reason, I can't help but think that perhaps they felt it would be helpful for me to get away so I could heal from the awful nightmare I have been living for the past six months. At no time would they ever say that to me. In fact, my parents have never said anything to me about the fact that my baby is dead. To them and everyone else in my world, things might be difficult and tragic, but life goes on.

For me, with the death of my baby while still nestled in my womb and only one day before what should have been his birth, all my hopes and dreams of becoming a mother to my precious child were instantly dashed. With that recollection, I roll over and bury my head beneath the blanket. I need a few minutes before I can bring myself to face the world.

❧

The tide is creeping closer to the shore as the sun begins to set in the West. The ocean is calm with its rippling waves. Several pelicans sit out at sea. A sailboat glides along the water.

We have just finished a three-mile walk along the beach and are about to settle into our chairs by the cabana to enjoy a refreshing iced tea before we dress for dinner. While I feel exhausted, Marie is filled with energy and wants to talk.

"Can you believe that Daddy has sent us here for my birthday?" Marie questions. "I still don't understand why he chose us and not the others for a winter vacation in the warmth and sunshine."

Does she truly believe that is why we are here? Is she covering up for the fact that I am depressed – that everyone in our family has been worried about me? Does she really think that I am able to engage in a celebration when I can barely get out of bed in the morning? Or maybe it never occurred to her that perhaps Daddy's ulterior motive was to give me a chance to get away and recover. Can she possibly believe this is about a wonderful birthday holiday for her, with me along for the ride? That is probably the case since Marie rarely thinks about me and my feelings – or anyone else's for that matter. It is almost always about her. Is she that wrapped up in her own self that she doesn't take the time to care about anyone else?

She continues, "Daddy probably wishes he could be here with Mother, but with things as they are, he won't be taking time off from the business for a while. Our poor Daddy works so hard!"

At least Marie notices that our father is doing all he can to ensure that his business thrives at a time when so many people are still looking for the next piece of bread to eat. The Great Depression has seeped into the core of our country. It has permeated the hearts and souls of almost everyone I know.

Before we left, I heard on the radio that the unemployment rate has risen to 25% in the United States and is worse in Europe. Sometimes I feel like there is so much more that I should be doing to help, but I find myself rationalizing that serving food to the long lines of poor people at the soup kitchen is at least making a difference to someone. Truth be told, these days I don't have the energy to do much else.

When I look into the eyes of all those desperate women, men, and children, all I can think about is how dreadful and hopeless their lives must be. How are they enduring their daily hunger and their fear of losing everything they have? I am hardly surviving my own heartache, and I have plenty of food on my table each day.

People talk endlessly about the great loss everyone has experienced since the stock market crashed, and yet, as ashamed as I am to admit it to myself, there are those times when all I care about is me. I feel alone on a deserted island with my own struggles. Everyone has been affected by what is going on in our country, but if I am truly honest, my own pain rises above that of all others.

My world has felt dark and dreary for months now. It is an enormous effort to get dressed and out of the house most mornings. No one seems to understand. Even Raymond has picked up the pieces and has moved on, anxiously hoping I will soon become pregnant again.

There have been countless moments when I behave irrationally. How many times in the past few months have I heard a knock on the door and felt sure that someone was bringing my baby back to me – alive and well? Who would ever believe anything as bizarre as that, and yet it keeps happening over and over again. Sometimes I think I am losing my mind altogether.

"Lizzie, did you see how many single men there were walking around at the pool yesterday?" Marie interrupts my thoughts. "I noticed at dinner that there must have been at least fifteen men to every woman. We're in the right place for me to enjoy myself. All I need is to meet some young guys who want to have a good time, and I will be set.

"And, hey," she lowers her voice and whispers, "Did you happen to see the adorable waiter at the table next to us? Honestly, could he be any cuter?"

Marie is constantly talking about boys. After a while, it gets tedious. I usually do the best I can to humor her, though these days, I am not in the mood. I cannot help but think that she should be settling down already. Marie is just interested in going from one guy to the next and is not at all concerned that she is the only one of her friends who is not married yet. I keep quiet and she prattles on.

"Remember we're going to have new people joining us for dinner tonight. I'm curious as to who they'll be and where they're from. Maybe we'll get lucky and someone our age will sit with us. If things work in my favor, there might be a good-looking guy who ends up sitting next to me. The majority of people in this hotel are old enough to be our parents. I'm ready for an exciting adventure and hope I can find it here."

On and on she drones. Perhaps if I close my eyes, I'll fall asleep and drown out Marie's endless chatter. She most likely won't even notice.

ᛂᚱ

"I'm not sure what I should wear to dinner, Lizzie," calls Marie from the bathroom. "I hope 'Mr. Blue Eyes,' the handsome guy I told you about earlier, will be our server tonight. I want to look pretty, just in case. Oh, I forgot to tell you about the dream I had about him last night."

Before she could go on, I quickly respond. "I doubt that it matters what you wear, Marie. Regardless of what you put on, your beauty is bound to attract all the waiters in the dining room. And by the way, what would William say if he knew you were thinking about another man?"

"Elizabeth, the fact is that he's far away and in his own little world. I'm on vacation and want to live it up a little."

"Are you sure he wouldn't be upset? After all, you've been dating only him for over a month now."

"Actually, I'm not sure that I care at this moment in time," Marie declares as she saunters into the room with a big, defiant grin on her face.

⁓

Marie is wearing her hunter green, tightly-fitted, bare-backed evening gown which she picked from the several she brought. With her exquisite eyes that perfectly match the color of her dress and her soft, auburn curls, heads turn as we step into the anteroom.

I immediately recognize two of the girls who normally work at the front desk. Tonight they're in formals, and they greet us with glasses of champagne and an assortment of hors d'oeuvres. This is probably the favorite part of their jobs since, from what one of them mentioned, they are occasionally asked to dress up and socialize with the hotel guests.

The minute we walk into the immense ballroom, I am impressed by the elegant setting. White Irish linen tablecloths drape the tables while the glasses and silverware glisten against the fabric. On each table sits a shimmery vase filled with luscious red roses. The music from the ten-piece band fills the room with classic melodies, and the extravagant ice sculptures stand tall and resplendent in the center of the room. I have never seen anything like them.

Once again, I am struck by the fact that we are vacationing in pure luxury and decadence. Built in the style of a Mediterranean village, this vast hotel is filled with furnishings that are century-old antiques – lavish and expensive. One of the men at the front desk told me it cost three million dollars just to build the structure, not including all that was added to the inside.

Scanning my surroundings, I see ornate urns sculpted into columns, cedar ceilings with hand-stenciled beams, hand-carved cornices, and velveteen wallpaper. This is a place to remember.

Meals in general are hard for me. After all these months, I am still having a difficult time eating much of anything. My stomach often turns at the sight of food. I've probably lost at least ten pounds in addition to losing the weight I had gained during my pregnancy. Eating is the last thing I'm interested in these days.

Here at the Hollywood Beach Hotel, the lunches and dinners are served in such a genteel fashion that it is hard not to be tempted by something. Daddy would love this place. In his position in the company and with him and Mother being the socialites that they have become, he has grown accustomed to opulence.

As we are taking our seats, Marie utters under her breath, "Well, well. It appears as if we have struck gold! Look at who's going to be our waiter tonight. 'Mr. Blue Eyes' himself, in all his glory."

The young man, whom my sister has been lusting after for the past twenty-four hours, approaches our table and makes a point to smile at Marie. "Good evening, ladies, and welcome. It will be my pleasure to serve you tonight." He pours our water, gives us menus, and asks if we would like a cocktail.

With Prohibition having been abolished just last month, this is a whole new world for us. "I'll have a gin sour," Marie requests, without giving it a second thought. It doesn't seem to matter to her that she won't be celebrating her twenty-first birthday until this coming Thursday. She obviously doesn't care about the law. Besides, how does she know about drinks like the one she has ordered?

"Marie, really, should you be…" but before I can get another word out, she gives me a look that tells me that I had better say nothing further. I order a glass of red wine, and the waiter again smiles and gives Marie a wink.

Her face turns a radiant crimson - a noticeable shade brighter than her newly sunburned look. I almost feel invisible. It no longer matters to her that anyone else is in the room. Marie immediately begins her seduction dance, which she has most likely been plotting from the moment that she first noticed 'Mr. Blue Eyes.'

Four empty chairs surround our table. The Smiths, who had been sitting with us since our arrival last Saturday, have gone back up north to Milwaukee. Tonight new guests will be joining us. As I look up from my menu, I see a family of four approaching. At first glance, it appears that the older couple is around my parents' age, and the two handsome, identical-looking boys with them are close to Marie's age.

Like all the other men in the dining room, the father and sons are dressed in tailcoats with white waistcoats and ties. The mother has on a classic, maroon-colored gown and a white fox wrap around her shoulders, with a matching hat. They ooze elegance.

"Pardon us. I hope we are not interrupting you," comments the father in the group. "May I have the pleasure of introducing myself and my family?"

"Please do," I respond, welcoming them. His formality strikes me instantly. I hope that these people aren't going to be as stuffy and dull as the Smiths were. They sat with us for what seemed like days on end, and their conversation completely bored me.

Marie, who is forced to postpone her flirtation with our waiter and divert her attention momentarily, instantly grins and greets them. I am sure it is because of the incredibly attractive twins who stand before us.

"Hi! I'm Marie Mansfield, and this is my sister Elizabeth Archer. I call her Lizzie."

"I'm pleased to meet you both. My name is Henry DeWitt. My wife, Rose, and our two sons, James and Joseph."

Even though Marie is preoccupied, I can tell by the way she is looking at the boys that she thinks this promises to be more entertaining than originally imagined. Within seconds, Mrs. DeWitt is seating herself next to me. James sits on the other side of Marie with Joseph next to him. Mr. DeWitt sits down right by his wife's side.

As I study the boys' faces, I realize that I would have no idea which twin is which if they were to get up and move around. Clearly, their every feature is identical. I've never seen two people who look so much alike. I cannot help but wonder how people tell them apart and also how it feels to look exactly like someone else.

We all exchange little details about our families back and forth as we begin to get to know one another. They come from Detroit where Mr. DeWitt works in car manufacturing with Hudson Motor Car Company. From what he has indicated so far, apparently he is one of the big bosses of the business.

Mrs. DeWitt is quiet and mostly listens as her husband talks. As soon as he finishes, Marie asks the twins about themselves. One thing I can say for my sister, she is not shy.

"We are sophomores at the University of Michigan," offers Joseph. "Luckily, we're on winter break and will be here until the end of the week. Then we have to leave this paradise and head back to school."

James jumps in and adds, "This is our first time in Florida, and we're both looking forward to swimming in the pool. We arrived late today, so all we had time for was a run on the sand and a quick dip in the ocean. We heard a woman, who said she lives here in South Florida, tell some man that she can't understand how any of us northerners can go in the water when it's so cold. Both of us laughed at that. We think it feels like a bathtub. In fact, we..."

Joseph doesn't give James a chance to finish his thought when he interrupts, "Coming from the freezing temperatures in Ann Arbor, this weather is outrageously beautiful. Don't you agree?"

Before either Marie or I can answer, Mr. DeWitt pipes in and says, "What the boys aren't telling you is that they're really here to check out the girls."

Everyone chuckles, but I can tell that James and Joseph appear a bit embarrassed. I'm getting the feeling that their father always teases them. Maybe I was wrong about him being so reserved. Based on this last comment and a few others he has made since his introduction, perhaps he isn't as formal as he first appeared to be. I just know Daddy would never say anything like that about my brothers, especially in front of them. My guess is that Mr. DeWitt says whatever is on his mind. He and Marie should get along well.

"What the boys also haven't told you is that they are stars on Michigan's track and field team. They each hold records at the university, and they're only in their second year.

"This past summer, they trained with some of the young men who might end up in the '36 Olympics," Mr. DeWitt continues on. "They're also straight-A students and are members of Phi Delta Theta, just like I was. Since there are two of them, it's double the pleasure and the pride."

By this time, both James and Joseph are squirming in their seats and rolling their eyes.

"Father, please. Surely Elizabeth and Marie would be much more interested in hearing about something else rather than us," Joseph admonishes.

James changes the subject and asks what we think of Hollywood-by-the-Sea.

Marie quickly answers. "We haven't explored much except the Hollywood Broadwalk, which is the promenade out back. You probably noticed it when you went out for a swim. We ended up walking along its entire length.

"You both might even want to run on the Broadwalk. We saw lots of people exercising out there. It's similar to the famous Atlantic City's Boardwalk – except this one is called the Broadwalk. Have either of you ever been to Atlantic City?"

The twins shake their heads. "No, but it's on our list of places to go."

Marie continues, "The other day when we were walking, we discovered the Hollywood Beach Casino about a half-mile north of the hotel. It's not a casino with gambling as we thought it might be when we first saw the sign. Instead it is a large bathing pavilion with a big pool, cabanas for people to rent, and showers for them to use after they swim.

"However, from what I hear, there is some gambling going on at this hotel." With that, she grins and keeps on chattering.

"We like browsing in the beachfront shops – the ones out back that are shaded by the striped awnings." Marie turns to Mrs. DeWitt as she says this.

I guess Marie realizes that the twins wouldn't be at all interested in shopping.

"Have you seen them yet? Maybe you might like to go shopping with us. They have some chic clothing stores," Marie offers. Mrs. DeWitt perks up, smiles, and nods her head in agreement.

Joseph changes the subject and asks if Marie attends a university. She begins to talk about how school never interested her and within minutes, she is off explaining her most recent job experience.

"Daddy never wanted me to work, and for a long time he was adamant that I didn't. After all, it isn't like our family needs the money. It was scandalous to him that I would ever consider it, since so few women work. I think he felt as if it wouldn't reflect well on him if I had a job. For weeks on end, I pleaded with my father and tried hard to break him down. He finally consented."

I am horrified that Marie has boasted like that to the DeWitts. *What is she thinking?*

She continues, "My favorite job was my last one when I worked for Mr. Adams in the railroad business. I was his personal secretary and used to love when he would storm in and demand my undivided attention. I felt so important! The only problem was that he seemed much more interested in cornering and kissing me than in appreciating my stenography skills."

Why does Marie say such things? What could the DeWitts possibly think of my sister? She does not seem to care. All that matters to Marie is that she has the floor and people are paying attention to her. Where did she learn her manners; or better yet, where was she when our parents were teaching us manners, since the rest of us are not anything like her?

During all this time, I can tell that Marie continues to be somewhat distracted whenever our waiter appears on the scene. It is obvious that he is immediately drawn to her. She does everything she can to flirt with him without giving much thought to her behavior or how she looks to those at the table. I am sure they notice, but everyone is polite enough to pretend that they don't. I see that Marie blushes whenever he brushes against her as he clears our dishes.

The conversation changes focus and becomes much more serious when Joseph brings up the Great War. He has just completed a world history class and wants some clarification. "In your opinion, Father, which would you say played a more significant part in the war – imperialism or nationalism?"

Mr. DeWitt thinks for a moment and then replies, "I believe they were equally important. Hostilities had been building for decades prior to the war. In my opinion, militarism and alliances were also contributing causes. You know, Joseph, there are always so many factors which enter into wars."

Following that brief discussion with his sons, Mr. DeWitt begins sharing stories about his time in France during the war. He tells us what it was like to have been a twenty-eight-year-old married man, who had twin babies, and was sent far away to fight a battle in another country.

"I was established in business and had already experienced some success when, without warning, I was called to serve in the Army. I wasn't the only one. Most of the young fellows I knew were drafted, except for my good buddy Edward who was practically blind. We had little notice, but within weeks, we were shipped off to boot camp, which seemed like another world.

"I was fearful of what going to war meant. It didn't take me long to realize how spoiled I had been by my parents, how sad I was to leave my beloved Rose and my little boys, and how much I missed my entire family.

"As early as basic training at Fort Lewis, I found myself longing to be back in Michigan and wishing for the comforts of home. The food was awful, and the routine was grueling. And yet, that was easy compared to what came next. When I left the United States for France, I remember being afraid that I might never come back. There were moments when I panicked at the thought of facing combat.

"I was a city boy -- a good, peace-loving one at that -- and not one raised to carry a gun and use it. My life had been easy up until then. I had my future all figured out, and this was not in the plan. Despite that, I had no choice but to turn my energies toward survival.

"We were only in France for a matter of days when we were sent into battle. Within a few hours, I was confronted with the possibility of killing someone or being killed. I remember my insides churning. There was no place to run. This was suddenly my reality."

James interrupts, "Father, it's surprising to me that you've never talked to us about this before."

"I didn't want to burden you when you were young. Now that you are older, I am much more comfortable sharing some of this with you."

Mr. DeWitt carries on, seemingly oblivious to the rest of us at the table. "I experienced feelings that were confusing to me. I will never forget the adrenaline rush I would get when we were out in the fields searching for the enemy. Sure when I was little, we used to play cowboys and Indians, but this was the real thing.

"I remember one time when I was next to one of my buddies from our unit. A bullet whizzed right by me and hit him in his thigh.

15

Next thing I knew, there was blood everywhere. A moment later, another bullet buzzed by and pierced him smack in the chest. He rolled over and within an instant, he was gone. Although bullets were streaming through the air, all I could think about was this man's family back home – his little daughter whom he had told me about the night before. How would his family manage? What would it be like for his wife of only a few years to hear the news? What would my dear Rose do if it were me next? How would it be never to watch my James and Joseph grow up – for them to have no father?

"Another time, we were warned that the enemy was approaching. My unit was out front, and everyone knew we needed to be on guard for what might be a huge battle. One of my officers had called me to his side and was giving me orders, when all of a sudden, shots came from all directions. All I thought about in that moment was finding shelter. I quickly jumped into a trench and realized later it was that simple act which saved my life. Blood covered the earth. I saw arms and legs hanging by threads. Men were strewn all over the field. Body parts were scattered everywhere. I was sick to my stomach and within minutes, I turned to the other side and heaved."

On and on Mr. DeWitt goes describing one bloody incident after another. Why is he talking about all of this now and especially here at the table? To protect myself, I drift off into my own world, unable to handle the gory details he is describing. I never was all that interested in war stories, and his descriptions are much too horrific for me.

All this war talk leads me to think about those mothers whose sons died while defending our country. These thoughts bring me back to my own sadness.

I glance around the table and see that James and Joseph seem enraptured hearing about their father's combat experiences. Marie, on the other hand, looks as if her eyes are beginning to glaze over. I can tell from her expression that she cannot tolerate these graphic stories either.

After a little while longer, Mr. DeWitt seems to notice that we are not paying much attention to him. He takes a deep breath and says, "Forgive me. I should not be having this conversation at dinner. I hope I haven't upset either of you."

Just as he says that, Mrs. DeWitt, who had excused herself to go to the powder room when her husband had first started telling his war stories, comes back to the table. As soon as she sits down, she turns to me and says, "Elizabeth, why don't you tell us a little about you?"

My reply is brief, since I am exhausted and ready to say goodnight. It has been a long day and evening, and I am mentally drained. But I do feel that I should tell them something about myself since I had been quiet most of the evening.

"I'll be married to Raymond for seven years next month. We met two summers after I graduated from high school, when I was up at the lake about an hour from where we lived. I belonged to a girls' club, and each August we would rent a cabin for a week. Raymond ended up staying across the lake with a group of his friends from college. During the day the whole bunch of us would go boating, play tennis, and bathe in the sun. At night we would meet at the big club house and dance and talk around the campfire. Raymond and I fell in love that summer and were married a year later."

Mr. DeWitt asks me if we have children. My heart sinks. All I can respond is, "Not yet." With that, everyone at the table becomes silent.

Thankfully, Mrs. DeWitt glances over at me and smiles in a knowing, caring way. I am not sure why, but I immediately get the feeling that she is a compassionate person. Maybe I'm reading into it because I want someone to share all of this with. Maybe it is my desire for a friend who shows an interest in me. Maybe I am just desperate for some empathy.

It takes a few seconds before the conversation resumes. After dessert is served, we excuse ourselves and go up to our room.

ᥱᥣ

As we sit down by the water's edge, Marie is clearly interested in one thing – her date later tonight. Our conversation is all about our waiter Johnny who, after two days of serious flirting on my sister's part, finally asked her out. She has to wait until his duties are finished for the evening and, at this rate, I am wondering if she can.

Marie's rambling sounds to me like high school girl talk, but that is how she is when it comes to men. While she goes on with her scheming and thinking about meeting Johnny later, I climb further into my hole and wish I could be left alone with my own sorrow. It is difficult to manage my feelings as she talks about her forthcoming date.

All I want is to be by myself. My mind continues to dwell on my loss. No matter how beautiful our surroundings are here at the beach and how delightful it is to be out of the nasty winter up north, I still can't seem to shake my depression. Being patient with my sister is not easy for me.

"Lizzie, do you think the DeWitts will still want to sit with us after James and Joseph leave for school?" asks Marie.

"I have no idea. We'll have to wait and see. They appear to like our company, and Mrs. DeWitt acted as if she enjoyed shopping with us yesterday. I was surprised at how open she was and how much freer she seemed when she was away from Mr. DeWitt. Did you notice that, Marie?"

"What I noticed was how much money she spent on that Allen A knit, two-tone, green bathing suit and then the red slinky one, the *maillot*, which the saleslady described as being designed in France. She sure doesn't seem the type to wear something that skintight and cut so very low in the back. I wish it was me who had bought it. Can't you just see me in that?" Marie asked without waiting for my reply.

"And yes, she is definitely fashionable, but would she dare come down to the beach wearing a bathing suit that fits her so snugly? I wonder what Mr. DeWitt thinks of it. He doesn't seem like the kind of husband who would let his wife parade herself in public and flaunt her body. In private, well, let's leave that to our imagination," Marie quips with a twinkle in her eye.

Marie continues on in her usual fashion. "Mrs. DeWitt does everything to please Mr. DeWitt. I notice how she waits on him in a way that is so different from what we are used to seeing. Instead, Mother makes clear what she wants and doesn't necessarily cater to Daddy. We both know, though, that it rarely matters because our father does whatever he pleases anyway.

"Mrs. DeWitt is much more subtle, and she never expresses an opposing opinion, at least not in front of us."

I can't resist commenting. "I've never heard Mother stand up to Daddy on any other issue except when it was about 'the children.' When we were growing up, he didn't have the time to devote to us and didn't seem all that interested in our day-to-day happenings. Even when he took notice, Mother was always the one to convince him to listen to our pleas and agree to do things her way when it came to any of us. And look at how he was with you when you wanted to go to work. No matter how opposed he was and how hard he fought, Daddy eventually lost on that account."

తా

The DeWitts have invited me and Marie to join them for the Sophie Tucker show. I had heard about her for years but have no idea what to expect. She is billed as the "Last of the Red Hot Mamas," which could mean just about anything to me. Today one of the ladies at the pool was talking about how people from all over the country have come to the Hollywood Beach Hotel just so they can see this vaudeville star - a brassy, Jewish lady. I am surprised that she is allowed to perform here considering that no Jews are permitted to stay at the hotel.

There is some time between dinner and the show, so we are sitting out on the pool deck chatting. James and Joseph are with us. It is their last night here, and from the few things I have heard them say, I can tell that they are ready to head back to school tomorrow morning. I would imagine that both of them are anxious to be away from their hovering parents. After all, they have had a taste of freedom and probably want to get back to their lives at the university where they can do as they please.

I must give them credit for their patience and willingness to be in adult company all week long. They probably would have been completely bored if it weren't for my sister, who made them laugh night after night with her unbelievably thoughtless and outlandish remarks and her flirtatious ways.

Marie is going to miss them. Last night when we were talking in our room, she said, "Have you ever seen two such handsome boys? Lizzie, I bet they could win the World's Most Beautiful Men contest. When they're out on the sand running for miles at a time, I see how all the women stare at them. One would be great to look at, but two is truly a treat! We sure got lucky having them at our table."

This is her last chance to be with them, and Marie is taking every advantage of it. "Did you ever pretend to be the other twin when you went out on a date?"

James laughs out loud as he remembers back. "One time my brother had a date with this girl named Eleanor from our class in high school. She had invited him to a party her friends were giving where all the girls decided to ask the guys. Unheard of, isn't it? He accepted, although he didn't want to go. I kept teasing him about it and could tell that he was getting more and more upset. Then we had a bet about something, and he suggested that the loser would have to take Eleanor to the party. I was so convinced that I was right that I stupidly agreed to the bet. Sure enough, I lost and ended up taking her. She never knew the difference."

Joseph interjects, "Well, it turned out that you had fun because you spent half the night with her girlfriend Florence."

Marie's curiosity gets the best of her. "What's it like to have someone who looks and acts exactly as you do?"

"Since it's all we have ever known, I'm not sure I can answer that," James replies.

"When we look at each other, it's like looking at ourselves. That probably sounds strange to you. One time when I was younger, I remember waving to Joseph, only to realize that I had been looking in a mirror and was waving to myself."

I can tell that Marie is intrigued by the twins and so am I. What would it be like to have a person who is with me almost every minute of each day -- always available and ready to hear what I have to say – someone who understands how I feel?

I wonder if either of them knows how fortunate he is to have the other. I am going to miss them, too, since James and Joseph definitely added a spark to our time here.

෧෨

It is 4:00 p.m., and Marie has gone down to the pool. I am in my room resting after a tough walk on the sand. The turbulent sea and strong winds are in full force today, and trudging along the shore took a lot of energy.

Today marks six months since the baby's stillbirth. Each month's anniversary leaves me feeling especially blue.

A knock at the door startles me. "A telegram for Mrs. Elizabeth Archer," a booming voice announces.

I immediately feel a sense of panic. What could be wrong? Who would be sending me a telegram unless someone was deathly ill or something drastic had happened?

As I jump up from the bed, I feel my heart beating rapidly and pounding through my chest. When I open the door, the bellboy questions, "Mrs. Elizabeth Archer?" and hands me a pale yellow envelope. He turns and walks away as I stand there with my hands shaking. I close the door, sit in the chair at the desk, and brace myself for whatever bad news I might be facing. I reluctantly open the envelope.

ELIZABETH, I AM MISSING YOU MORE THAN I EVER DREAMED POSSIBLE. PLEASE COME HOME SOON. ADVISE OF YOUR ARRIVAL. I LOVE YOU. RAYMOND

A huge feeling of relief floods over me.

While sitting and staring out at the tumultuous ocean with its waves rushing onto the shore, my thoughts float to what I left behind. Raymond, who is now working at least fifty hours a week at the radio manufacturing plant, has let me know he misses me.

Before I left, he told me how sad he is and how he longs for the fun and affection we used to enjoy. Ever since the baby died, we haven't been the same. Laughter has disappeared from our home. No longer do we joke around with each other. Our life together is quiet -- much more than ever before.

Losing the baby was probably as disappointing for Raymond as it was for me, but somehow he seemed to accept it and move on. He only cried that first night after the long and difficult birth which ended in the baby being stillborn. After that, he never shed a tear - or at least I am not aware of any.

For that one day immediately following the stillbirth, Raymond was willing to talk to me about our baby dying. He seemed sensitive to my needs. In fact, he even got rid of the things we had bought in preparation for the baby, so that I would not have to face them when I came home. I have no idea what he did with all the clothes, the dresser, and the crib. I do not even care. All I know is that when I arrived home from the hospital, I walked into an empty room – one that had been a nursery-in-waiting just days before.

After that, Raymond would no longer discuss the fact that our child had died. Whenever I would bring it up, his response was much the same, "Elizabeth, we need to move on – to think about our future and not look back. There is nothing we can do about our loss. We can only hope and pray that we will be parents one day soon."

As much as I wanted to talk about my feelings with him, I could tell that it would have been a big mistake. I almost think that he is incapable of going to that place of pain. All he wants to do is get me to cheer up and keeps saying, "Sweetheart, you will feel much better if you get out, see some friends, and forget about what happened."

℮⁄ᷓ

Each day after Marie and I walk and eat lunch together, she goes off with a few girls her age that she met down by the pool. I am not sure what they do all afternoon, but she comes back happy and full of useless conversation. She is having the time of her life.

Now that she and her 'Mr. Blue Eyes' have become attached to each other, she spends all her time with him when he isn't working. That leaves me pretty much by myself many days and nights. Even when Marie is with me in our room, I can tell that she is preoccupied and surely does not want to be listening to me talk about my sadness. If only she could understand how I am feeling, but she is still too immature and has no way of relating to what I am experiencing.

After all, she has just turned twenty-one years old, the baby in our family. Our other sisters and brothers coddled and sheltered her from the basic realities and hardships of life. She has no idea what any of our lives are like. She's much more concerned about what to wear or whom she might meet than about the rest of us. The bottom line is that she truly only cares about herself.

I wish it could be different. When we first arrived here, I was hopeful that Marie would take the time to listen to me. I must accept that it is not going to happen. I can see that she isn't capable, and is, in fact, way too selfish.

❦

Tonight at dinner, Rose asks me if we could spend some time together once Marie goes off with Johnny and Mr. DeWitt leaves to play cards, as he has gotten into the habit of doing every evening. I've heard him mention that he has become part of a group of men who hole up in the Men's Living Room, smoke cigars, and gamble the nights away.

I gladly accept Rose's invitation to be with her. I relish the idea of company.

Since we have been sitting next to each other at all our meals, I have grown quite fond of Rose. I notice that she's somewhat quiet when she is around Mr. DeWitt, but when he's not with her, Rose opens up and is a different person.

I'm sitting at the desk in my room writing some postcards to the family and waiting for Rose to come upstairs. In the last two weeks that we've been here, I have grown to like the chintz bedspreads splashed with cherry red, sunny yellow, and emerald green roses and the matching drapes on the window that looks out to the sea. I have turned off the lamps by our poster bed and have lit only the sconce on the wall. The dim light feels just right for tonight.

It is now nine o'clock, and there is a knock on my door. This is the first time Rose has been to our room, but since I knew Marie would be out, I invited her up to my home away from home - Room 732.

At first, it is a little awkward. I have never had anyone visit here, but Rose quickly makes herself at home as she sits on the green overstuffed chair in the corner of the room close to our bed. I am a little surprised when she throws off her shoes and digs her feet into the plush, gold pile carpet. Our window is open and in the background, I can hear the crashing of the waves. I lie down on the bed across from Rose and feel the breezes from the ocean wash over me.

"I haven't spent a night with a friend without Henry around in years," she exclaims. "This reminds me of how my sisters and I used to lie next to each other and talk the night away." She takes off her knitted blue cardigan sweater and puts it on the edge of the bed. Pulling her feet under her, she makes herself comfortable.

"How many sisters do you have?" I ask, since she had never mentioned them before.

"There were four of us, but my sister Greta died when she was eighteen. Lucille and Louise are twins and are younger than I am. They married brothers from Indiana and moved there right after their weddings. I don't see them nearly enough. Thank heavens for letter writing. At least we keep in touch that way. Both my sisters are struggling since the Depression began, so I feel sad for them."

"How did you meet Mr. DeWitt?"

"It's a long story. Are you sure you want to hear?"

When I nod my head to signal that I do indeed want her to tell me, she begins. "Henry and I came from two different worlds. My family arrived here from Poland by boat. I was born right before my parents boarded the ship. The rough and rocky seas left them fearful and quite sick, but as religious Catholics, they trusted in God to bring them here safely.

"Life was tough right from the beginning. Neither my mother nor my father assimilated into the culture. They never learned the language and always felt like outcasts. My father died of influenza after we had been here about ten years. Initially, both of my parents found jobs in factories, where my mother continued to work long after my father passed away. We barely managed to make ends meet. My sisters and I did whatever we could to earn a few pennies after school and on weekends.

"At age sixteen, I took a job as a domestic in Henry's parents' huge home. I went to school by day and worked long hours there at night, tending to the house and then cleaning up after the family's dinner. They had a full-time maid and a cook, but I was there to help with various other chores since there was always so much to do.

"Henry had six younger brothers and sisters, all of whom were living at home. His mother entertained high society women and held big, fancy luncheons at least once a month. Everything was formal and beautifully prepared. I was seeing a glimpse of a world previously unknown to me. I liked what I saw."

Once Rose said that, I began to think about what it would be like to come from a poor family and work for wealthy people. Before this conversation, I had never considered how our own maids must feel. Mother always treats them respectfully, but still it must be difficult for them to see all the affluence that surrounds us in our home.

"Henry was already working in the office at the auto plant where they mass-produced vehicles. Sometimes when he was home, we would end up in the same room after dinner, and he would talk to me. He seemed interested in my schooling and would ask me questions about my classes. I found myself getting flustered whenever he spoke to me, regardless of the fact that we weren't talking about anything personal.

"I was attracted to him, but by the time I had begun working at his parents' house, he was already focused on marrying the daughter of his father's best friend. Henry was caught up in the whirlwind of wedding plans that surrounded him, but I never saw him showing much enthusiasm over his forthcoming marriage.

"Once he married Ethel, the two of them would come back to the house for dinner at least three times a week. At nineteen, he was just a kid himself. He always seemed happy when he was around his family. After a few months, Ethel was no longer nice to anyone and behaved in a particularly rude way toward me. She did not act like the same cheerful person whom he had married only a short time before."

I wonder how Rose had felt when Ethel treated her so poorly. It must have been difficult to be around someone who was acting like that.

"During the first few months after their wedding, Ethel and Henry were extremely affectionate toward each other – two young teenagers in love. He would hold her hand or put his arm around her – a surprising display of affection that was generally frowned upon by the adults. I would see his father give Henry disapproving looks from time to time. After a little while, though, I noticed that the doting and tenderness toward each other had disappeared.

"A year later, Henry asked me if I would like to work in his office as his secretary. By then I was finished with school, so I agreed."

"Were you glad that you could finally take a regular job?" I ask, curious as to how that felt for her.

"I was grateful because no one in my family had done anything but menial labor or factory-type jobs, so it was a step up for me."

I notice that Rose shifts in the chair, hesitates, and takes a deep breath. "Elizabeth, I'm not sure why, but I feel as though we've been developing a special friendship during the time that we've spent together here at the hotel."

I nod immediately because I have been feeling an unusual bond developing with Rose -- something I have not felt with any-one since high school. Ever since marrying Raymond, I hardly ever see or talk to my girlfriends except when we're together with our husbands. My life has felt void of this kind of relationship for many years, and now talking to someone like this seems natural and comfortable.

Rose continues, "I want to tell you something, but it might shock you. It concerns part of my past that I'm not proud of and that almost no one in my life knows anything about. I feel as though I can trust you and hope that you'll understand."

"I'm flattered that you feel this way, Rose," I say quietly, honored that she is putting her faith in me.

"Henry and I worked together every day for a year. At first we had a professional relationship. He was my boss, and I was his secretary. As the months went on, he began to talk to me more and more about his marriage and how miserable he was. He told me how he had never wanted to marry Ethel but that it had been expected of him from the time they were children. Their families had assumed that they would wed and had laid the foundation for it to happen. He ended up getting caught in their web of dreams.

"I was falling in love with Henry. I would find myself staring at him when he walked into a room. Each time he came close to me, my breathing would change and my heart would beat faster. I knew that this was not good – that he was a married man; however, I couldn't turn off my feelings, hard as I tried.

"I would dream about him at night. Then I'd wake up in the morning and realize I was paying special attention to how I was dressing to go to the office. It was becoming difficult to stay focused on my work."

As I listen to Rose, I start imagining where her story might be leading. I brace myself for what's coming next.

Rose takes a deep breath and continues, "I could tell that he was also attracted to me. He would make overly-friendly remarks which were anything but what one might expect from a boss. He always had a big smile on his face when I would come into his private office.

"One morning I arrived at the plant before Henry did, which rarely happened. When he came in, he looked despondent. He walked straight into his office and shut the door, something that was most unusual for him. Later when Henry called me in to take dictation, his eyes were red and swollen. I could tell that he had been crying. That shocked me, since I had never seen a man cry before. I knew something was seriously wrong, but I couldn't imagine what it was.

"He told me that when he got home from work the day before, he found their gardener in bed with Ethel. The shock of that sent him into a fury. The man bolted out of the house dressing as he ran. Henry was so enraged that he couldn't talk to Ethel. Instead, he ended up sleeping in a separate room that night, and Henry never saw her in the morning when he left.

"As I sat across from him, I could feel myself wanting more than anything to wrap my arms around Henry and comfort him. I knew he was hurting, and my heart ached for him."

I notice that Rose shifts in her chair once again and stops talking for a minute. She seems lost in another world. I sit quietly waiting for her to go on.

"To this day, I have no idea how it happened, but before I knew it, the two of us were in an embrace. He told me that while he knew it was all wrong, he realized that he had been in love with me for a long time. One thing led to the next and soon, we were making love."

Rose looks up at me as if to see how I am reacting to all that she is sharing with me. I sense that she feels a bit uneasy, but I give her a reassuring smile and she continues her story.

"From that day on, he and Ethel began to make plans to get a divorce. It was a scandal in their world, but his parents supported him. Almost no one divorced back then. His father ended up losing the friendship with Ethel's father, but thankfully, his son was more important to him than his friend was.

"As far as Henry and I were concerned, we did all we could to hide our attraction and desire for one another. Work took on a new meaning for us, since when we were together the flames were ablaze. It was almost impossible to keep our hands off one another. We constantly ended up behind his locked office door.

"Then one day I realized that my menstrual cycle was late. Up until then, I had always been regular. Within a short period of time, I knew that I was pregnant. I wasn't sure what to do. Henry's divorce was not yet final. The only one I could tell was my mother. Because of her old-world religious upbringing, she let me know that I must go somewhere else, have the baby, and then give it away.

"I agonized for a few weeks about what to do and whether to tell Henry. When I finally did, he was kind and loving, but he agreed with my mother that I could not keep the baby. I wrote to my aunt in Ohio, and she offered to have me come there until I gave birth. And so, on a gray and rainy July day, I left Detroit by train and went to Athens, Ohio, where I stayed for the next seven months."

I sit in shock, amazed that Rose is sharing such personal details with me.

"I helped my aunt take care of my young cousins, so my days went by fairly quickly. Yet, I was lonesome and miserable knowing what I was going to have to do in the end. As my pregnancy progressed, I became sadder and more depressed. I didn't know how I was going to give up this baby whom I would soon bring into the world and who was the child of the man I loved.

"My uncle treated me wonderfully. In the end, it was Uncle Timothy who made all the arrangements with the Children's Home Society of Ohio for the adoption.

"I was allowed to hold my precious daughter for about five minutes before a nurse came and took her away. She slept in my arms as I clutched her close to my heart. To this day, I remember her perfectly-shaped, rosebud lips, the dimple in her chin, her full head of golden brown hair, her pure white skin, and her tiny fingers and toes. I dream about her often. I felt devastated when the nurse separated us and walked out of the room with my baby. I would never lay eyes on my child again."

Something about all that Rose is telling me strikes a deep chord within me. I feel her pain in a way I would never think possible. Until now, it hadn't occurred to me that there are many ways in which a mother can lose a baby.

"Once I came back to Detroit after the baby was born, I was terribly upset inside, feeling grief-stricken and heavy-hearted. Henry did the best he could to try to cheer me up. For him, giving the child away for adoption did not hold much meaning. He barely seemed to have given it a second thought."

When she says that, I immediately think about Raymond and how he acted when we lost the baby. I also now realize that I am not the only one who has experienced this kind of suffering and loss.

"The only other person in Detroit who knew what had happened was my mother. She never mentioned the situation to me again once I left for Ohio. It was like the seven months away were erased from anyone's thoughts but mine.

"I went right back to work for Henry. His divorce had become final while I was away, so after a little while, we decided to get married. In 1913, we had a small but lovely wedding in his parents' beautiful backyard. When I got pregnant a little over a year later, I understood the meaning of hope. Within two years of marrying Henry, James and Joseph were born; my life turned around. Having the twins helped me to go on living. I invested all of my love and energy in them, and for me the sun began to shine again.

"I'm probably telling you this story mostly because today is the birthday of my daughter. A year never goes by when I don't silently celebrate her. Unlike me, Henry was able to move on. He never seemed all that affected and didn't understand my sadness over the loss of our child. It was a subject that we almost never discussed and most likely never will again. Because he hadn't seen her and was far removed from the reality, he didn't seem to care like I did. He was so in love with me and only wanted to make me happy."

Pools of tears well up in my eyes. Rose has no idea how moved I am by what she has told me and how many emotions this is stirring in me. She also has no way of knowing my story unless I tell her. I have never told anyone what happened to my baby, and yet this seems the perfect moment to share what is in my heart.

Before I do, I get up from the bed and walk over to Rose. She looks different, almost relieved. It is as if a heavy veil has lifted. Rose stands up and we embrace.

"Elizabeth, you cannot imagine what it means to me to have been able to tell you all of this and for you to be here listening, not saying much, but showing me by your attentiveness that you care. I have never before told anyone about my daughter and didn't expect that I ever would. Thank you for listening to me."

We face each other for a while – both of us feeling a sense of disbelief over what has transpired. I sit down at the edge of my bed right next to the chair where Rose has once again situated herself. Now it is my turn. I am gathering my courage to begin.

The more I think about it, the more aware I am of how important it is that I finally have someone who is with me and who will be open to my pain. Talking about this is a huge risk, although after what she told me, I am no longer afraid. And so I begin.

"Like you, Rose, what I'm going tell you is something I've never talked with anyone about since it happened. For me, there has been no one who was willing to discuss this with me.

"A year ago October, I became pregnant. Raymond and I had been trying for several years and had had no luck up until then. Both of us wanted a child more than anything else in the world, so when I finally conceived, we were joyous. As the months went on, the two of us were busy anticipating what special things we would do with our child and how our lives would change once our baby was born.

"Raymond helped me decorate the nursery. He hired an excellent craftsman from his factory to build a crib and a dresser. Mother and I went shopping for baby clothes. We were all set and impatiently waiting for the day when I would give birth.

"Because Raymond's family's close friend was a doctor, from the start I had been going to him for my care. We chose not to have a midwife. I planned to give birth in the hospital instead of at home."

As I am talking, Rose puts her hand on my knee. There is something about her touch that signals to me that I am safe. I feel reassured and go on talking.

"In the days before we were expecting the baby to be born, I didn't feel well. In addition to being cumbersome and huge, I wasn't myself. I went to bed early one night and when I woke up the next morning, I noticed that there was no movement inside me. Raymond had left the house for work before I woke up, so I never said anything to him or anyone else that day.

"As the hours passed, I became filled with absolute dread and fear. I realized that there was something terribly wrong. Still I didn't tell Raymond when he came home that night. I wanted to believe that maybe this is what happens right before it's time to give birth.

"But by the next morning when there was still no movement, I was panicked and told Raymond. He rang up the doctor, and within minutes we were on our way to the hospital. By the time I arrived, I had already begun to go into labor."

I stop at this point. The memories going through my mind feel like knives in my heart. I take a deep breath and continue.

"What took place during those next twelve hours is somewhat of a blur to me. I do remember the nurses talking to me as if I would soon deliver a healthy baby. The doctor didn't say anything to lead me to believe that what the nurses were saying was anything but true.

"The baby was finally delivered after many grueling hours. I was sedated and did not wake up until several hours later. When I awoke, the room was silent. Raymond was not at my side. A nurse walked in after a few minutes and quickly left to get the doctor. A short time later, he came to my bedside along with Raymond and told me that our child was stillborn. I never even had a chance to see my baby."

The tears flow down my cheeks, and I begin to sob. This is the first time I had said these words aloud. Rose is witnessing my pain and sorrow. She reflects my despair. She says nothing. She does not have to. I know she understands. It takes me a while to compose myself and when I do, I go on telling her my story.

"For days I languished in the hospital. I was surrounded by women who had given birth to healthy babies. I could hear infants crying in other rooms. I saw people walking down the hall carrying flowers for the new mothers. I was completely and utterly alone. The celebrating around me felt agonizing.

"Yes, Raymond and my mother came to see me. He was in shock but at least on the first day, he showed sadness and tremendous disappointment. But after day one, he began talking to me about moving on – about how important it is to look to tomorrow and not dwell on the past.

"My mother said nothing about the baby and to this day still hasn't mentioned him. At first, she talked about the weather and about my going home and about how Raymond needs me to take care of the house and to make his meals – as if I must have a purpose in my life and that will fulfill it. I could tell that she didn't know what to say to me. She was never one to discuss feelings anyway, so it is no surprise that in all this time she hasn't been able to, even though I have needed her more than ever before."

Rose takes my hands in hers. She comforts me with this simple gesture. This is such a difficult thing to be talking about and yet, I know that I must.

"No one else has said a word to me about my baby who died – not a single soul. It was as if my pregnancy never happened. Raymond's parents live out of town, and on the rare occasion when we speak to them, the subject seems taboo. My brothers and sisters have been anything but supportive of me. I still don't understand how none of them has made an effort to talk to me about losing my child. Forget my father. He is as incapable as the rest of sharing any feelings or emotions.

"Our friends haven't been any better in terms of caring for me. They stop speaking and clam up as soon as I walk into a room. It's almost as if everyone is talking about me behind my back, but not to me. I feel as though I'm totally alone in a vast wilderness consumed with my distressing thoughts and sorrowful feelings. There is nowhere for me to turn for comfort.

"What I understand now is that no one knows how to broach the subject. Instead of trying, they remain silent. Probably before this, I would have done the same thing. Now I understand how the simplest acknowledgment in a distressful situation like this makes a big difference."

Again I stop for a minute. I know I must continue, but it is so hard to say all these things to someone else. Rose waits patiently for me to speak.

"All of the couples we're friends with have children. None of them has a sense of what I'm experiencing. The women gave birth to their babies and began to nurse them from the start. I gave birth to a dead baby and had to face the sad truth that there would be no child to suck at my breast.

"Meanwhile, my milk was coming in, and my breasts became engorged and painful. At least for me, it was a physical reminder that there had been a baby – that I had given birth – even if it was to a stillborn.

"I have wanted to be a mother from the time I was a child. As a result of the stillbirth, I feel like I am less of a woman. In my mind, it is as if I am a failure for not being able to accomplish that one simple act. Other women may feel differently, but what purpose do I have in my life if not to be a mother?

Rose looks at me with an understanding and kindness in her eyes. She does not say a word. She doesn't have to. Just talking to her is a tremendous solace to me.

"While I was walking along the shore earlier today, I practically ran into two little girls frolicking in the surf. I looked up and there sat their mother watching from a few feet away. Nestled in her arms was a little baby. My heart stopped beating for a minute. Feelings of jealousy flooded over me.

"That happens all the time when I'm with my nieces and nephews. Since I lost the baby, family gatherings have become increasingly more difficult for me to attend. While I love all of these children, it hurts too much not to have my own. I'm sure that my brothers and sisters see a huge change in me and aren't happy about how I am with their children, but I don't know any other way to be these days. My heart is broken, and I can't seem to move past that."

Now it is Rose's turn to put her arms around me. The comfort of her being there and knowing that someone finally has heard me and understands my pain begins to seep in as she holds me close to her.

While tears stream down my face, I feel the despair that I have lived with slowly lifting. It is as if by speaking the words that have been buried deep in my soul for the past six months, something has shifted for me.

Rose has listened, and by her presence and caring, I feel differently than I have in all this time. I don't need her to say anything else. Relief followed by calmness washes over me.

In a matter of a few short hours, and because of the conversation Rose and I just had, I am beginning to understand the importance and the gift of being able to unburden oneself. Instead of carrying this hardship alone, by speaking it aloud, the heaviness in my heart starts to lessen.

As I sit here absorbing these new and liberating feelings, I think about Raymond and realize that I am ready to be where I belong – back in his arms once again. Unexpectedly, the words that Rose described earlier about how she felt when she finally had her twins are helping me to think differently about my life.

I will be eternally grateful for this conversation with Rose here in Room 732. The time has come for me to go home. As I begin to contemplate my future, I am once again filled with the hope that one day I will become a mother.

PROUD TO SERVE

UNITED STATES NAVAL OFFICERS' INDOCTRINATION AND TRAINING SCHOOL 1943

February 6, 1943

Dear Anna,

When we aren't in close touch, I find myself missing you so much. Many nights I lie in bed listening to the lulling sounds of the sea and can only think about you. Sometimes I wonder how much longer I can tolerate the distance between us. It feels like forever already, and that makes me sad.

Doubt that I'll ever get used to being away from you even though we have spent so much of our marriage apart. Some days I worry that this war will never end. From what I just saw while at sea, doesn't look like it'll be over any time soon. The fighting on all fronts seems to be getting worse instead of better. The news is discouraging. Want to come home to you and the girls already. Can always and will always hope for that.

Now that I'm back on land in the USA, look forward to once again receiving your mail regularly. Your much-welcomed letters finally caught up with me and arrived yesterday. While on board, seems a long time between mail deliveries. Have to depend on the supply ships to deliver, and rarely does that happen in any orderly way. Sometimes we get more recently written letters before older ones – odd how it all works.

Has been well over a month since I held an unopened envelope from you in my hand and enjoyed the anticipation before reading what you wrote. While on the ship, the pages were getting worn-out and dog-eared from my reading them over and over again.

Hit the jackpot today with the ten letters from you, a few from Mama, three from Mac, and two letters from Virginia and Irene. Love hearing the news from home. Wish I was there with you. Feel far away from our life together.

Hard to imagine that you are working at the aircraft production facility in town. How is that possible? If it helps the war effort and brings in some extra money for the family, then guess you have no choice. Just that it doesn't seem like a job for you. No woman should have to work outside of the home. It's beyond me to think of you having to report there every day and do what you are doing. There's something so wrong about that, Anna. Am working hard to accept the reality of this, but in the end, I do feel proud of you for taking on this difficult job.

Trying to picture you punching small alloy rivets into aluminum aircraft skin. Since when did you ever know what those things were — let alone be responsible for putting anything like that together? Who's there to teach you? How can you manage that difficult labor? You're way too delicate for that kind of work.

Sounds like the women in the neighborhood are right alongside you. Sure wish for those rare days of long ago when we were all together sitting on our front lawns watching the kids at play, beers in hand, no cares to speak of, no wars raging throughout the world.

Glad Virginia landed a job as a secretary in the office of the munitions factory. At least she's doing women's work and is enjoying it. Guess she's learning a whole new set of skills. Good for her. Does her boss treat her kindly? Bet she's a great worker. Remember how organized she always was, so that must help her get the work done.

Don't love the idea of Irene delivering mail. Must be grueling for her during the hard winter you're having. Not sure how she does it carrying that heavy sack of mail, being so tiny and frail. How did she ever land that job? Need to send both of them a letter soon. Filled with pride over our daughters and know you must be as well.

Surprised to hear that Mrs. Littleton is doing her share by organizing the war bonds drive in town. At least she has joined the ranks. Wonder what made her get involved like she is. Have to give the woman credit for her effort. Never would have guessed her to be the type to do anything on such a grand scale. Always seemed like a meek, little old lady – kind of an odd duck. Remember the first time we met her in town with her tiny pup in that silly basket on her bicycle?

Must say that I'm grateful to finally be stateside. Last tour in the Battle of the Atlantic cost us way too much. Lost too many ships – too many good men. The constant watch and fear of U-boats was endless. Shelling was going on everywhere. The rough seas and bad storms seemed to have had no mercy at times. Had a few days that practically wiped out most of the crew, but we're tough and did our job regardless. Scary part is that it isn't over yet. The battles continue on with no let-up in sight.

Now that I'm away from the intense fighting, can't help but think of how hard it was to witness all the destruction. But we were doing what we set out to accomplish. Am damn proud of the United States Navy! Our men are well-trained and know what it takes to perform the tasks at hand – all in the name of protecting our country and fighting for freedom.

Not sure why they assigned me to do this training except to know that when we're all done here, I'll probably be going back on board, and these guys will be spread out all over the world. Can't question it. Have to be thankful for this reprieve and hope that the war will end soon so none of us has to go back over to Europe or to the Pacific and so that no more lives are lost.

Before we arrived, one of the other officers had told me I was going to be at a hotel, but I was sure he was pulling my leg. You know how the guys are – always joking around. What were the chances of my ever landing in a fancy place like this – on the ocean in South Florida of all things? Was amazed when I got here. Never did I expect to find the surroundings to be quite as beautiful as they are.

Being stationed at this luxurious hotel that we're using for our officer training and indoctrination center is like being in heaven altogether. Who would've ever thought I would be this fortunate? Of course without you, nothing is perfect.

Must describe to you where I'm at. Riding east toward the ocean from the train station, we were on Hollywood Boulevard, a beautiful palm tree-lined road. As we got nearer to the end, there in front of us stood this huge building – the Hollywood Beach Hotel, where we are stationed. Had to cross a low bridge over the Intracoastal to get there and as we drove closer, we saw these lush, neatly-manicured gardens in front of the place. Don't think I've ever seen anything quite so grand. Hard to believe that this is my home for now. Almost feel guilty when I think of all those who are out there in battle where I could easily be.

Interesting history from what I hear, and you know how much I like history. Before the hotel could be built, they first had to drain mangrove swamps and get rid of the pineapple farms and palmetto fields. Then roads were built over sand,

and the bridge was installed. Supposedly the whole project cost millions. Took months to get to the point where they could begin construction on the hotel itself.

Started to work on that part in spring of 1925. Pilings were driven. Had just begun on the foundation when a railroad freight embargo halted most construction in South Florida. Joseph Young, who was responsible for the concept and for building the hotel, refused to be stopped by the embargo. He negotiated the purchase of two freighters and sent them to Belgium to get cement. The project continued.

People in town called it the "'ninety-day wonder." Hundreds of workers were hired to get the hotel built in three months. From what I've been told, workers were on the job twenty-four hours a day using lights at night in order to see what they were doing. Before long, the walls were up.

Hope I'm not boring you with these hotel details, but after where I've been, this is fascinating to me. Want to share it all with you.

The hotel opened in time for the 1925 – 1926 season but wasn't entirely completed until February of '26. Then, of all things, the Great Miami Hurricane in September of that year washed directly over and through the hotel. Sand piled into the lobby while the ocean rushed into the building. From the sounds of it, there was sand everywhere on the first floor. Because the hotel was so well-built with poured concrete, it wasn't destroyed. Only the windows on the east side were demolished. Stores and other buildings all around it were wiped out by the hurricane, but not this baby. The brand-new pipe organ and the rest of the furnishings were completely ruined.

In order to clean out the sand that covered the first floor, they brought in mules that had been borrowed from the farmers in the nearby city of Dania. The workers attached wooden buckets to the mules. Then once the men filled these buckets with the sand, they took them out back to dump onto the beach. As soon as the hotel was cleaned out, it was refurnished. The Hollywood Beach Hotel went back to being a high-class vacation spot for the rich and famous.

Have to wonder what took place in these rooms before we came. Based on how the huge dining room looks, the elegant dinners and dances must have been quite a sight to see. Hear they partied well into the night. Can still see many remnants of beautiful fixtures, wallpaper, and statues everywhere we go.

My bedroom has plush gold carpeting and fancy lamps on the nightstands and even has a small but sparkly light fixture on the wall. There's a bathtub in every room, plus I'm on the side of the hotel that overlooks the sea. Can sit at the desk or on my bed and watch the ships and tankers out on the water. Have a bird's eye view up here on the seventh floor.

This place is much nicer than anywhere I've ever been. Talk about living the good life. Haven't had this kind of privacy ever. Feels like this is how kings and presidents must live.

You would love it here. I'll send you some postcards from the Hollywood Beach Hotel days that we found, so you can get a better idea of how it looked. Just wish you could be with me to enjoy this scenery and share my bed.

The general manager of the place, Oscar Johnson, a nice and decent fellow with a cigarette in his mouth at all times, decided to retain the maid services once the naval training center took over. Have no idea how or why but am not complaining. This guy will do anything for us. In return, we keep him supplied with his smokes.

My boys won't have the same luxury of having maids as we officers do. They will have none of the extravagances, in fact. For them, it's basics only. Heard that all the Beauty Rest mattresses in the guys' rooms were replaced with bunk beds. Plus, in some cases, there are five men in a fairly small room.

They do have the benefit of the refined atmosphere – just being here in such a beautiful place. For all of us, it's hardly real. Living in this elegant hotel on Hollywood Beach for me is a far cry from my usual naval stints. Never in my life would I have expected this and still can't believe I landed here.

Heard that last year there was a big party with the townspeople. They called it a "shipwreck party" to symbolize the hotel going nautical. The floors turned into decks, the walls became bulkheads, and the stairs were ladders. Said goodbye to an era of elegance and a peace-time mecca – all for the United States Navy and this awful war.

Lots of changes here to ensure safety. Air raid watchers are on alert constantly on the roof of the building. There's a chain-link fence that surrounds the whole hotel complex. Security is tight. No one can go beyond the first floor without proper credentials. Radar has been installed on the top two floors. Sure it's a big switch from how things used to be, but then our world is a different place from what it was a few years ago.

Organizing everything this week. Getting to know staff and figuring out my way around here. Approximately 1,500 men or more will be in this class, and there are fifty of us officers here preparing to work with the new seamen coming in this week. Know a few of the guys from one or another of the ships we've been on together. Always good to see a familiar face – especially now during this war. Gets lonely otherwise when there's no one to talk to that knows who I am.

Classes consist of training these new officer candidates to be leaders. Should be an interesting experience for me. Don't know how it'll be to work with these elite guys – the ones who were lucky enough to go to college and all. Wonder if they'll act like rich, spoiled brats. Doubt that they'll be hardy stock like our enlisted men. We'll most certainly be whipping them into shape. They don't have a clue what's in store for them. We need to get these guys ready to serve as part of our great Navy.

Heard the teenagers who work in the snack shop downstairs call the men here the "ninety-day wonders" – just like what the hotel was nicknamed when it was first built. Meanwhile the guys all love seeing the elevator girls in sailor suits. That's probably the highlight of each day for them. Don't worry. I'm looking the other way.

You would love the beautiful beach. When I sit out there in the early morning hours as the sun rises and the tide makes its way either in or out, it's you whom I think of and want by my side. Wonder how long I'll last before I get tired of looking at the ocean instead of being on it. You know me and my love of the sea.

Keep writing to me. Your letters are my lifeline.

Love,
Hutch

༺

February 20, 1943

Dear Mac,

Grateful that you are alive! Wondering how your recovery is going. Glad that they put you on one of the U. S. Navy hospital ships so you can get the care you need. Hear the medical team is among the finest around. Hopefully they're treating you well and are able to help you with all of your wounds. Can't begin to guess how you're managing with the number of injuries you have. Any idea how long you'll need to be under their care and attention before they let you go home? You have sure had your share of suffering the past few months.

After all the years we served, the few since war was declared have been the toughest, don't you think? At last count and as far as I can tell, we've lost at least half our original buddies. What a brutal war this has turned out to be.

Don't know how this happened, but am now in Florida, of all places. Got word last month that they were shipping me back to the States to work with soon-to-be officers. Will be here for at least three months training the next group of guys in navigation, and then don't know where they'll send me.

Big relief to be away from fighting at sea. For once, have a bit of a break. Still not sure why they chose me to do this, but won't complain at all. Do miss the sea, though. Know you can understand that. It's in our blood.

Training of the new class is beginning. When we picked these guys up at the train station, could see terror in some of their eyes – excitement in others. You know how the usual first few days are – with the processing, issuing uniforms and other clothing, medical checks, and lots of waiting around.

Overheard a few talking after the initial indoctrination. Didn't like being poked and prodded, heads shaved, and having orders barked at them from every direction. They better get used to it. This is a whole different ballgame. They definitely need to learn the ropes if they're going to succeed in the Navy. Know you agree.

While these guys didn't enlist, can't help but remember when we did. Do you? We were such big shots at the ripe old age of seventeen. I'd been influenced by my father and later by my older brothers – seeing them in their crisp, summer whites or dress blues – like right out of a recruitment poster. For as long as I can remember, they talked about their adventures in the Navy. Loved their stories of life on the high seas. Never tired of listening to them go on about their ships, their love of the ocean, and the camaraderie of their naval buddies. I was ready to become one of them. Talking you into joining with me took no effort.

The first trip with you, me, and Albert down to the recruitment office sure made us feel like we were such hot shots, didn't it? Remember how we snuck out of our houses? Our parents had no idea. Can still picture us getting there by hitching and then watching that glorifying movie about the Navy and knowing we didn't need any additional convincing. From that moment on, you and Albert seemed as ready to sign up as I was.

Amazing how we each went home that day and never said a word to our families – not until after we were sworn in. Your poor mom got so upset at first when you told her. She sure wanted you to go to the recruitment center and tell them you had made a mistake. Remember how your dad had to hold her back on that one?

Must give her credit for the way she changed her attitude once she thought it over. Your mother understood that she needed to support you. She was smart enough to know how important it was for you to join the rest of the country to fight for what's right.

For me, it happened as it was supposed to – following in the footsteps of my father and my brothers. No one ever questioned it – just the way it was in our family.

Remember Albert's parents' reactions? At first they were in shock and didn't give him a fight, did they? Then came the worrying and his mom becoming unbelievably relentless. Drove him nuts. She would go on and on, and he would have to leave the house to escape from her constant badgering. Poor woman must have suffered so much over that. Even though we were young, I will never forget how she was. Come to think of it, surprised I noticed — although with Albert continually talking about her distress, guess it was impossible not to have paid attention.

Speaking of those days, got word that Albert will be reporting here next week. Haven't seen him in years. Keep thinking about how great it'll be to reunite. We experienced lots of crazy shit together, didn't we? Wish you could join us once again. Can you imagine the stories we could tell if we all ended up in the same place? Maybe someday. First order of business — just get well!

We had no idea what to expect during our first weeks in the Navy. We were so naïve. No way we could do half of what was expected of us in the beginning. Remember collapsing into bed each night with sore muscles, aching backs, and tired feet? It didn't take long, though, before we became masters at sit-ups and push-ups — not exactly like we had a choice.

Noticed one of the new guys was practically in tears on the first day when we started the marching drills. By the end of it, he could hardly walk. He turned to the guy next to him, and I overheard him saying, "Sure wish I was back at Oberlin College." Will have to whip him and the rest of them into shape. Definitely have my work cut out for me. Like the way it was with us, these guys have no idea what's ahead for them.

At the end of day one, gave them the lecture about becoming useful men and ending up as leaders in our country. Trying to keep them pepped up and prepared to become officers.

Remember how Lieutenant Wilder once inspired us? We were so enthusiastic about our careers in the Navy.

Got to get going and face the boys. Couldn't resist sharing the old memories first, though. Seeing all these young kids has taken me right back to where we were all those years ago. Can't help but think of you and remember how it was for us.

Some things never change no matter where we are. Reveille at 6:00 a.m. with the blasting bugle on the loud speaker and "Come alive – hit the deck – everybody up," signaling the beginning of yet another day. I'm off to start mine. On the double.

> *Take care of yourself, Mac.*
> *Hutch*

ᕲ

February 27, 1943

Dear Mama,

How's my Pearl, the girl? Missing you and wishing I could walk into your kitchen right this second and have a piece or two or maybe three of your famous peach pie. Can taste that and your delicious meatloaf with mashed potatoes and gravy. I remember your amazing meals day after day growing up. Chow here doesn't come close. Wish we could hire you to cook for us. The guys would drool if they got the chance to taste your cooking.

Funny what I miss when I'm far away. Somehow days go by and all I end up thinking about is home. Never get used to being separated from all of you.

Anna is holding up okay, isn't she? Know you see her all the time. Appreciate that you can be there for her. You are so strong, Mama. Even though you have had to suffer through so much in your lifetime, you have always been there for us. You may not realize it, but your support has made a big difference in our lives.

Know everyone is anxious for news about what's going on in the Atlantic and Pacific. Luckily, am out of that scene for a while – at least until I'm done here with the training of this class of guys. Hoping the war will end by then, and we can come home. Praying for peace.

Last Friday, went with a few trucks into Miami to pick up supplies for the guys. Got to see some of tropical South Florida. Nice to be in a place that is hot and sunny during this time of year. Got tired of freezing our butts off out at sea. Know you're having some nasty weather still. Sure don't miss all that snow. Never was a big fan of winter, although it was all I knew for so many years.

Had a real shocker on that little trip through the city. A few of us stopped to pick up lunch. First restaurant we went to had big signs over its two doors. One said WHITES ONLY, and the other said COLORED ONLY. Never before in all my travels did I see anything like that. Sickened me to the core. Refused to eat there, so we moved along. At a drinking fountain, we again noticed a similar sign. Drove back through Miami Beach and on one of the hotels, there was a sign that said, RESTRICTED CLIENTELE. In smaller print, it stated, NO COLORED, NO JEWS, NO DOGS. We kept on driving. No one in the truck said a word. None of us could believe what we saw.

Just a few weeks ago, I heard talk that there is some unrest among the troops because the Navy only lets the Negroes prepare and serve food and tend to the officers' living quarters. They aren't allowed to be sailors like the rest of us. Didn't give it much thought then, but something about these signs has gotten to me and has started me thinking.

Mama, what is this world coming to? You and Pa always taught us to love our brothers and sisters regardless of their skin color or religion. What kinds of people do this to one another? How is it that anyone thinks this is okay? Looks to me like we need to have a battle right here on our own soil and straighten this terrible thing out. Thought our Civil War took care of this many years ago. Turns my stomach to think about all this going on now.

On a happier subject, Anna told me you've been busy knitting scarves and hats for the troops. Nothing feels better to us guys than to receive some of the handmade items that are sent to us from folks back home. Course down here, fortunately don't need any of that. All I need is a bathing suit.

Finally heard from Mac last month. Don't know if anyone told you. He got injured by the Nazis and ended up on a hospital ship. Took some nasty blows. Hoping that he'll make as full a recovery as he can and will be home soon. Have you seen his mom at church lately? If so, how is she doing? Try to reassure her that Mac will be fine.

Got word that Albert will be here in a few days. He, too, has been in the thick of battle since the war began. Am sure he'll be relieved to have a break from the fighting. Heard his ship was in the Pacific Ocean and had been constantly going from one combat zone to the next. Do you ever see his family?

Been working harder than ever to get these boys in line and prepare them for what is yet to come. Have had almost no breaks since it's such an intense training for the guys in navigation. Days are long. Nights seem short. Best moments are when I get back to my room in this beautiful hotel and sit on my bed, have a smoke, and look out at the sea. Never tire of that view. Am up on the seventh floor, so I can see the ocean for miles on end.

Maybe one day you'll get to see the sea. Know you never think of leaving town. With all my travels, it's hard to believe that you have never been further than ten miles in any direction from Cheyenne, Wyoming.

> *Until next time, I remain your loving son,*
> *Hutch*

❧

March 3, 1943

Dear Mac,

Been thinking about you and hope you're starting to feel more like yourself. Looking forward to hearing good news from your end. Can't picture you down for too long – not you, Mac. Surprised to hear that you met up with Lee but saddened to hear that he lost his arms in battle. Wonder what his life will be like after this. The toll this war is taking on our guys is too much. Must be terrible to see our buddies coming in with such awful injuries. Since you're living it, I especially feel for you.

Albert arrived on Monday. Was happy to see him and thought he'd be glad to be here with me. Big shock when I walked into the room and went to greet him.

Not sure what's going on with Albert but noticed a strange look in his eyes. Could tell he's on edge. In fact, he seemed nervous – almost jittery. Not like him at all.

Tried to talk to him, but most of his answers were short and he seemed angry. Not the fun-loving Albert we once knew, that's for sure.

He has just returned from that awful battle with the Japs at Guadalcanal. Impossible to get him to speak about it. When I asked, he cringed and put his head down.

In fact, the little he talked at all, he kept muttering the name of Ashlyn. Not sure who she is or what that's all about. Too strange for words. Tried to get him to explain, but Albert was lost in another world – someplace I was unable to reach.

When they marched the guys into the mess hall, Albert and I stayed back for a bit. Did everything possible to have a conversation with him, but he didn't seem all that interested. Sat together for the prayer and meal. Noticed he didn't eat the way he used to in the old days. Remember the huge appetite he always had – how he would wolf down anyone's chow who didn't want it? Not this time. Hardly ate half his food.

Tried to reminisce with him about the good times we had together, but Albert wanted no part of that either. He didn't even smile once. Something is going on. Never saw him like this before. Could tell that all he wants is to be left alone.

Just watching how he is acting concerns me and makes me think there is something seriously wrong with him. Maybe I should talk to someone here about Albert. Will keep you posted.

Sorry to dump this on you, Mac, but had to tell someone. Knew you would want to know. Miss you.

Get well,

Hutch

❧

March 8, 1943

Dear Virginia and Irene,

Good to hear from both of you. Hungry for any news I can get from back home. Appreciate all you write to your dear old dad. You girls are the best daughters – always have been.

Sounds like you're both keeping busy with work. Still having trouble thinking of you carrying around bundles of mail all day, Irene. Must be building up some fairly hefty muscles. Don't get too bulky. When George comes home, he'll want his pretty, petite lady to be the way she was when he left. Take my word for it. Am sure he's missing you as much as you're missing him. Does he write much? Where is he stationed these days? What about his buddies? Is he with anyone from home?

Was surprised to hear they are now rationing sugar, butter, and coffee. Lots of sacrifice is being made all over the country. Can hardly get used to the fact that almost none of you can get your hands on any meat anymore. Guess they're saving it for us. After all, we men need our meat and potatoes. Life sure isn't like we knew it, but then after the Great Depression, it could be a lot worse. At least people have food to eat – even if it isn't exactly what they want.

Proud to hear that you're both working on the paper drive. Suppose you save every scrap from the office, Virginia. No wasting of anything at all anymore. Know that you can't go out and buy any shoes or clothes these days with rations on those things, too.

Grandma told me that she's been teaching both of you to knit. Never imagined that either of you would have the patience to sit and learn to do that. Probably now that there aren't any boys around to go to dances and have fun with in the evenings, you have lots of spare time. Bet the scarves you make for the men overseas will be the nicest of anyone's.

Pleased that you're both doing what you can for the guys at war. Know you can't wait until the day when life returns to normal. Glad you go down to the USO to help out. The whole country is making an effort to win this war one way or another. Feels good to have the support from everyone.

Could tell that Grandma likes having both of you with her. She's doing all she can to help. Am sure she's more than pleased that you're joining her in this.

The picture you sent me of the two of you is a big hit. Word is out that your old man has two great-looking daughters. Everyone wants to stop by to look at you. Room 732 is the spot to come for guys to take a peek at two beauties. You have made me, Chief Hutchins, popular among my boys. Good going, girls.

Heard that your ma has a bad cough. Make sure she takes her cod liver oil, and while you're at it, take a few swigs your-selves. Dress in warm clothes and stay indoors as much as you can to avoid the bad weather. You, Irene, have no choice but to be out in the sleet and snow. Hope you haven't had to give up your boots for the rubber drive. Don't want to think about you not being warm enough when you go from house to house. Shudder to think of my baby out there in the elements. No woman should have to be doing that.

How lucky I am to be stationed in Florida for a while. Weather is wonderful, especially considering that it's the beginning of March. Sun is shining; air temperature is about seventy degrees. Went for a swim in the ocean early this morning. Speaking of swimming, there's the Hollywood Beach Casino, a huge U-shaped complex nearby that has about one hundred cabanas and an Olympic-size saltwater pool. At one end there is a three-level diving board. Try to go there off-hours when fewer people are around and swim at least a mile each time – good place to get my exercise.

Have a great room in this lovely hotel. Loving this life. What a switch from what I'm used to on board. It hardly seems real or possible. Am working long hours, but it's more difficult on my brain than on my body. Feels good to be out of the arena of battle for the time being.

Am constantly thinking about the boys your age and those a little older who are off fighting in the war. Most of them had no preparation for what was to come. Just months ago, they were police officers, carpenters, janitors, and farmers. Some are young fathers who've been forced to leave their children. Now they face a huge transition into a new life – one that requires such tremendous responsibility.

Here we have guys who come from much different backgrounds. They're college-educated. Many of them have wealthy parents and never had to take orders from anyone. Working hard to help them understand the importance and seriousness of what they're facing. Want them to know how it feels to honor and serve our country. For some, they're first generation Americans who hopefully understand what the United States of America stands for and why their parents left other countries to come live here.

These future officers have a pretty tough schedule with lots of hard work and studying. The day begins with four hours of navigation classes that take place in the Bamboo Room. What a contrast from when this was a ritzy hotel; the room used to look down on people dancing. Still have beautiful murals all over the walls, but what goes on in there is so different now.

The guys spend time learning about the mysteries of some of the super-secret bombsights – this time in the grand ballroom where famous opera stars like Grace Moore and Lawrence Tibbett used to give concerts. Pretty special to be learning and teaching in this environment with all the ghosts of the past. Different times in those days.

The course is rigorous. Students are exposed to so much that's intensive and complicated. Good thing these are smart guys. They need to learn aerology, which helps them to better understand how to calculate the best way to bring their plane over the target in good or bad weather. They also get instruction on how to use the new weapon that calculates the trajectory of bombs, given the crosswinds, altitude, and airspeed. More information than this is classified, so it's all I can say about that for now. Another class they take is in learning how to recognize the types and names of various planes. I'm teaching the men lessons in free gunnery, from skeet-shooting to turret gun operation – something that I've specialized in for all my years in the Navy.

The majority of the guys have never been on a boat, so preparing them for ship life and for being on the ocean for months on end is also part of what we need to do. Wish that they didn't have to fight in this war. I can always be hopeful that it'll come to an end soon. Have some nasty enemies out there. Need to be ready for whatever these sailors will face.

Miss the two of you so much. Thinking of your bright smiles and good hearts keeps me going.

Love you both,
Dad

࿇

March 15, 1943

Dear Anna,

Grateful to you for your faithful and loving correspondence. You have no idea what it means to get your letters and know that you're there on the other end of all of this – waiting for me to come home. Keep wishing and hoping that that's going to happen soon.

Can hardly understand when you have the time to sit and write to me the way you do. Don't get me wrong. Definitely appreciate it – just trying to figure out how you fit it in. You have so much going on now with putting in such long hours doing that difficult work.

Pleased that you are also volunteering at the USO with the girls. The packages you put together make a big difference to the men, but when do you get the cleaning and cooking done? Does my honey collapse into bed each night completely exhausted? You never had enough time to get everything you wanted done when you were just at home doing your chores. How are you managing all of this? Still say you shouldn't have to be working. Kills me to think of that. Once this war is over, you will never have to work again.

Baby, I miss you so much. Sometimes I close my eyes and picture your sweet smile. Can only think about what it would be like to hug you and have you back in my arms. When I crawl into bed at night, I lie there and remember how we used to be together, what your body felt like touching mine. Yearn to fall asleep with our legs wrapped around each other. Miss your lips on my skin. Long for your embrace. Life is lonely without you near me. Would say more if it weren't for the censors.

Don't want to get too carried away. Not good for either of us since there's nothing we can do about our distance from each other. Have to keep ourselves on task.

You're the only one I can tell about how ready I am to be home. It wouldn't be right to let anyone else know when my job is to keep up the spirits of this officer student body.

Heard from Mac a few times. He is starting to get better. He's learning to walk with crutches. Said that within the next month or so, they will fit him with a prosthesis for his leg and will help him get used to it. Then he can go home.

His attitude is remarkable. Keeps mentioning how fortunate he is to be alive – how so many of his buddies didn't make it through that last battle. Still, his life will be different in many ways as a result of his injuries and all that he's experienced.

Am sure that Jenny and the kids will be glad to have him home. She'll take good care of him and will nurse him back to his old self – both in body and spirit. He's fortunate to have her. Has she said much to you about how she's doing with all of this? Must be hard for her to think about him like he is now, without a leg and all.

Mentioned in my last letter to you that Albert is here. Hardly know what to say about him. When he's out with the men doing marching drills, he's ruthless. He treats them like hell and is determined to make them into men. He doesn't care that they're book-smart. He acts heartless – brutal, sometimes, and almost inhumane. They must shudder when they see him coming.

When he isn't doing training with the men, he's like a different person. He's jumpy. Last night, I went down to his room to visit – hoping to get him to talk to me.

Had to knock at least four times before he finally answered. When I walked in, there were empty beer bottles and cigarette butts strewn all over the floor. He was in the midst of drinking a beer and didn't offer me one. Was almost as if I wasn't there. Suggested that I help him clean up a bit, and he brushed me off. Tried to convince him to go down to the beach for a walk, but he wasn't budging. When I said something a bit too loud, noticed he seemed alarmed.

Don't know what's going on. Am terribly concerned and wish that there was something I could do. This is not the Albert we know. Couldn't sleep last night thinking about him. Looks like he has a bad case of battle fatigue.

On a happier note, training is beginning to fall into place. Has taken a while for these guys to shed their pampered ways and get accustomed to the routine. Most came with absolutely no discipline, and many were scared and had no idea what was ahead for them. We're breaking the majority of them in and are starting to shape them up. Won't be long before we'll be proud to call them officers.

Must say, though, that a few are still having a rough time – seem to be fearful of what's ahead with this war at full blast. Wait until they embark on their ships and are far from home with big guns and anti-aircraft fire exploding around them. They don't have a clue how they'll be feeling then. Probably better that way. Need to continue working hard with them to ensure that they'll have success in the Navy.

Glad to say that the marching and drills are looking much better. Think they've almost conquered the push-ups, sit-ups, and running. Having the guys do lots of the exercises on the beach. Next mission is to get them to succeed at the obstacle course we've devised out on the golf course. Got to toughen up these boys and get their bodies ready for what's ahead. Also need to help them learn how to make the seamen under them follow orders. Trying to teach by example. Not an easy task.

Must make sure to prepare the sailors for land and sea. Most have never been on a ship before. They're definitely a lot smarter than the average guy on the street and that helps a lot. Majority of these men catch on quickly to anything and everything we present to them. Good news is that they seem eager to work hard and learn whatever they need to know. For their own sakes, they had better.

Sure takes a lot of patience and energy to get them all on target. Am dog-tired each night when I get into bed. Sometimes I barely take my uniform and shoes off before my eyes close.

Don't get me wrong. Feel proud to be a sailor in the United States Navy and am doing all I can to pass along those feelings of honor onto my men. Can't help but think of my brothers who lost their lives in battle for our country. I'm doing it for them and for dear old Pa who led the way when he joined the Navy in 1882.

Sometimes I wonder how Mama can stand it. She always appears strong, never showing us her pain or sadness. Yet it has to be difficult for her to have lost her husband and two of her three sons. Wonder if my being a sailor is a constant reminder – or if living with the reality of their having died while serving in the Navy is enough.

Will look forward to hearing from you in the days to come. Your letters are the bright spot in my day. When I get the mail, I usually wait until later in the evening when all my work is done to read what you've written. I take your letter down to the beach, sit by the water, have a smoke, and open my letter from you. Then I go on the Broadwalk, take a walk, and think about all that you've written to me. At least that way, I can enjoy you in the solitude of my own thoughts.

Can't wait until the day when you are back in my arms. Picture your beautiful brown eyes, long blonde curls, and sweet smile. Want you right here by my side. Get so lonely at times and wish we could see each other for even a day. Maybe I'll get lucky after this and will have a little time off to be with you.

Love,
Hutch

❧

April 10, 1943

Dear Mac,

Glad to hear you are feeling stronger and have received your prosthesis. Bet the adjustment to wearing it is a challenge. Have full confidence in you and know that you'll do what you must in order to walk again. You've never been one to shirk any job. This one may be the toughest of your life! Am picturing you putting up a good fight.

Great news that you're going to be heading home sometime in the near future. You probably can hardly wait to wrap your arms around Jenny and the boys. Hear that little Tommy is the spitting image of you. Smile when I think of that. Heard that Ronnie was drafted into the Army. Hey, Mac, how did that happen? One of yours in the Army and not the Navy? Anna told me that Frankie is hell-bent on someday becoming a doctor. That would be amazing, wouldn't it? A kid of yours going to college. Wow! These college kids are something else – so smart and ready to learn. Frankie always was a bright, curious little boy. He'll fit right in. Good for him.

Amazing training going on here. Teaching the fliers the shortest course to Berlin, Tokyo, and other important locations in all directions. So much more learning happening here than just aerial navigation.

They have begun to do intense tactical radar training at this site, which goes beyond the regular navigation – calling it an elite school. Pretty impressive stuff. Officers have been arriving for this intensive course of study. Heard they have former university professors as well as those from the Battles of the Coral Sea, Midway, and others who are able teachers. Would like to be a part of those special courses, but the Navy has other plans for me.

The course is rigorous. Night time study is from 7:00 p.m. – 10:15 p.m. Then for those who need or want more time, the officers have established "late lights" in different rooms so they can continue to study after taps. Many of the sailors take advantage of that.

No one passes without a grade of 80%. These soon-to-be officers are serious about their studies, so that isn't a problem.

Can tell they're "college" men who are used to hitting the books – not like some of us used to be.

Some are doing actual navigation flights during the day and night. They've got three students plotting one leg each of a long triangular course over water. Lost a few guys already while practicing and learning. Those were tough moments for everyone here. Have to do it though because how else will they learn to take off from their carrier and then return with no landmarks to help them steer their course?

Good news is that the guys do get occasional breaks. Because this place was once a fancy hotel, there are tennis and basketball courts, plus they can play baseball and handball. At least they get that outlet once in a while.

Then on Saturday nights, the men can go to a dance at the nearby country club. Girls come from all over South Florida, so there is a pick of lots of pretty ladies. They're as starving for guys to dance with as the sailors are for someone to hold in their arms. Never go myself. What would I do there? Some of the married men are less faithful, but that's not for me. I just want my Anna.

During this last month of the training course, the guys will get an overnight leave on a Saturday night. That's huge, as you know. Otherwise the rest of the weekends, they can stay out until 1:00 a.m. They need to blow off steam. Got to give them that. They work hard here.

Gave half the company liberty on Saturday. Let loose the sailors all decked out in their summer whites and their "Dixie cups" on their head. Off they went to Miami and Ft. Lauderdale. Suppose I shouldn't have been surprised when most of them came back sporting tattoos. Had to shake my head at the ones with their girlfriends' names, knowing the chance of those girls becoming their forever love is slim at this stage in the game. Best to stick with tattoos of the United States Navy with an anchor behind it or else a heart with Mom on it like mine. It will never lose its meaning. Should have warned them. Never expected that these college-educated sailors would consider tattoos – being as sophisticated as they all are – or so I thought. They'll learn.

Wanted to fill you in on Albert. Anna told me that his family has not heard from him at all. His mom, in her usual fashion, is worried sick. This time I can understand it. Our pal is in bad shape these days. Guess Mary Beth is beside herself. Anna said that when she saw her in church last week, she was a wreck. It's no wonder. They all have to be so concerned about what's going on with him.

Haven't given up on Albert yet, but must say that it is getting harder to watch him like this. Keep trying to talk to him. Was reminiscing with him (actually just me telling him stories) about that time when the three of us played mumblety-peg. Will never forget how the two of you came so close to your foot with your knives and how positive I was that I could do the same and better. Remember my scream when the knife went right into my foot? Stupid kid that I was!

Also was sharing with him about the dances we used to go to at the high school gym. Reminded him of how the girls were lined up on one side, and we were on the other. Once that music started, we made a beeline dash to get the girl we wanted. Then there was that one night when we three ended up walking home with Anna, Jenny, and Mary Beth, and here we are married to them.

Sad part is that I barely got a rise out of Albert, which is pretty frightening. Not sure what to do. Any ideas? Makes me worried for him. Have reported this to the medical personnel. Don't know if they can or will do anything, but someone needs to know.

Take care of yourself and give me the latest update on your health.

> *Thinking of you,*
> *Hutch*

❧

April 26, 1943

Dear Mama,

Wanted to send a quick note to you before things get too hectic here. Have been thinking a lot about you and the sacrifices you have had to make all your life as a result of being a wife and mother to military men. Know it wasn't easy and still isn't. Am sure you worry plenty about what will happen to me with this war going on in so many corners of the world.

Just want to let you know how much I appreciate your prayers and support. Throughout my life, you've taught me the meaning of family love. You have always been the most caring and generous mother. Am blessed to have you as my dear Mama.

It is you who gives courage to Anna to be strong and look at the positive side of things. Sometimes Anna seems to be sad and scared. She tries not to show it, but it seeps into her words on the page without her being aware of it. Not much I can do but reassure her that I will be fine.

Because of the way you raised me, I feel like one of the lucky ones to have my faith – in my religion, in my fellow man, in our country, and in all that we sailors are doing to fight for freedom from fascism.

Deployment will take place within the next two weeks. The ship I will be on is sailing toward South Florida as I write. Should arrive by the beginning of the month. Once it gets stocked and ready, I'll be on my way out into the Atlantic.

When my men took the oath of office, I was on the verge of crying. Since when did I become a softie? Feel confident that once these seamen board their ships, they will do what they have been trained to do and will focus strictly on the task at hand. Praying that this awful war ends soon with the Allied forces as the victors. Want these guys, whom I have grown to care about, to come back home safely to their families and with their heads held high.

Mama, thank you for all you've done to help me be who I am. I like to think that Pa, Edward, and George are looking down on me with pride. Just as they did, I will continue to serve the United States of America with honor as I face this next assignment.

> *With all my love,*
> *I remain your son,*
> *Hutch*

May 3, 1943

Dear Anna,

For these past few months, being on shore and training the men has been my focus. Slowly, I must shift my mind and begin to think about the next stage of this operation – going back on board and heading into battle – to protect the waters, to back up the troops on land, to be all that the Navy is known to be.

I know it is not easy for you to face my leaving, and it isn't for me either. Got used to being in close touch with you and hearing about your daily life. As you know, once at sea, the letters back and forth will be a lot less frequent. Will have to go back to our old way of connecting – looking up at the moon each night at exactly nine o'clock and knowing that you will be looking at the same moon at the same time sending me the same loving thoughts as I will be sending you.

Make sure that the girls stay strong. Please be there for Mama as I know it's never easy for her when I leave for sea. She has been through this so many times during her life between Pa, George, and Edward. She's a brave woman, but still it has to be difficult for her to live with this all over again. She never acts like she's worried, but it would be impossible for her to be anything but concerned. She has lost way too much already in her life.

Heard that Mac has finally arrived home and am so glad about that. Have you seen him yet? Would guess that it's taken a lot of hard work and energy for him to get used to his new leg. If anyone can do it, my money is on Mac. Jenny must be thrilled to have him back with her and the boys. Wish I could have seen that reunion.

Soon it'll be our turn. Hopefully it won't be long before I return to your open arms. After this, I'll be ready to begin living a civilian life. Am looking to be done with my service – almost having thirty years in the United States Navy under my belt. Will be proud to retire and begin a new life where I can wake up by your side each and every day.

Think about that as the days go by. Trust that I'll come back to you and will give you the biggest hug you've ever had – not to mention all the kisses that will follow.

Will write whenever I can and hope that my letters reach you as I hope yours will find their way to me.

Love,
Hutch

CHANGING TIDES

HOLLYWOOD BEACH HOTEL
1960

Sunday, July 3, 1960 3:30 p.m.

At last, we have finally arrived at the Hollywood Beach Hotel. It took us a while at the airport because a piece of our luggage was missing. Donald went to find a skycap to help him look for it while I stayed with the rest of our suitcases. Just as the two of them walked up to where the bags were, someone who had picked up ours by mistake was returning it. What a relief!

I'm not sure what we would have done if that suitcase was lost. It had our underwear, shoes, and bathing suits in it and, most importantly, my birth control pills. Now that my doctor finally feels that the pills are safe enough to take, it would be a disaster if I had to be off them for a week. Donald would not be happy, since he wants to wait at least six more months before I get pregnant. I wouldn't mind if it happened now; however, he has his plan and I don't dare mess with that. On vacation of all times, he would be less than thrilled to wear rubbers. He has never liked using them.

The taxi ride here gave me a chance to enjoy some of Miami's sites. I've always dreamed of seeing palm trees, but they are so much more beautiful in real life than I ever imagined. I'm so happy to be here!

Our room is on the seventh floor and faces the water. We can see the deep blue ocean in either direction. What a spectacular view!

Donald used to come to South Florida with his family as a young child and later as a teenager, therefore he isn't as enchanted with it as I am. He probably thinks I'm crazy with the way I keep gushing over everything.

After we checked in, several people entered the elevator with us. One of the men pushed the buttons as people called out their floor numbers. We were the last ones left on the elevator after it stopped at the lower floors, so when the door opened, we didn't pay attention and got off. We dragged our luggage (I think we packed way too much) to our room and when we got there, our key wouldn't open the door. Donald kept trying and nothing happened. Then I looked up and realized that we were at Room 632 – not 732! We had to make our way back to the elevator and go up one more floor. I couldn't stop laughing. Donald didn't see any humor in the situation. He becomes serious when he focuses on a mission. It's probably how he got to where he is in life.

He's unpacking his suitcase now and, in his typically meticulous way, is putting everything neatly into the beautiful oak chest of drawers. He can't stand to have anything out of place. We are different in that respect. My mess, as he refers to it, bothers him, but I'm content with how I keep my things. Donald is forever telling me to straighten up my drawers. That's how he is about everything in the house. He wants his surroundings to be perfect and is not happy when they aren't. I do the best I can.

When he finishes, we're going down to the beach for a swim. I work much faster than he does. Since I'm done, I am sitting down at the desk facing the ocean where I can write until he's ready.

I started this journal on the plane and hope I'll have lots of time for writing during the week. June bought it for me as a going-away present. I have wanted to get a new one for a long time, so I was really happy when she gave it to me.

It has been a while since I've written in a journal. It's weird how I go in spurts with my writing, but I'm always glad once I start and then am motivated for at least a month or two. My problem is that I generally don't finish them. I have a stack of incomplete journals buried somewhere in my closet.

When I do write, it's usually because I am having a problem. Sometimes when I'm really frustrated and angry with Donald, I pick up my journal and get all my negative feelings out and down onto the page. Once I do that, I generally feel much better – at least until the next time.

Hopefully during our stay here in Florida, I can sort out some issues that have been festering and which seem to be surfacing more often. While we are in transition, this vacation might be a perfect time to reflect and come to some understandings about my life.

But for now, I had better stop writing and put on my bathing suit. Otherwise Donald will be angry if I'm not ready when he wants to go.

6:20 p.m. We walked around and checked out the surroundings. I've never been anywhere as luxurious as this. The large second floor lobby with its shiny terrazzo floors is absolutely dazzling.

Built in the 1920s, the elegant, old world atmosphere remains. Pictures hanging in the halls give me a sense of how it used to be here. I saw men in suits and top hats and fancy women dressed as if they were modeling in a style show. Other pictures show people strolling in the flowering gardens and deluxe cars lined up in front of the hotel.

When we were exploring, I noticed that someone from the hotel put out large baskets filled with fruit on every floor for guests to help themselves. The hotel also serves cookies and tea each day at four o'clock. They don't miss a trick! In fact, I was surprised that we even have a television set in our room. That says something about how fancy this hotel is.

The sign on our bathroom door lists our room rate as sixty dollars per night. That's pretty steep. Donald's parents certainly splurged on their graduation gift for him. Nothing but the best for their son! Where I fit in is something else altogether.

Donald told me that he plans to take one day off this week to play golf at the hotel's course, which is supposed to be quite spectacular. He never asked if I would mind if he played, but then he never does. I clearly have no choice in the matter. Somehow or other, he always manages to do what he wants and rarely asks for my opinion or, heaven forbid, my permission. The same is definitely not true when it comes to what I would like. I always need to ask Donald before I do anything that involves him or our time together.

Since we'll only be in Florida for less than a week, I wanted to be with him the entire time. Now I'm going to have to make the best of every moment we have together during our stay here.

Because Donald will be golfing on Tuesday, I'll have a lot of alone time on that day. No sense in getting all upset about something like him leaving me for five or six hours. Like a lot in my life, so much is out of my control. Once we leave here and move up to Boston, our lives are going to be drastically different than they've been. I have a feeling that I'm often going to be by myself, so I might as well get used to it.

We went out to the beach after we settled into our room. Since I have never seen an ocean in real life, let alone been in one, I was surprised at how salty the water tasted. We didn't go too far out because it came up above my waist when we had only walked a few feet.

I asked Donald if the water is always this deep. He gave me a scientific explanation about how the tides are caused by the gravitational pull among the sun, moon, and earth. He explained that the size of the tide depends on where the sun and moon are in relation to the earth. He also told me that the tide changes and that there are two high tides and two low tides in each twenty-four hour period. Donald knows so much about everything. I'm fascinated with his mind and all that he teaches me. I never knew anything about the tides until today.

We realized that with the rough water and sweeping waves, we weren't going to be able to swim. Instead, Donald and I stood in the water up to my shoulders and talked for a while.

Out of nowhere, he started to get romantic on me. He grabbed me, wrapped his arms around my back, and held me close to him. Next thing I knew, he was kissing me. At first I was embarrassed with all those people around, but he didn't seem to mind. It took no time for me to forget where we were. I was delighted to be in his arms in the middle of the Atlantic Ocean. What a treat! He can be incredibly loving and sweet at times.

We have seven o'clock dinner reservations tonight. When we checked in earlier, the concierge told us there is assigned seating for dinner. That surprised both of us. We don't understand why we have to sit with strangers when we eat. I thought Donald and I would be at a table by ourselves each night and would have romantic meals in the candle-lit grand ballroom. I hope that we will at least meet some nice people as long as we have no choice in this.

Donald has just told me we need to leave for the dining room. I had better stop writing.

11:10 p.m. Wouldn't you know that the couple who sat with us at dinner has two yellow Labradors and three cats

– a calico and two Siamese? As soon as Donald told them that he had just graduated from vet school, they perked up. Most of the conversation from then on centered on their cats and dogs. I guess I had better get used to it since my life is going to be filled with animal stories from now on.

I've never had a pet before and can't wait to finally get one. With my sister Judith allergic to dogs and cats, it was always out of the question. My parents probably wouldn't have wanted one anyway. My mother was never too thrilled about cats and disliked dogs. In fact, she always crossed to the other side of the street when she saw one – even if it was on a leash. My dad is anything but an animal lover. I'm just glad he likes Donald, who loves animals.

I want a small puppy, but Donald won't hear of that. While he likes all dogs, I get the feeling that his least favorites are the little ones. I don't want a big dog and wish he would compromise and get a medium-size one – although that will never happen! In that respect, he is so much like my father. He always has to get his way.

Donald says we'll need to acclimate ourselves to our new life in Boston before we start with a pet. He told me we should wait until I get pregnant, have the baby, and am home every day. He thinks we need more time with a puppy to train it, and that it doesn't make sense to get one while we're both at work. I suppose he knows what's best, but still I am tired of waiting and will probably need the company. I can only imagine that a little puppy would be comforting and loving.

Because I'll be working in the office at the clinic with Donald, his dad, Jeffrey, and Alan -- the whole Friedman clan except for my mother-in-law, thankfully -- I'll be around lots of dogs. Those will be other people's pets, though, and I want my own. That's the least of it. I wish we weren't moving to Boston!

I don't want to think about all of that tonight. There's plenty of time to write about our move this week. For right now, I just want to be on vacation!

Back to this evening. I could tell that the couple sitting with us has a lot of money. Theresa was wearing a huge diamond ring and a broach with smaller diamonds and emeralds — at least it's what I think those green stones were. Vincent, her husband, was wearing cufflinks engraved with a big V and a flashy gold pinkie ring with his initials in diamonds. They both must be about fifteen or twenty years older than we are. He's a trial lawyer and a partner in a large international firm in Manhattan. According to what Theresa said, they are "patrons of the arts," which I would guess means that they must be really rich. Thank goodness, they talked about their pets because I'm not sure we would have had much else to say to them otherwise — not that I did any of the talking. My in-laws probably would have loved them!

Donald is so much better at making conversation than I am — especially after all the wine and other drinks we had. These people can sure hold their liquor. I couldn't keep up with them and neither could Donald. We were both pretty tipsy by the end of dinner.

I listened to how Donald kept the discussion going and wished I could have offered more. Sometimes I find myself feeling inadequate. I was uncomfortable a few times during the night and tried not to show it. I mostly smiled and did my best to be pleasant.

Vincent is a tough, take-charge guy. When the menus came, he told us not to bother looking at them. In fact, he whisked them up into a pile. We had no choice. He insisted that he order for us. I was shocked and not at all happy about it.

My dad used to do that when our family would go out to a Chinese restaurant. I always wanted to get General Chang's Chicken, and he would never let me order it. He would tell the waiter to bring won ton soup, egg rolls, and chicken chow mein – plain and simple. I never did get what I wanted.

Vincent definitely knows how to take over. He made my father, Donald, and my mother-in-law look tame in comparison. When the server came back, Vincent spoke right up and gave him our order. I wasn't sure how Donald felt, but neither of us said anything. Vincent must be ruthless in a courtroom.

Dinner was delicious, although I never would have ordered most of the foods we had. There were a few dishes I could have done without like the jellied strained gumbo and the bouquet of fresh Florida vegetables with a poached egg on top. Oh, and I wasn't thrilled when they brought out the ox tongue either. I passed on that and on the liverwurst.

I'm not used to such elegant dining and unusual foods. We must have had at least seven courses between the supreme of Florida fruit, the prime rib, mashed potatoes, asparagus, Caesar salad, peach brandy cream pie and chocolate fondue, preserved pears, Swiss Gruyere, and sorbet in between courses. I've never eaten so much in my life. They kept the rolls warming at our table in a dish with hot charcoal on the bottom. This is the first time I've ever seen anything like that.

I'll probably gain five pounds this week if I keep eating like I did tonight! Our waiter told us that they hired a new pastry chef and brought him all the way from Switzerland. If the pie was any indication of what's to come, we are in store for some luscious desserts.

They served a different wine with every course. Vincent chose those as well. Before dinner started, he ordered us each a highball, and we finished the evening with brandy on the rocks. It was obvious that he knew exactly what he wanted and didn't consider what we might have preferred.

I found Theresa interesting to observe. She completely let Vincent run the show. The only time she spoke up was when she requested the York ham instead of the ox tongue for the cold service course. It didn't matter anyway because Vincent ignored her and went on ordering. I could tell she wasn't happy about that, but she didn't say a word. It reminded me of how I am.

I need to stop writing. Donald has turned off the television and wants to go to sleep. He doesn't care that I might be in the middle of a thought.

❦

Monday, July 4, 1960 11:30 a.m.

Yesterday when we were talking to the concierge, he had mentioned that the Hollywood Beach Hotel had been used as a naval training center for officers during World War II. I woke up today remembering a dream I had had last night about the sailors who were once here at the hotel. There were all these handsome men walking around decked out in their fancy uniforms decorated with stripes, medals, and ribbons and wearing cool white sailor hats.

What a great fantasy! It must have been the wine that had me dreaming about good-looking men when I have Donald right here at my side.

The hotel delivered a newspaper to our room this morning. How neat is that? Neither of us ever reads the paper, although I'm pretty sure that Donald's parents do. I glanced at the front page and saw an article about how they are hanging the new flag with fifty stars at the United States Capitol for the first time today. That makes me feel patriotic. Happy Birthday, USA!

When Donald called down to the desk earlier to ask for more towels, someone answered and said, "Hello, Dr. Friedman, may I help you?" How can they tell who is in which rooms just by picking up the phone? It surely makes the service we're getting all the more personal and special.

After breakfast, we came down to the pool. Donald is swimming laps now. I've decided to sit out and relax. The morning sun is pretty hot, so I don't know how long I'll last out here considering I'm broiling already. We walked on the Broadwalk earlier. Donald said it reminds him of the way Coney Island looks. There are all kinds of cute souvenir, t-shirt, and clothing shops which I'll go into at some point this week – maybe tomorrow when he goes golfing. We also saw the Hollywood Beach Casino, but it was way too crowded for me to ever want to go there. Thankfully, the pool here at the hotel is perfect for us.

While Donald is busy swimming, I do want to write about the issues that have been simmering regarding my mother-in-law. Perhaps if I get them down on paper, I might be able to sort out my feelings and figure out how to approach some of the things that loom ahead once I get to Boston.

First and foremost, the stuff with Donald's mother makes me miss mine more than ever. While she was alive, I used to talk to her about some of the problems I was having with my mother-in-law. My mother was open to listening and was tremendously supportive of me. Somehow she helped me find solutions to problems and positive ways to look at things, so that in the end I felt better. Because my grandmother wasn't an easy mother-in-law either, my mom could relate like no one else I knew!

Although almost fifteen months have gone by since Mom died, I still think about her each day and wish I could sit across the kitchen table from her and talk like we used to all my life. Maybe if I had been prepared for her death, it would have been easier, but it all happened suddenly. I only wish she had said something to one of us when she first found the lump in her breast. We'll never know how long she had it or what the outcome would have been had she gone to a doctor immediately.

When she finally did go to Dr. Johnson, she was terrified. Even though he insisted on operating immediately, it didn't matter. The cancer had already spread.

I wonder why I'm thinking about all of this now. I never expected to when I sat down and began to write. When Mom first passed away, I wrote about her in my journal for the first several months and then I stopped. Judith, June, and I still discuss her often, but Dad has barely said a word to any of us about her since the funeral. Maybe it was too painful for him, but I never could understand how he held it in. Whenever my sisters or I brought up any mention of Mom, Dad changed the subject. I guess he had to do what worked for him.

The fact that he has been dating Evelyn for a few months now probably takes a lot of his pain away. Even though she was my mother's best friend and someone we've known all our lives, it's still way too awkward for the rest of us to be with her when she's with my dad. It doesn't feel right to see my father holding hands with Evelyn; and I have an especially hard time when I see him kiss her — even if it is only a peck on the cheek. I doubt that I'll ever get used to it.

My sisters and I cannot imagine our father living with anyone but my mother. According to what my dad says, Evelyn wants to wait at least a year to get married since her husband Al died only five months ago. However, it looks like they might not wait that long for my dad to sell his house and move into hers. My skin crawls when I think about that. I am sure it's going to happen one of these days soon. I might as well try and get used to the idea now if I can.

I miss my mother and all of her loving ways. She and I were always close. Thinking about her makes me sad, but it is helpful to write all of this anyway. I am about to...

4:15 p.m. Donald interrupted me earlier because once he was done swimming laps, he wanted to get something to eat right then and there. They served a delicious buffet lunch by the pool. We didn't even have to get dressed and go into the dining room. We stayed out until about two o'clock, and now I have gotten way too much sun for today.

He is amazing with his workouts and loves having the exercise room on the eighth right floor above us. I don't know anyone who sticks to a rigid routine like Donald does. He is obsessed with doing something each day to keep his body in shape. It will be interesting to see if his brothers are like that, too. I'll learn how they are soon enough when I am surrounded by them on a daily basis. In the meantime, exercising is the last thing I would want to do on my vacation or any time, for that matter, but it obviously makes Donald happy.

Tonight we'll see fireworks! I'm glad that Hollywood Beach is having them just a few blocks away. That way, we can sit at the pool to watch and don't have to leave here and fight the crowds.

Fireworks remind me of when I was little and used to go with my parents to the park near High Street each July 4th.

One year when June was about four or five, we ended up leaving because she was so afraid of the booming sounds. Her screams could be heard over the loud, crackling noise of the fireworks. From then on, my mother stayed home with her and Judith, and I went with my dad, Al, Evelyn, and their three boys.

To this day, June still doesn't like loud noises and never goes to see fireworks. I've always been the opposite of her. This is one of my favorite holidays! I enjoy the bright, colorful sparkles spreading across the evening sky – the louder, the better!

10:40 p.m. We got back to our room a few minutes ago. Donald is showering, which means I have a few minutes until he gets out. We sat at the pool tonight with this sweet couple. They're here from Wisconsin on their honeymoon and were super friendly. Carolyn is my age and like me, she works in an office at a university. We both thought that was quite a coincidence. Melvin sells pharmaceuticals, so he and Donald talked about medical stuff.

We enjoyed each other and being with them made watching the fireworks even more fun than usual. I was glad to meet someone our age, since we are stuck with Theresa and Vincent at dinner.

ℰⓈ

Tuesday, July 5, 1960 11:25 a.m.

I just got back to the room after taking a two-mile walk along the shore. On some sections, I ended up walking on a slant, which was not easy to do. Donald has been insistent that if nothing else, I at least walk to keep myself in shape.

When I finished, I took a dip in the ocean to cool off. It turns out that the water was too warm to be refreshing, so I just sat under my umbrella for a while. I was surprised when a girl about my age, who was meandering along on the sand, stopped and talked to me for a few minutes. Later, a man, who had to be at least fifty years old, walked by and asked if I was having a good day. People seem unusually friendly out at the beach.

It is a brutally hot day with no breeze at all. It must be awful out on the golf course. Thank goodness I don't have to be out there. Right now, I'm content to be in my air-conditioned room.

Even though I was upset about Donald going off to play golf, I'm surprised at how much I am enjoying this time to myself. It has been ages since I've been alone with nothing I had to do and no one telling me what to do. Those last few weeks turned out to be incredibly busy at the dental school office. Making sure the grades got posted and all the professors completed their responsibilities before they left for summer break ended up to be a lot of work for me.

I didn't realize how I was going to feel as I wrapped up everything. Since I've been working there for the past four years, and most of my co-workers have been there equally as long, it was difficult to leave them. I had found a niche where I was comfortable. I fit in and felt good about myself. The people I worked with were terrific, especially my sweet boss Dr. Benjamin, who respected me and constantly praised the quality of my work. I enjoyed going into the office every day.

I was touched that the entire office staff took me to lunch and was sad to say goodbye to all the secretaries who have become my friends. I didn't expect to cry, but I did when they gave me the beautiful stationery, a roll of stamps, a paperweight with the Ohio State University logo on it, and those magnificent yellow roses.

I'll stay in touch with all my high school friends as well as with Linda, Patsy, and a few of the others from the office. It surprised me to see how some of them were acting as the time got closer to my leaving. It almost felt as if someone had died. From the time I started there, my co-workers were aware that after graduation, Donald would be going back home to work in his dad's clinic. Yet, they didn't make it easy for me to say goodbye. I figured it would be difficult, but I never expected to feel as sad as I did when I walked out the door for the last time.

I hope that everyone will write letters to me. Maybe we can talk to each other once in a while, but with long distance calls costing so much, Donald probably won't let me spend the money. Aside from talking to his parents when they call every Wednesday night and every other Sunday when we call them, we almost never phone anyone else in other cities.

What worries me now is what it will be like to be living in Boston. I dread working in my father-in-law's office, since I'll be the inexperienced one. The other women will probably think I only got the job because I sleep with the boss's son. I'm feeling nervous about everything and sad to be leaving my place of comfort.

Of course, Donald is delighted to be moving back home. After all, he isn't the one going to a place where there's a mother-in-law who doesn't value or care about him. He's going to be with his family who loves him. On the contrary, I'm facing his mother, who has made it known that she doesn't particularly like me and also that I don't fit in with their family.

From the first day I met her, I've felt like she thought I wasn't good enough for her son. It bothers both his parents *that I don't have a college education. My mother-in-law thinks Donald married beneath his "station in life" and that he should have found someone who could offer her dear son much more than I do. The worst part is that she has been obvious about it all along! At least Donald's father has made a noticeable effort to be sweet to me. He's that kind of guy.*

Donald never seemed to mind that I didn't go to college. For whatever reason, it isn't an issue for him. Unfortunately, my mother-in-law let us know more than once how she feels. Donald shrugs it off. He says I'll do fine and that I should just smile and be happy. Does it even matter to him? Does he ever stop to think about how I feel? I doubt it!

Ever since first meeting her, I've tried to give my mother-in-law the benefit of the doubt and thought it might be me who was being overly sensitive. But the reality is that my family does not meet up her to standards. I hate to think of her as a snob, but that's how she appears.

Writing this brings back a funny memory of what happened the first time Donald brought me home to introduce me to his parents. I knew how important it would be to make a good impression on them. Donald had warned me that his mom was tough. I planned to be on my best behavior and do all I could to win her over.

His father hadn't come home from the office when we got to the house, so I didn't meet him right away. Maybe it would have been better if he had been there to make the conversation a little easier.

Before we arrived, his mother had put out a lovely spread with pastries on a silver platter and nuts and candy in separate little pewter dishes, which she later mentioned had come from one of their European trips. Colorful, bone china tea cups and saucers sat waiting to be used. Big, juicy red grapes were piled in a crystal bowl right next to the pastries.

Since I have no willpower when it comes to any kind of pastry, and especially cheese Danish which she had, it took everything for me to wait and not help myself to one right away. I sat there patiently as we waded our way through the formalities of getting to know each other. Finally, Donald took a handful of nuts. His mom offered me a cup of tea and suggested I eat something. Even though I tried to be "dainty," I gobbled down the Danish in about a minute and then took another one. We hadn't had lunch. I was starving and was tempted to take some of those delicious-looking grapes, too, but I didn't want to look like a pig in front of her.

At some point, Donald excused himself to go to the bathroom and at that same moment, the phone rang. His mom went into the kitchen to answer it. I looked around and saw that there was no one else in sight and quickly grabbed three loose grapes that were lying on top in the bowl. I put one in my mouth and couldn't believe what happened. The grape was plastic! I was horrified imagining if I had done that while Donald's mother was sitting there. Maybe from the start, she thought I was uncultured, but that would have proven it all the more! I can laugh about it now. I told Donald later that night, and we had a great chuckle. He promised not to tell his mother.

I remember when Evelyn and my mom's other friends were planning my wedding shower. Donald's mom said she was going to come to Columbus for it, which I hadn't expected since I didn't think she would consider it important enough to be there. After all, it meant her taking off a day from her charity work.

She arrived the morning of the shower and went right to the hotel where she was staying. Donald borrowed a car from a friend, met his mom there, and then drove her to Evelyn's house where he dropped her off.

I had only been with her a few times before that, so I wasn't sure how she would act. She was friendly enough to everyone but was far from warm and engaging. My mom was terrific and made sure Donald's mother met all her friends. She sat right beside her when we ate, in order to make her feel comfortable. All the while, I got the feeling that my future mother-in-law was looking down on us. My sisters felt the same way, although in all fairness, they might have been influenced by what I had told them prior to their meeting Donald's mother.

I know now that my mother-in-law and her friends would never make a shower in anyone's home. They don't do things like that. For them, entertaining belongs in restaurants and country clubs.

When it was time for the shower in Boston that Donald's aunts made for me, his mother behaved differently. She acted bubbly and exuberant the entire day. It was obvious that she was happy to be with her family and friends who are all college graduates. I got the feeling that she wasn't particularly thrilled to be introducing me, my mom, and my sisters to everyone, but she was on her best behavior.

I must admit that I felt totally out of place at the country club and honestly don't know if I will ever get used to that scene. The women could not have been nicer – each was polite and welcoming. They all seemed to adore Donald and were happy that he had found someone he loves. They treated me kindly and were much more welcoming to me than the way my mother-in-law has acted from the start. For that, I was grateful. My mom and my sisters were a little surprised by the classy, upscale atmosphere of the club. None of us had ever stepped foot into a country club before that day.

Months later at our wedding, my mother-in-law acted terribly. Even Donald was upset with his mother because of her awful attitude. She refused to join Donald's father when he got up and toasted us. Then when Donald and I cut the cake and after when he threw my garter and I tossed my bouquet, I noticed her off in a corner talking to one of her friends. It was obvious that she wasn't interested in any part of the festivities.

She only danced one time all night and that was for the bridal dance when she was called on by the bandleader to dance with her son. For the rest of the evening, she sat at the table with her closest friends and didn't mingle at all. Whenever I looked over at her, I saw a scowl on her face.

Not once the entire evening did she bother to come over to me. In fact, she never said a single word to me at our wedding. I did see her talking to Donald one time, aside from when they were dancing and she was in the spotlight. She made her feelings about us getting married clearly known that night.

It's hard to deal with my mother-in-law, who undoubtedly doesn't like me. I wonder if there will ever be anything I can do that will be good enough for her. I keep trying, but it usually dead-ends into a total flop.

What bothers me is that she has not ever taken the time to get to know me. I can only hope that at some point once I'm living near her and seeing her often, she will make an effort to find out what it is about me that Donald loves. I wish she would realize that I'm a good person with solid values and am someone who cares deeply about others. I would like to have a pleasant relationship with her. Maybe with some luck, that can happen; however, I'm not going to hold my breath.

Needless to say, I'm a wreck inside thinking about living in the same city with that woman. What will it be like when I am with the Friedman family all the time? Are they going *to leave me out and make me feel like I don't belong? Is Donald going to protect me from his mother if she treats me unkindly?*

My sisters think that perhaps his mother is angry at me for taking her son away and might even be jealous because Donald loves me. It's certainly a possibility.

I have to stop making myself crazy and trust that what Donald says is true. He feels certain that once I'm around his family, all of them, including his mother, are going to love me. We'll see about that.

In the meantime, on another subject that I also haven't had the time to write about, I ended up packing everything into boxes and getting ready for the move all by myself. Donald had way too much to do before graduation. He was hardly around during the last two weeks, since he had to take a few finals and finish up in the clinic. Of course, in his typical fashion, he also managed to fit in a few rounds of golf with the guys before they all parted and left for different cities.

Graduation itself was thrilling, even if it was long and tedious. I was excited for Donald to have accomplished his goal. Donald's whole family was there, and they were so proud of him. I could see his parents glowing. Since his brothers had both also graduated from the College of Veterinary Medicine at Ohio State University, they were happy to be back there and were delighted to welcome him into the profession.

My dad had never been to a college graduation until this one and was impressed with Donald achieving all that he has. He didn't seem to mind that the ceremony took several hours.

Donald's family and mine had lunch afterward at the Kahiki, a new Polynesian restaurant that happens to have great food. However, getting our families together is always awkward and stressful because of how my mother-in-law acts toward me and my family. She has that patronizing way about her. Dad doesn't seem to let it bother him, but June and Judith certainly don't like it. Thank goodness someone understands and sees what I know to be true.

Right after graduation and all the activities surrounding it and with Donald's family in town, we only had a few days to complete everything left on our list. Before I knew it, the moving van came and loaded up our stuff. On Saturday after it pulled out of our driveway, we headed to the hotel near the airport where we stayed that night. Our timing was perfect, but I was devastated to leave – not unhappy about coming to Florida – just about leaving Columbus, Ohio, the only place I have ever lived.

Saying goodbye to my family was not easy. My dad, who rarely shows emotion, seemed visibly upset. I think he's going to miss me. He can be difficult and demanding, but I know he loves me. When he hugged me as we were saying goodbye, he said, "Janet, you're going to be fine. Just keep a stiff upper lip."

While all this leaving is hard, what is much worse for me is moving to Boston where I don't know a soul except for Donald's family. There will be so much togetherness with Donald joining his father's practice and me working in the clinic all the time. While that would be enough, the idea of his mother's involvement in our lives makes me nervous.

My mother-in-law chose our apartment for us! I had told Donald that we should go up there and look ourselves. In his usual, controlling way, he was adamant and wouldn't hear of us taking a trip to Boston. He felt sure that his mom could do it and that she would find the right place for us. In the end, Donald and his mother won, as they always do. His mother picked out the place where we are going to live!!!

I have no idea what it will look like except that it has two bedrooms and is on the second floor of a low-rise building with ten apartments in all. It's also only two-and-a-half miles from his parents' home. Does that mean that they'll be stopping by our place all the time? I certainly hope not! The only positive that I can think of so far is that we are allowed to have pets there.

∾

Wednesday, July 6, 1960 8:45 a.m.

Donald decided to go for an early morning run along the beach and then to play some tennis with Vincent. At dinner last night, Vincent challenged Donald to a match. They had been talking about how well they each play, and Vincent bet Donald that he could beat him. I hope Donald wins because the bet was a bit too steep for our pocketbook.

Anyway, I will meet him downstairs in an hour, which gives me a little time before I have to go. I wrote out some postcards for June, Judith, Linda, and Patsy. They'll be jealous when they see where we're staying.

We went down to the beach last night after dinner, took a walk, and sat on the chairs of one of the smaller motels along the Broadwalk. The evening was eerie. There were black, low-hanging clouds, darkening skies, electrical light storms, and thick humidity. It was almost impossible to distinguish the sky from the sea, and we could only tell where the horizon was from the lights on the boats.

We sat there for about an hour talking. During those weeks when we were getting ready to leave Columbus, we had never taken the time to talk to each other about the things that we were doing. So, Donald told me stories about some of the guys from his class, and I told him about what it was like to say goodbye to everyone at work. I have been feeling completely out of touch with him and didn't like how that felt at all. It's one of the reasons why this vacation has been so important to me. I also told Donald a little about my day since he was away for most of it, and, of course, he filled me in on his golf game.

I was surprised and happy yesterday when Carolyn came by. It was around one o'clock, and she wondered if I knew how to play Canasta and whether I wanted to join in a game with two women she had met out by the pool. Since my mom had taught the rules to me and my sisters when we were teenagers, we used to love playing. I was delighted to be asked.

Carolyn remembered that Donald was golfing. Melvin was content lying at the pool, which meant she was free and hoped I would join the game. I didn't need any coaxing.

However, I was glad that I had some time to write before I went downstairs. What I realize whenever I write in my journals is that I'm a much happier person for doing it. I like giving myself the space to think about my feelings and then let them flow from my mind, through my pen, and onto the paper. It often helps to center me. Today, I especially felt relieved to explore the issues I have with my mother-in-law. Somehow writing about them left me feeling a little lighter.

After Carolyn asked me to join her, I wrote a note to Donald, went down by the pool, and ended up staying there for the rest of the afternoon. Annette, one of the women we were playing Canasta with, told us that she had spoken to a few men who have worked at the hotel for years. One of them told her that after the war, this place was purchased by an anti-Semitic gentleman (if you can call him that). Supposedly, some wealthy Jewish people from Washington had wanted to stay here, but they were refused admittance because they were Jews. So, to spite the owner, when it was put up for sale, they bought the place and kept it for a year or two. Then Ben Tobin, a real estate developer, purchased the hotel from them, and now he owns it. I thought that was an interesting and ironic piece of history, but I'm curious as to whether it's true.

When Donald returned from golfing, he immediately came to find me and wanted me to come upstairs with him even though I was in the middle of a Canasta game. I felt funny having to quit, but I knew that I had to go and be with him. He becomes so insistent at times, and this was clearly one of those times.

Had I known how exhausted he was from his long day out in the heat and that he only wanted to sleep, I might have put up a fight and not gone up to our room when he "beckoned" me. I can always dream that I will stand up to him one day!

He is never one to nap, but he decided to lie on the bed and close his eyes for a little while. He wanted me by his side, so I lay down and rested, but I wasn't tired and didn't want to be doing that. It's hard to say no to Donald, though. He gives me that look, and I know I need to do what he asks.

Sometimes being married to Donald reminds me so much of how it was with my parents. My mother never got her way. I wonder if it bothered her as much as it has been frustrating me. My dad always made demands and decisions and didn't let my mom have much of a say in anything.

The only time I saw my father mellow was when my mother was so sick. Then he would sit at her bedside, hold her hand, and make sure she had what she needed. Before that, my mom was always the one caring for and catering to him.

Anyway, back to yesterday. When Donald woke up, he was affectionate and cuddly. Perhaps he felt a little guilty leaving me for the day – although that was most likely my imagination – maybe how I would have felt. To think that Donald even considered me would be unrealistic. Whatever the reason, he started to rub my back and before I knew it, he was undressing me.

While he isn't always the most thoughtful husband in the world, especially when it comes to things he wants to have or wants to do, when we make love he definitely does care about me. He seems as interested in making me happy as he is about ensuring that he is satisfied. He's always been that way and for that, I am most grateful.

We ended up having some steamy sex. He was in such a loving mood and at first was only concerned about getting me all hot and bothered. He started kissing me on my neck, over my breasts, and slowly worked his way down my body.

Do I dare to write all of this? What if someone were to read it? Donald would be horrified if he ever knew I was describing our lovemaking. He would probably demand that I never write in a journal again. Somehow, though, part of the fun is the thrill of putting things down on paper that would be frowned upon by another. It's like my own secret with myself.

When I was about twelve years old, I had a pink plastic diary that had on its cover a girl with pigtails and a poodle on her skirt. She was talking on the phone. The diary had a lock on it, so I always felt secure knowing that no one could open it. I kept the diary between my mattress and box springs. At night after my sisters went to sleep, I would take it out to write in it. They never seemed bothered by the light. What I didn't realize was that June wasn't always sleeping when I thought she was. She must have seen me writing in my diary.

One day, I noticed that it was not in the exact spot where I had left it. When I took it out, I saw that the lock had been broken. Days later after I was at my wit's end trying to figure out who had violated my privacy and opened it, June confessed that she had taken a bobby pin, picked the lock, and read what I had written.

It took me years after that to feel safe writing in a journal again – not that there had been anything too earth-shattering in the one June had read. I wasn't a teenager yet, so what could I possibly have written that would have mattered much?

When Donald and I got married, I spoke to him about respecting my privacy, and he swore that he would not pry and would never open my journals. I completely trust him and don't think he would read what I've written; however, every once in a while this week, he has asked me what I'm writing about. For sure he would not be happy if he knew that I was writing about how angry I get at him and his bossy ways or even about his mother, for that matter.

5:00 p.m. Donald decided that he wants to go to see "Psycho" a movie that came out last month. Patsy had seen it and mentioned to me that it's pretty scary. I don't like those kinds of movies. As usual, though, Donald didn't give me a choice. He told me he was going to ask Carolyn and Melvin if they want to join us. I hope they do because I like them a lot, and if we're with them, I won't be as upset about going.

We had a great day today at the beach, although it was extremely hot. There were beautiful blue skies, gentle breezes, fluffy, white clouds sitting way out over the horizon, and mobs of people enjoying the day in the best possible spot around. I liked watching a sailing regatta out at the sea. The colorful, striped sailboats glided along the water right in front of us. One couldn't ask for more exquisite scenery.

Then the strangest thing happened. We were sitting down by the water, and I looked up and saw a big, dark thing being washed ashore. Within minutes, a crowd gathered to watch the unusual invasion of an octopus. A few men tried to drag it back into the water, but it seemed to instantly react to being touched. A huge circle of blackish-brown bubbles from the octopus surrounded it. I suppose the octopus didn't like people messing with it. This was the first time I had ever seen an octopus and was fascinated watching it struggle for its freedom. Eventually, the tide took it back out into the ocean.

Donald just told me I need to start getting dressed for dinner. I thought I had more time, but he never likes to be a second late. Tonight is the fancy dinner of the week when everyone dresses in formal evening gowns and tuxedos. I'm sure I'll feel like we're at some special banquet. So far, this place is amazing with the finest dishes, silverware, and linens I've ever laid my eyes on. The service is impeccable. What a wonderful place to be! I'm being treated like a queen.

Thursday, July 7, 1960 2:35 a.m.

I cannot believe how absolutely furious I am. I thought I could sleep, but that isn't happening. I don't know where to start. I'm sick of the way Donald treats me. It is as if he is the only one who matters in our relationship! I don't understand how he can feel like it is always okay to be the one to make all the decisions. He never gives me a chance. I hate that about him!

At dinner, Vincent told Donald that he needs to even up the score. Vincent was not at all happy about Donald beating him at tennis. Without any warning, he turned to Donald and told him that they had a date in the morning. He had already arranged a golf match with a tee time at ten o'clock.

I could hardly believe my ears! Donald and I had decided that we were going to do some sightseeing – go down to the Miami Seaquarium and then out to dinner someplace on Miami Beach. Within minutes, those plans went out the window. Instead Donald quickly took up Vincent's challenge and agreed to play golf – as if he and I never had made plans to spend the day together.

I was speechless and felt my blood immediately begin to boil. After all, we are leaving at noon on Friday. This was going to be our last full day here.

Based on what Carolyn has told me about the way Melvin is, I am sure that he would have been considerate and would have asked her if she'd mind if he went. Actually, now that I think about it, he probably would have refused to go altogether. That's what a kind and thoughtful husband would do. But not mine! No, he does what he wants and doesn't think twice about anyone else – namely me.

I'm fine when Donald isn't around, but that isn't the issue. It's just that we don't get that much time together, and we did have plans, after all. What bothers me is that Donald makes all the rules - that he is the one who decides what we do. He is never happy unless he's the boss. I don't need to be in charge, but I would like it if once in a while he would ask me what I wanted to do or what I would like to eat or what movie I would like to see. Since I have always given in to his every demand, I wonder how it would be if I ever tried to stand up to him.

Anyway, back to earlier tonight. After that fiasco at dinner, I was furious and would have loved to have gone upstairs and screamed at Donald. That's a fantasy, but I was raging inside. But no, he had made plans. We were going to the movies - like it or not. Thankfully, we were with Carolyn and Melvin.

I did my best not to act angry and to have a good time, which we seem to do when we're with them. They laugh a lot – much more than Donald and I ever do. But I'm way too furious now to write about that.

After the movie, which was frightening (but I must admit quite well done), Donald decided he wanted ice cream. He stopped and asked everyone he saw coming out of the movie theater if they knew of a good ice cream parlor. He was persistent – the way he always gets when he makes up his mind about anything. Tonight it was ice cream. Another night it could be a steak or watching a game on television or anything that strikes his fancy. He is a man who knows what he wants, what makes him happy, and what he has to do to get his way. He doesn't think about anyone else the majority of time. This aggravates the hell out of me.

The rest of us would have been content to get a cup of coffee at the restaurant nearby since we had had such a huge dinner, but no, not Donald. He wanted ice cream! We ended up taking a cab all the way to Dania, which is the next town over, so we could go to Jaxson's, the place that a few different people had recommended. Granted, it was adorable with all kinds of eclectic collectors' items like old license plates and street signs. Plus they had an assortment of great candy and stuffed animals for sale and served popcorn and hugely obscene portions of delicious ice cream.

Once we were there, even though I was steaming inside, I made up my mind to focus on enjoying myself. I would have enjoyed it much more had Donald been considerate of the three of us from the start. Carolyn and Melvin went along for the ride. They are the best-natured people and didn't seem upset at all. Of course, compared to Donald at this point, anyone would be easy!

I couldn't wait to get back to our room. It took everything I had to act normal and not start anything in front of Carolyn and Melvin. I would never want to do that! My mother always told me not to air my dirty laundry in public. She never shared any of her problems with her friends and let me know that it's better that way.

As soon as we got to our room, I went into the bathroom, brushed my teeth, and got ready for bed. I didn't say a word, but I was fuming. Donald was unaware and didn't even notice. Instead, when I came out of the bathroom, he was on the bed, lights turned low, and stripped down to his boxers with a hard-on. He was waiting for me and was all ready to make love. He had only that on his mind. What was he thinking and why didn't he get it? I sometimes wonder what world he is living in.

I told him I had a headache and got into bed and rolled over to the edge of my side of the bed. He slid over to me and put his arms around me with his erection practically sticking into my back. There was no way I would respond. He tried to sweet-talk me, and I told him I wasn't in the mood and to leave me alone. He turned over in a huff, and before I knew it, he was sleeping soundly.

That was hours ago, and I'm still up stewing over all of this. I stayed in bed for a long time, but I finally decided to go into the bathroom, turn on the light, and write.

I'm not sure what I can or should do about how I'm feeling. I don't want to start a fight with only a little over a day left of our vacation. I would never win anyway. Somehow he always manages to get the last word in and browbeats me into agreeing. It is maddening, but he's much better at this than I am.

I wish I had someone I could talk to who could help me figure out what to do. Thank goodness, I can at least write in here. Still, I don't know how I'll feel in the morning. For now, I need to try and get some sleep.

1:40 p.m. I've been spending the day at the beach with Carolyn. She has gone up to her room to get the book To Kill a Mockingbird that she wants to give me, since she thinks it is worthwhile reading. I'm content to be out here by the water.

I barely slept last night. The last time I looked at the clock, it read 4:26. When I did finally fall asleep, I had quite a dream. I was standing on a ladder above Donald. I had a big bucket of muddy-looking brown paint in my hand. I looked down, told him I was done taking his shit, and poured the paint right onto his head. He stood there and looked up at me with the paint dripping from his face, down his neck, and all over his clothes. He was in shock.

Right at that moment, Donald woke me up. He was as sweet as can be – as if nothing had happened last night. Of course, maybe he never realized that I was angry with him. He often sees only what he wants.

When I thought about my dream, I smiled to myself, remembering how great it had felt to pour the paint on him. For once, I had had the upper hand. I started to think about all that I have kept inside and would love to say to Donald. I would be happy if just once he would listen to me and do what I want.

Meanwhile, I am walking around feeling angry. I am sick of trying to please him. Throughout my life, I have been like this – always doing for others – considering everyone else and not putting myself first. I sure as hell hope that one day I will be strong enough to stand up for myself. Is it too much to wish that something would be different for me?

As a child, I did whatever my dad wanted me to do. It was always important to me that he approved of my behavior. I wanted to make him happy. Now I realize that I've carried this over into my marriage. Suddenly, it's beginning to become clearer to me.

I must begin examining my actions in all of this. I am letting Donald get away with too much. What could I be doing that might have an impact – that might change things? Perhaps the next time he tries to tell me what to do, instead of letting him get his way, I will stand up to him. It might be worth a try. How would he respond? What could he possibly do to me? My dream of pouring the paint on him might be a sign of something good to come.

Before Carolyn comes downstairs, I want to write about what happened this morning when I was down by the water's edge. As I meandered along being soothed by the waves lapping onto the shore, I noticed a woman whom I had seen pass by me a few times this week.

She stopped to show me a beautiful shell she had found. She told me it was a whelk and asked me if I would like it. I was surprised by her generosity and gladly accepted. I've found a few special shells since I've been here, but none as lovely or intact as this one.

As we talked, she stood with her back to the ocean and was blocking the sun for me with her wide-brim hat. It almost looked as if a halo had formed around her. Something about that struck me.

She started to ask me questions about where I was from and if I was on vacation. Then she wanted to know if I had a family. The next thing I knew, without my even asking, she began to tell me her story.

I understand that people sometimes end up telling strangers things they might never say to those they know. I just wasn't expecting this woman to open up in the way that she did.

She began by showing me the tattoo of faded blue numbers on her arm. I had seen them on Mr. Schwartzman, the butcher, and also on Grandma's friend Mrs. Goldstein's arm, but I never looked at them closely and would never have asked them about it.

"Even though I'm not Jewish, I was in a concentration camp —Auschwitz," she explained. "Soldiers broke into our home and found the Jewish child my parents were hiding. They ended up taking my entire family. I was only fourteen years old and was tortured mercilessly. In the camp, I carried sacks of potatoes on my back for hours. Our daily meal consisted of one piece of bread with the wheat shafts still in it and an awful drink called 'ersatz,' which vaguely resembled coffee.

"My aristocratic father, single heir to a textile dynasty, lost everything to the Nazis during the war. We went from riches to rags in a matter of moments. Much of my family was killed, including my parents and siblings. I ended up having no one – not even my friends from my hometown."

She continued, "Years later after I survived the terror and torture of the Holocaust, I migrated to the United States. I was alone and wanted to begin a new life.

"I eventually married an extraordinarily wealthy man. We had five homes around the world and lots of money. One day I came home and found my husband in bed with another woman. As soon as I saw that, my hurt feelings took over. I stormed out, leaving for good, and took off for Florida. I arrived in Miami with only $33."

She was alone, without anyone to turn to for comfort. She explained to me how she began to pray out of desperation. Although she didn't know to whom she was praying, at some point things began to come together for her.

"I found my faith when I found God. My life changed as a result of understanding that I was not alone. I was no longer a ship without a sail."

We talked about the ocean and how her walks along the shore are healing. I was moved by her resilience and the strength of her spirit. She is a gifted singer, and this weekend is her debut in a small side room in the Deauville on Miami Beach.

We had been talking for about a half hour when Carolyn came to join me. As she approached us, the woman said goodbye and took off. I never learned her name.

I couldn't wait to tell Carolyn. She probably would have thought I made up the story had she not seen me talking to the lady.

After everything this woman had experienced and shared with me, I was inspired by her words. I understand how her strong belief in a higher power has made a difference in her life.

And more importantly, what I realized after listening to her is how her inner strength led her to be independent and to take care of herself. Also, I was particularly struck by how she was positive and grateful in the face of all that she endured.

One of the things I'm left with is how minimal my problems are in comparison to this stranger's. Her story is one that I'm going to remember. After all, at such a young age, she lost her entire family and then later, her husband. Yet, she found a way to pick up the pieces and forge ahead.

10:40 p.m. When Donald came back from playing golf today, I could tell that he was upset. From what he said, Vincent had been a bear. It appears that he is extremely competitive, and right from the beginning of the day, he let Donald know that he intended to win.

It was hot on the golf course and by noon, Donald wanted to stop and get a drink. Not only would Vincent not take a break then, but he also refused to go for lunch later. He was on a roll and only cared about winning. By the time they finished, Donald was starving, thirsty, and although he played a good game, had lost to Vincent – who only then began to gloat. Donald said it was a miserable day. Vincent had totally taken charge.

I listened. It occurred to me that since meeting Vincent, this is probably the first time in Donald's life (except maybe with his mother) that Donald wasn't the one in control.

We began to talk about what we were going to do for dinner. Although we hadn't explored Miami and done what we had planned, we were at least going to go out to eat this evening. All I could think about was the craving I had for Chinese food. Donald said he was thinking he would like Italian.

I couldn't believe what came out of my mouth next. "We always do what you want. This time I'd like to do what I want."

Silence.

Although he was taken aback and didn't say much in the end, we wound up at House of Won, and I had General Chang's Chicken for dinner. I anxiously anticipated having to "pay" for getting my way, but Donald was just fine and we had a wonderful evening.

There's hope.

IN SERVICE OF
FLORIDA BIBLE COLLEGE
1973 - 1974

September 1973

As I lie in bed, I can tell by Christy's breathing that she has fallen asleep. Cathleen is still awake and about ready to climb into bed. I hope to get to sleep soon myself because it has been a long day. My mind won't shut off tonight. I hate when that happens.

"Margaret, are you up?" whispers Cathleen, as she bends down to crawl into her bottom bunk across from me.

"Yes. I was lying here wondering if I will ever sleep tonight. My mind is going in all directions," I quietly answer.

Cathleen then confesses, "I hate to do this to you, but I really need to talk. Would you be okay staying up with me for a little while? We can go out in the hall, so we won't wake up Christy."

"Let me put on a robe and I'm ready."

Christy hangs her head down over her bunk bed and interjects, "Hey, please don't leave me out of this."

We have been roommates for only a couple of weeks and are slowly beginning to feel more comfortable sharing and learning about each other. While it has been a bit of an adjustment for each of us to be away from home in a new environment, having one another to talk to is making a big difference.

Cathleen begins speaking to us and immediately gets into her family issues. "This afternoon I received a letter from my brother Ken. It's the first time anyone in my family has written to me since I've been here. Ken wanted me to know that my father has gotten himself into some serious trouble. For many years, he's been going out at night to play cards. Lately, he has been on a terrible losing streak. One thing has led to the next, and now he is about to lose his business. From what Ken says, my father has accumulated about $17,500 in debts.

"Ken only knows all of this because he started working for my father a few years ago. They're in the trucking business, and things were supposedly going well for them for a while. Now there is a crisis. If my father doesn't get enough money to pay off what he owes, he could go under and that would mean Ken would lose his job, too. Ken is convinced that my father continues to gamble in order to make money to pay off his debts, even though that's how he got into trouble to begin with. It sounds like he is far from being on the winning end at the moment."

I know Cathleen is one of six children - three sisters and two brothers and that she is the second youngest, but I have no idea what her family is like. Being an only child, I can't relate to how it must be to live in a house filled with others all around the same age.

I had created my own fantasy about what went on in their home. I had imagined the fun that must have taken place – always having a sister nearby to gab with or someone to help her get dressed for a date. I had pictured their family sitting around a big table, joining together in prayer before they eat and enjoying a lively discussion during the meal. I had assumed that their house would be filled with laughter and lots of joy. I had envisioned her parents spending most of their time going from one child to the next, helping them with homework, listening to stories about their friends and school days, and being completely involved in each of their children's lives.

I had also imagined that her older siblings were always watching out for their younger sisters' best interests. Her brothers probably also had lots of good-looking friends who would come over to their house, which would add to the excitement.

Living with only my mother is such a contrast to what Cathleen's family must be like. I've always dreamed of not only having a father who cared about me but also siblings who would be company for me. Unfortunately, neither of those things will ever happen. There is a part of me that wishes I had been born into a big family like that.

I suddenly realize that I have drifted off into my own thoughts and have stopped listening to Cathleen. I immediately shift my focus back to her.

"It's so hard to say all this out loud to the two of you, but I honestly can't keep it in. I've been beside myself since I received the letter and knew that I would not be able to sleep if I didn't tell you what's happening. I'm embarrassed and feel funny about exposing my family's issues and problems to both of you. I hope you aren't going to think I'm awful for telling you all of this. There's still so much more I want to say and not any of it is pretty. In fact, I'm ashamed of it all."

Cathleen's voice quivered as she spoke. I could tell that it was incredibly difficult for her to confide in us, and yet, she had to tell someone before she fell apart. I couldn't imagine ever sharing something like what she had told us with anyone, but then again, I've never had anything at all like this in my life.

"My mother has no idea what's going on. She's been an alcoholic for as long as I can remember. Through the years, I've found bottles hidden under her bed, behind the couch, and in the linen closet. She has at least a few Cokes every night, but I also figure she must add alcohol to her glass because she never lets any of us take a sip. She smells of liquor whenever I'm near her.

"I would come home from school in the afternoon, and my mother would always be upstairs sound asleep in her room with the drapes drawn. If we dared wake her, we'd be in serious trouble.

"For most of my life, my brothers, sisters, and I were pretty much on our own. Luckily, I'm one of the youngest in my family, so my older siblings took care of me. They were more like parents to me than my own parents were. My dad was always working or out with the guys at night. My mom was pretty emotionally deadened as a result of her drinking."

I notice that Cathleen seems to be getting more upset as she talks to us. The sadness in her eyes and the pained expression on her face shows me how difficult this is for her. Yet, she goes on with her story.

"Since I'm away from all of that and in a completely different environment, I can see what a free-for-all it was living in my house. Sadly, my mother didn't pay much attention to what any of us did. I never felt that she was concerned about me. She was anything but a devoted, caring mother like I had always wished for. She didn't show up for school conferences with my teachers and never came to any of my programs or plays. Neither of my parents went to my brothers' sports games either. They didn't seem to care.

"My parents would be furious with me if they knew what I've said about them. But what I'm going to say next is much worse. I keep asking myself if I should be revealing this to the two of you. I hope and pray that you don't think I'm a terrible person once I tell you the rest."

"We're here for you," I reassure Cathleen. "And we are grateful that you feel safe enough to share with us. Please know that what you say will stay in this room. Understand that you can trust me and Christy. The Lord is here with you as well."

Christy then adds, "Cathleen, thank you for being brave enough to open your heart to us. What courage it took to say what you have so far."

Cathleen thanks us and goes on, "Before I came here, I was completely the opposite of who I am now. I would never be where I am tonight if it weren't for Betty Sue, who was in my English class at Lincoln High School. She was the one who invited me to go with her to the Christian Youth Ranch at the beginning of the second semester of my senior year. You know Betty Sue, the one who lives on the sixth floor, right?"

We both nod. Cathleen continues with her story.

"Starting in about tenth grade, I totally got into the drug scene. It was pretty much a given in my house. My sister Trudy was the first one who introduced me to pot. We were in our backyard when she pulled out a joint and offered it to me. She and I giggled the afternoon away and then went inside and raided the refrigerator.

"Not long after that, my sister Diane joined us. Later on, I learned that she was the one who always had the drug anyone wanted and was, in fact, dealing drugs; she might still be. Diane and her friends walk around stoned most of the time. They are all hippies and constantly talk about free love, peace, and ending the war.

"Richard was a little more subtle about being high in front of me. I guess he always felt like he was the big brother and maybe didn't want to be responsible for my downfall. It took him a while to catch on that I was right in there with Trudy and Diane."

I don't know anyone who did drugs in my school. Maybe I'm naïve, but what Cathleen is talking about now is all new to me.

"Ken was the outsider from the start. He did not and still doesn't do drugs. He and my little sister Tracy are the good ones in the bunch. She's only in ninth grade and hopefully will not go down that path of self-destruction. I'm working on her and trying to lead her to the Lord. Richard, Trudy, and Diane are pretty much wasted all the time and barely make it to work each day. All of my siblings are still living at home.

"Ken also told me that Richard got his notice to report to the Army. That will shape him up, and now he's going to have to clean up his act. But Richard says that if they do a drug test, he'll fail and then what? Will they still make him go? Will he be in trouble? With the war in Vietnam going on, I don't see how he can get out of it. The service will probably be the best thing for him in the long run. Still, it's scary to think of him out there in battle. I worry because so many of our troops are getting killed. This war frightens me.

"Anyway, my parents were and continue to be totally clueless about anyone in our family doing drugs. My mother is too drunk to notice, and my father is never around. We're on our own for everything.

"Until I found the Lord, my savior truly was Betty Sue. She always had a peaceful, almost blissful look about her. All I knew was that she seemed to like me and kept trying to get me to go with her to Ranch where she went each week. The first time I went, I had gotten high before leaving my house. I had no idea what a Youth Ranch was or exactly where we were going. I never bothered to ask her. I thought we might end up riding some horses. Whoa! Was I ever wrong about that!"

A thought crossed my mind as I remembered my experiences at the Youth Ranch. I quickly let it go and continued listening to Cathleen's story.

"The first thing I noticed was that everyone seemed friendly and upbeat. When they started singing, they all appeared to be filled with joy. I sat and watched. There were people up front playing the guitar and singing Christian songs, while those of us on the floor clapped to the music and sang along. This was all new to me.

"Someone told us about the gospel of Salvation and how we could know that when we died, we would go to Heaven. My parents were not into going to church, and religion was never mentioned in our house, so this was all new to me. Bible stories weren't something we heard in our family. They never read anything to us when we were little. In fact, the only stories that were ever read to me were by my teachers in elementary school."

As I sit listening to Cathleen, I am struck by how different our lives were. Attending church and Ranch was such a huge part of my week. It's hard to imagine all my junior and high school years without either of them in it.

"That evening at Ranch was so much fun. I thought I might be enjoying it because everything I did when I was high was great, but when I went back the next week without getting stoned first, I was even happier. The rest of that week, I chose not to smoke pot. I started talking more and more to Betty Sue. She shared the good news of Jesus Christ and discipled me in my growing from a newborn babe in Christ. Within a month, everything had changed for me.

"No longer was I interested in anything that was going on with my siblings and their drugs. They kept trying to entice me to get high, but by then I understood another way to experience happiness. I knew that Christ had died for my sins; it all made sense to me. I was moving on and far away from my life filled with drugs.

"June came around and I graduated from high school. By that time, I already felt sure that I wanted to come to Florida Bible College here in Hollywood. Prior to that, I had thought about going to college somewhere but never filled out the necessary applications to get into any school. It's funny how things work out. Jesus was watching over me, and I didn't know it.

"Betty Sue was going to the two-week summer camp here at Florida Bible College and then the one-week of school orientation following the camp. I wasn't sure what I was going to do. I only knew that somehow I hoped to get into the college. I had no idea how I could pull it off.

"One day I went over to Betty Sue's house and her dad, who's a pastor, and her mom spent time talking to me. I couldn't get over how loving and caring they were to her and also to me, who was a stranger to them. I had never felt that tended to at anyone's home before – and definitely not in my own house.

"Her parents told me they would help with the paperwork and encouraged me to fill it out and send it in. Her mother addressed an envelope to Florida Bible College and put a stamp on it. They felt sure that I would be accepted to the school based on my high school grades.

"Then they let me know there was a bus that would take everyone to South Florida for the summer camp, but since Betty Sue was going to stay there for college, her father planned to drive her down. They offered to give me a ride and let me know that if I went with them, I could pack more of what I wanted to bring with me. Her parents also said that they would help me find a job to pay for my tuition. It all sounded too good to be true. No one had ever been that kind to me.

"After they did that, Betty Sue's father called the school and made arrangements for me to attend the camp. Not only that, he also assured me that based on his conversation with the dean of the school, I would be accepted to Florida Bible College for the fall semester.

"Anyway, that was the day I knew I would be moving out of my house forever and would be leading another life. By that time, I was thinking that I would like to go into the ministry. I believed in my heart that I could make a difference in someone else's life. I had already started to help Tracy, as I had mentioned earlier, and felt good about that.

"I left Betty Sue's at the end of that day and went home to talk to my mother and father. My parents didn't care one way or the other what I did with my life. They never had any religious upbringing, and they didn't give us any. My mother's religion is her alcohol, and my father's is his gambling. That hasn't changed.

"While I was happy that I made up my mind, I felt sad when I left knowing it didn't much matter to my parents whether I was here or at home. There were no tearful goodbyes and no wishing me well. My father wasn't even home when Betty Sue and her parents came to pick me up. Ken and my sister Tracy were the only two in my family who even let me know that they were going to miss me."

Christy climbs down from her bunk and puts her arms around Cathleen. I sit and watch as Cathleen breaks down and cries. Christy embraces her. I get out of bed and go over to join them. I suggest that we pray for Cathleen and for all of those in her family who are in trouble.

After praying, I can see that Cathleen feels better. She tells us that she is exhausted, so we decide to go to sleep and talk more in the morning.

It is impossible for me to sleep after hearing all that. If I thought my mind wouldn't shut off before, forget it now. In contrast to Cathleen's life, I feel grateful for mine and for the wonderful mother I have. She has always been my support and has given me an abundance of love.

When my father disappeared off the face of this earth, we didn't know if he was dead or alive. I was ten years old at the time and kept worrying about him, and if he had died, where he had gone. I kept asking my mom if he was in Heaven and then began to wonder where I would go if I died.

Luckily, my mother was a Christian who had all the answers. She helped me to understand how the death of Jesus provides a payment for man's sins and makes eternal life available as a gift to those who believe. Once I understood that and knew I would go to Heaven, everything made sense to me.

My mother chooses to believe that my father died and is in Heaven as well. It is the only way she can experience serenity. If she is at peace, than so am I.

After going to church every Sunday and attending Youth Ranch, coming here was natural for me. My mother was sad to see me go, but she is happy to know that I am here where I am learning the Word of God. She knows that what I want in my life is to marry a godly man who is dedicated to following the Lord. How blessed I am that she understands my love of Jesus and supports my desire to find the right man to marry.

Christy also found out about Florida Bible College through Youth Ranch. The one she attended was in Tampa near her friend's neighborhood. Her family belongs to a Lutheran church and when they heard that she wanted to come to college here, they were not at all pleased with her decision. Since her parents are Florida State alumni, they wanted her to go there. Christy had a big falling out with them. Finally after a really painful time, they agreed to let her go where she wanted. The one thing her parents insisted on, since she decided not to go to FSU, was that she would have to pay all of her tuition and living expenses. She was totally on her own in that department.

When we first met, she told us that she doesn't care about that. She is happy to work like the rest of us and only dreams of one day becoming a foreign missionary. I feel sure she will make that happen based on the kind of person she is.

We three came from such different paths, but they all led us down the same road. I believe we are here for a reason. My hope is that by the time we graduate, we will be able to go out into the world and spread the Word of God's gift of eternal life.

❧

October 1973

Christy comes into our room all excited. There was a message for her on the message board downstairs near the mailboxes. It was from Doug and read, "Will you meet me in the second floor lobby at noon tomorrow after classes?"

"He actually wants to talk to me! How is this possible? I have wanted him to pay attention to me since I first saw him in Chapel on the second day of classes. Finally he has made contact!" Christy exclaims with glee in her voice. "What should I write back to him? Any ideas?"

"How about, 'Let's have emotions. I mean devotions.'" I suggest.

Cathleen groans, "Margaret, how can you joke about that? This is serious. It's Christy's golden opportunity to snatch up Doug. She needs to say something clever like, 'Sure, how about meeting me by the secret door?' There's a chance that might get him thinking."

"Oh my," Christy answers. "What if that door leads to some mysterious place? I never would have known about it had Marianne not pointed out the door to me last week. Now I'm especially curious. We need to find out if anyone has ever opened it and gone in. Anyway, that's a great thing to reply. Thanks!"

Cathleen then starts to talk about a few of the freshmen boys. "Did you hear that Fred and Robert have asked out girls from the Hollywood Youth Ranch? Those high school seniors are definitely interfering with our chances of getting guys. They need to stop flirting with our boys and stick to their own."

I respond, "Cathleen, there are enough guys to go around. We just have to make ourselves a bit more obvious and available.

"I hear that Rosemary down the hall has a date to go to the beach with Peter next Saturday. He told her that if the weather is nice and if there are decent waves, he'll teach her how to surf. Wouldn't that be neat?

"Personally, I'm looking to find a way to get Paul's attention. He talked to me the other day before Hermeneutics class. He asked me if I understood Luke 24:25-27, which we were supposed to have studied the night before. I wasn't completely positive that I did, although I sure tried everything I could to make it sound like I knew what it all meant.

"I have been thinking of what I might say to him to get a conversation going tomorrow when I see him in class. Maybe I could ask him if he could explain Peter 1:20-21. Do you think that would work?"

"Anything is worth a try," Christy replies as she busies herself writing her message response. Within a minute, she is out the door and on her way to post it on the board.

As soon as she leaves, Cathleen announces, "I need to get my uniform on and leave soon. I'm going to be working the late shift tonight, which means I probably won't be home until at least 11:15. I'll leave my books and my pajamas on my bed. That way when I come in, if you and Christy are sleeping, I can quietly change and go out into the hall to study."

"I doubt that I'll be asleep," I tell her. "I have so much to read for World Religion class, plus I'm already lost in Old Testament Survey and want to see if I can get a grasp on what we did in class this week. Languages were never my thing, and I'm definitely struggling with this one. It feels as if I might never get it, but I understand that I need to have faith and know it will all come to me eventually."

Cathleen comments, "You'll do fine, Margaret. You have your intentions in the right place, and you're smarter than Christy and I."

"Thanks, but that's so not true," I claim.

"I'm going to take some of my reading to do in case I get a break at the hotel. Every once in a while when I've finished turning down all the beds and getting the rooms ready for the night, I go into this small maid's quarters that the Diplomat provides and do a little studying. I hear that we'll never have time to do anything but work once the season begins. They say it gets real busy at the hotel then," Cathleen explains.

"I'm kind of looking forward to it, though, because I also heard that it becomes pretty exciting around there. I understand that lots of famous people entertain at the hotel. I'll never get to go to any of those shows, but I do love the idea that I might meet someone who's a star. Maybe I'll clean one of their rooms. Wouldn't that be so cool?

"I need to stop talking and get out of here. I don't want to be late, and unless I leave now, I will be."

Cathleen leaves and Christy returns. Out of breath, she zestfully shrieks, "You will never guess who I saw on the elevator when I was going downstairs! DOUG!!! I got all flustered and felt my face turning beet red. I hid the note in my hand because it would have been embarrassing for him to see me with it. I stood speechless for at least a minute. Doug said hello first and since he was with Roger, that guy from our Personal Evangelism class, they just went on talking. I realized that my body was shaking. I kept hoping that Doug wouldn't notice or hear my knees knocking together. I was a wreck!

"As soon as the doors opened, both guys waved goodbye to me and that was it. When I got off the elevator, I pretended like I was on a mission to go somewhere instead of to the message board. I noticed that they went right to the board before they turned around and went through the laundry room, probably on their way out to the beach. I wonder if he thought my answer would be there.

"Will tomorrow ever come? I can't imagine what I'll say to him when we meet downstairs. Now I'm not only eager like I was; I'm also pretty nervous. Somehow I hope that I don't make a mess of things. I've never had a boyfriend before. In fact, I've never gone out with a guy except in groups from church."

"You'll do fine, Christy," I reassure her. "This is going to be a lot of fun for you. Who knows? Maybe Doug will end up being interested in traveling the world and becoming a missionary himself. After all, lots of couples who meet here end up getting married. Wouldn't that be something?"

Christy frowns and replies, "My parents are probably still hoping that by some miracle I'll meet a Seminole, a jock who went to Florida State University, and fall in love with him. Since they weren't at all pleased about my going to school here, my guess is that they wouldn't be any too thrilled if I married a man who wanted to live a life focused on serving others. That isn't exactly what brings them happiness. They are much more into cars, boats, and living life in the fast lane."

Our conversation ends. Christy picks up her book to study. I find myself sitting here thinking about the messages I got from home that I brought here with me.

My mother told me before I left for school that it was going to be important for me to concentrate on my studies. While she knew I wanted a guy in my life, she tried hard to get me to think about going out with a lot of boys rather than immediately finding a boyfriend. She understands that what I want most is to fall in love and get married. I hope to live a more normal life than we led. Being an only child and just living with my mother had its pluses, but I desire something different from that.

I have always wanted children — lots and lots of them. I can see myself devoting my life to my kids as my mom has with me, except that I imagine that someday I will fill a home with at least five or six children. I'll teach all of them the importance of being good Christians. We will live a life of prayer, laughter, learning, and love. I already know that in my heart.

I'm glad that I got to do ministry work with the Redlands Junior High Youth Ranch while I was in high school. I adored being with those kids from my neighborhood junior high school. Each week we would sing songs, learn Bible stories, eat pizza, and joke around. Now I'm happy that I am doing the same kind of ministry work close to Florida Bible College right here in Hollywood. It's perfect for me. I'm clear that this is what I want to keep doing with my life.

There are so many ways that we can help others. Cathleen loves to participate in feeding the homeless, and Christy is happy to go with all the others down on the blue bus to the University of Miami where they witness. Some students prefer that above everything else. Not me!

Many of our classmates are walking along Hollywood Beach talking to people who are out there enjoying the sunshine. I'm thankful that FBC doesn't make us do that. They do encourage us; however, that's where it stops. I don't think I would want to pass out Heaven tracts to people and ask them if they think they are going to Heaven. While there is tremendous satisfaction when I can teach others another way and make them aware that Jesus died for our sins in the past, present, and future, walking up to strangers still isn't my favorite thing to do.

I do believe that it is important to spread the Word, however we do it. What I am completely sure about is that if I knew I had the cure for cancer, it would be my responsibility to pass it along to anyone and everyone. This is the very same thing. I understand how people's lives change when they accept Christ as their Savior and then know that, as a result, they will have everlasting life.

Still it would be hard for me to face rejection if someone didn't want to hear what I had to say. I would feel sad for them knowing what they are missing. Every once in a while, I hear some of my classmates talking about how unfriendly and angry an occasional person at the beach gets when he's been disturbed and asked to listen to the good news of Jesus. Some people feel as though they are being badgered because more than one person has stopped to talk to them. I'll leave it up to the others at the school who can handle the rebuff. It is not for me.

Somehow we each find our way and learn what works best for us. It is part of what I am coming to understand now that I'm here. There is no place I would rather be! I love this school and everything about it.

∼

November 1973

"I couldn't wait to get back today," Cathleen exclaims once we all sit down on our beds and start to talk about our few days away from each other. "The weekend at home was as awful as I expected it might be, except that I made the decision not to stick around for most of it. I ended up sleeping at Betty Sue's every night after the first one.

"Sadly, even though everyone was home all day on Thanksgiving, they mostly sat in the living room glued to the television. It was pitiful to see them argue over what program to watch and then act like zombies as they stared at the screen. It made me realize how little I miss TV and how glad I am that we aren't allowed to have televisions here at FBC.

"Once I arrived home and took stock of how dreadful things were, I saw that no one was interested in making a Thanksgiving dinner. I decided that I would have to shop and prepare the meal for everyone if there was going to be one. I felt it was important to have some kind of meaningful moment with my family. Tracy helped me do some of the cooking, and Ken set the table. The others could have cared less.

"It was an effort to get them all to come to the table. Once everyone was seated, I began the dinner with a prayer, which we've never done before at any meal in our house. Almost everyone at the table was either drunk or stoned. The only two who seemed at all interested and paid attention to me were Ken and Tracy.

"I'm fearful of what's going to happen to my family. They don't care about each other or anything else for that matter. Hard as I try, I'm not sure it's making a difference. I won't give up because I believe I can help them find the way. It might take time. My being home didn't matter to anyone other than Ken and Tracy. It was too sad for words."

Christy puts her arm around Cathleen, and I notice that Cathleen lays her head down on Christy's shoulder. "I wish it had been a better weekend for you. At least we're back together as a little family, and Margaret and I are here to support and love you."

My thoughts drift to how blessed I am to have a mother who adores me and puts me before anyone else in her life. Our weekend, which was a huge contrast to Cathleen's, was filled with gratitude for all we have. Everything my mother and I did was with Jesus by our side. We know that He is what brings joy and meaning to our lives. Thanksgiving to us was yet another reminder of how we are each safe and secure for eternity, being justified by faith, sanctified by God, and sealed by the Holy Spirit. I feel truly blessed and thankful for everything I have and know.

As I sit here thinking about all of this, Christy interrupts and says, "It's time for dinner. We better get going. I wish I had brought leftovers back, but my mom was afraid they would spoil. Thank goodness the cafeteria always has peanut butter and bread for sandwiches. At least that way, those of us who have no money to spare for meals can eat.

"I must confess," she continues. "I went into the Stuff E Nuff Shop before I left for home on Wednesday afternoon. I'm not sure what possessed me to walk into that store. It's always a problem for me because I end up buying something I can't afford. This time, instead of saving money for my meals, I foolishly spent everything extra I had this month on a white and lavender polka dot dress I knew Doug would love. I'm sure I'll survive until next week when the bookstore pays me, but once again, I didn't use my best judgment."

2∕∘

January 1974

As we all gather back in our room after Christmas vacation, I immediately notice a ring on Christy's finger. "Christy!" I shout. "Did you get engaged over vacation?"

With a big, beaming smile on her face, Christy announces, "Yes, Doug proposed to me the day after Christmas. He came into town early that morning and immediately went to see my father to ask for his permission for my hand in marriage. I didn't even know he was there."

Christy goes into every detail of Doug's proposal. Her father was a bit surprised, even though she had talked non-stop about wanting to marry Doug the entire time she was home. Her parents had only first met him the weekend they were here visiting in October. They liked Doug, but it didn't sound like they were all that thrilled for her to marry him. Nonetheless, her father reluctantly gave him the go-ahead. He could probably tell how happy and in love Christy was.

She describes how later on that morning her doorbell rang and when she looked out the peephole of the door, no one was there. I chuckle as she goes on to tell us that she opened the door and still didn't see anyone. Then when she glanced down, she spotted Doug on one knee with a dozen red roses in his hands. The first words out of his mouth were, "Will you marry me?"

Christy's face lights up. "I almost fainted. Talk about romantic dreams coming true! I was absolutely ecstatic and couldn't say yes fast enough. For the rest of the day, we sat and talked about our plans for the future. We're going to get married in May right around graduation time, so that we can move into the Towers. Since Doug doesn't have much family and mine is small and scattered, we decided that we would get married here at FBC. After all, they don't call it Florida Bridal College for nothing!

"Tomorrow I have to go to the office to find out about using the Red Room for the ceremony. My parents have given us a limited budget, so we'll have a simple wedding with a cake and punch reception out in the back area overlooking the ocean. They said we can invite everyone, so I'll put an invitation on the message board when we get them in April.

"I can hardly contain myself. I didn't sleep at all the first night. I kept waking up, turning on the light, and looking at my ring. We can't wait to announce our engagement tomorrow in Chapel."

"What terrific news," Cathleen shouts. "Congratulations! I can't think of anyone better suited for you than Doug."

I give Christy a big hug. The three of us have reason to celebrate.

∽

With the new semester starting, I find myself somewhat overwhelmed. I pick up my books at the bookstore and walk out with the following: *Bible Doctrines, Balancing the Christian Life, Galatians, The Revelation*, and *Strong's Exhaustive Concordance of the Bible*. These titles are a little daunting, but I can't wait to begin classes.

Meanwhile, they did a great job rearranging the bookstore. They moved it out of the front area into a larger space. Now there is so much more room for other things rather than just books. I noticed that they stocked the shelves with stationery, school supplies, cards, postcards, and book bags.

Christy told us that the old bookstore had been a men's tailor shop when this place was the Hollywood Beach Hotel. She said that her friend Sally, who has been working there since the school opened at the hotel, told her that they found old spools of thread, needles, and measuring tapes in cupboards and drawers. From what they gather, the wealthy vacationers must have bought suits and tuxedos at the hotel's stores and then must have come into the tailor shop to have them altered – all while on vacation.

Thinking about moving the bookstore to its new location reminds me of the conversation I had yesterday with Gary Brooks, who also has been here at the school since the beginning. He shared all kinds of facts about what the hotel was like before it became the bible college and then how FBC transformed it.

He told me that they were on a campus in South Miami on South Dixie Highway a few years ago in early 1971. Gary was at a program in Chapel when they received notice that the president of Florida Bible College was going to be making an important announcement. They had absolutely no idea what it would be, so they held tight and waited.

Gary described how the president came marching down the aisle waving a piece of paper in his hand. In a booming voice, he announced, "The Lord has provided the opportunity for us to have a beautiful building on the ocean. Florida Bible College has purchased the old Hollywood Beach Hotel and will be moving there within a matter of days."

He went on to say that classes were suspended for a bit while they packed all the books and other important things from the school and moved up to Hollywood. When they got here, they found the hotel in total disarray. It had been deserted for quite a while, which meant that there was a tremendous accumulation of dirt and litter. One of the things that surprised him the most was the fact that so much was left behind – as though the previous owners departed in a hurry – picked themselves up, walked out the door, and locked it – never turning back.

Within days of arriving there, the students began to attend classes. Gary went into detail about the condition of the place when they moved in. The kitchen was coated in grease and grime. From what he said, it took a large crew of students working for days on end to get it into a usable condition. The kitchen was huge. After all, in the hotel's heyday, it had served over a thousand people at every meal – and gourmet lunches and dinners at that.

The best part was that all the cleaning up provided jobs for the students who needed the work to pay for their tuition, room, and board. They felt it was God's will that they could help to refurbish the building so it would be a place fit for study, worship, and living. I was so happy to hear that.

"It sounds like it was such a mess," I said. "It's hard to understand how you could have moved in like you did."

"You don't know the half of it. I'll never forget all the dead pigeons that covered the floors when we first entered the building. Somehow they had flown in through the broken windows and couldn't get out. Being on the 'dead-bird-clean-up patrol' was about the worst.

"One night right after that, my friend Marilyn was sleeping with her window open in her room on the seventh floor. The building was supposed to have had air conditioning, but instead what it had was water sucked into the pipes and cooled. That was meant to be a way to make the building colder. It didn't really work, so in order to survive the hotter days and nights, we kept our windows open. Anyway, Marilyn woke up one morning with a sea gull standing at her feet. After recently having seen the movie *The Birds* and having been on 'dead-bird-clean-up patrol,' she was scared half to death!"

I shuddered just thinking about it and couldn't stay quiet. "That sounds awful! Poor Marilyn must have had nightmares for weeks after that."

"From what she told me, she didn't sleep in her room for the next month or so. I didn't blame her either," Gary declared.

He went on to tell me how the naval training center was located here during World War II. The U. S. Navy had set up a barracks in front of the hotel. I had always wondered what that old building was doing there, so he explained. He described how the college faculty had found a lot of old furniture in there. They took out the old navy surplus items like beds and used them. He said that a few of the boys at school, including him, initially slept in the barracks until they cleaned up enough of the rooms in the main building for them to move over there.

Some antique furniture, maybe from when the hotel was first built, was in the barracks as well. When students got married, the school administration allowed them to go in and rummage through it. If they saw anything that they wanted for their apartments in the Towers next door, they were welcome to take it.

Gary didn't miss a detail in describing how the building was converted to FBC. "Long ago, the large ballroom had been the main dining room and was elegant with its massive crystal chandeliers and flocked wallpaper. That's the room we now use not only for our church services on Sunday but also for Chapel during the rest of the week and the wonderful concerts we hold several times a year. Our current cafeteria with its floor to ceiling windows looking out at sea was originally another fancy dining room. Most of the beautiful linens and china as well as the elegant silverware were left behind, so some of it is what we use for our special banquets."

I was interested in hearing about the water issue because it's all the administration seems to talk about, so I asked Gary about it. I now know it has been a problem from the start. Gary indicated that they were always plagued with water leaking from the pipes. From the time they moved in, the students were told that if they saw any leaks, they needed to let someone in the office know immediately. That hasn't changed. Water still costs the school so much, and it's probably because all the pipes are old and deteriorating.

While he was telling me about the history of the building, I was thinking about all the people who came before us. Did they appreciate the beauty of the surroundings and the ocean, in particular? I never get enough of that and feel blessed to be living at the beach while going to school and learning about those things that matter most to me.

പ

February 1974

Christy's soft, sweet voice wakes me at 5:30 a.m. I am tired and don't want to move, but she reminds me that if I'm going to be ready for the day, I had better get up.

"Mondays are tough," she explains, "and we need enough time for our fifteen minutes of devotion together before we head downstairs."

Cathleen appears to want to sleep a bit longer, too. "It's kind of the school to start classes at seven o'clock for those of us who need to get to work in the afternoon, but it would sure be nice if we could begin just a little later on Monday mornings to ease us into the week."

The early rising doesn't stifle my enthusiasm. Today during Chapel, my little group will make our announcement about the yearbook and will encourage the girls to sell ads for it. The administration said we could have five minutes to give our special pitch. So, Betty Sue, Cathleen, Christy, Connie, and I are going to perform a skit that we made up. I can't wait to do this. After all, if we're good and make our point, then when Slave Day comes around, the girls will be the masters. From what I hear, the boys have lost a few years in a row, and we want to keep that record going.

As we get out of bed and begin brushing our teeth and getting dressed, Cathleen tells us about her late night and what happened with the Bibles. When she had found out that Desi Arnaz, Jr. and Liza Minnelli were going to be performing at the Diplomat Hotel this week, Cathleen decided that she wanted to share the Gospel and would give each of them Bibles with their names engraved on the cover. Since Christy works in the bookstore, Cathleen asked her to take care of getting that done for her.

"So, Jesus was with me, and I didn't have to go searching for which rooms they would be in," Cathleen tells us. "As soon as I reported to the front desk yesterday, I was told that I was going to be assigned to both Desi Arnaz, Jr. and Liza Minnelli's rooms to turn down their beds, put chocolates on their pillows, and make sure that their bathrooms were spotless. The management wanted their rooms to be perfectly lit with dim lights and 'a pleasant, calming ambiance' when they returned from entertaining.

"I made sure to take special care in straightening out and cleaning up the rooms. When I was all done and felt sure that things looked exactly as they should, I then placed the Bibles on each of their beds. I was delighted when I walked out of there knowing what a precious gift I had left for them."

As Cathleen finishes telling us about her experience, I start to think about the babysitting job I had last night. I didn't get home until midnight, which did not allow for much sleep. I had hoped to be home by ten o'clock, since I had begun at 6:15 p.m.

Before I arrived, I was told that the family had three kids, ages six, nine, and eleven. When I got to the condo where the Bornsteins were staying, the parents said I could take the boys to the building's pool downstairs, but I wasn't real comfortable doing that. They were disappointed, but it felt like it was too big a responsibility for me. I'm not a good enough swimmer to be in charge of kids in a pool.

I encouraged the boys to play some quiet board games like Sorry and Clue, but that didn't last long. If they couldn't swim, all they wanted to do was watch television. I finally gave in.

When the youngest one, Aaron, was ready for bed, I went into his room and read him a few of the children's Bible storybooks I had brought with me. Then I talked to him about Jesus, whom he had never heard of before. I suggested that he could go to Heaven if he just believed in Jesus. He went to sleep with a smile on his face.

I asked the older boys if they wanted me to read a few stories to them, but neither was at all interested, so I let it go. Maybe next week when I go there, I'll bring something more on their level to share with them. The best news was that I made $3.50. Mr. and Mrs. Bornstein gave me a little extra since I had taken good care of their three boys.

Christy was with Doug all day yesterday. She was anxious to tell us about their day. We didn't have a lot of time, though, because we still had to do our fifteen minutes of devotion before we headed to class.

Christy talks fast. "We had the best time. There were twenty-five kids from South Broward High School – all tenth graders. We divided them up into five groups and gave each one a list of things they had to find on the beach and instructed them to take pictures with their Kodak Brownie cameras. Each item had a spiritual meaning. I'm not sure that they necessarily got that in the beginning, but eventually, they all seemed to figure it out. They came back from the hunt enthusiastic and bubbly. After that, we set up an ice cream sundae bar and ate way too much."

I listen to Christy with delight. Her happiness is contagious.

"What I liked most," she says, "was watching Doug with the kids. He's such a high-spirited guy who has the best time kidding around with everyone and making them laugh. I can tell that most of the girls in the group have a crush on him, but he's hands-off!"

After that, Doug and Christy had a lot of studying to do, so they went to dinner and then to the Saints' Soda Shop for a Coke and some chips. They sat and studied for a few hours.

"I never get enough time with Doug, so I was glad we could be together for so many hours. Since he's had all the classes I'm taking, he was able to help explain a few of the questions I had on the North Galatian and South Galatian views. He cleared some things up for me, which was definitely helpful."

I interrupt her by saying, "I want to hear more, but we better get to our prayers or we'll be late for class."

∽

March 1974

"We had the best time with AWANA last night," Christy says. "Kids from all over Hollywood came as they do each week. This time they brought more friends than usual, which was great. The Word is spreading. It was amazing to see how well they memorized their verses. I was so happy we had enough Wordless books to hand out to everyone who came. Doug was the best at getting the kids involved in all the games, especially the rope-pulling event. He does such a terrific job of instilling in them 'Approved Workmen Are Not Ashamed.'

"You should see him as a clown doing ministry work. Last week he dressed up in funny clothes, put on a lot of makeup, and made balloon animals. With the small children at Kids' Bible Clubhouse, he presented to them how to trust in the Lord for their Salvation and how to tell others to do the same. It was a sight to see and made a lot of kids happy. Doug is just amazing.

"I'm also happy that the ministry work we're doing with Impact at the University of Miami is going so well. I remember that I was somewhat afraid at first, but now I am comfortable. I've been using the 'hand gesture' and informal surveys to share the Gospel. We are establishing Bible studies in each dormitory on the University of Miami campus. It feels so wonderful to be doing this."

"It sounds perfect," I respond. "It's terrific that you and Doug have found ways to do what's so important and be together at the same time. It looks like he might end up being willing to go with you all over the world doing foreign ministry – especially if you keep this up."

Cathleen pipes in, "I can't wait to see tomorrow's *Momentum*. This week our journalism class worked harder on the newsletter than ever before. For some reason, we had more trouble than usual getting all the information on the speakers that we wanted to include. But I had the best time going around and getting the scoop on what's happening here at FBC. Thankfully, I'm never in charge of the sermonette portion. I don't think I would be too great at that."

"Hey, I almost forgot. Did you hear what happened in Bible studies class today?" I asked. Both Christy and Cathleen indicated that they hadn't, so I continued. "Ronald Hughes was sitting next to Martin Taylor. Ronald fell asleep and was snoring softly. Martin waited about ten minutes and was amazed that Mr. Johnson hadn't noticed Ronald sleeping. So, Martin leaned over to Ronald and whispered in his ear, 'Wake up. Mr. Johnson wants you to stand and quote from Titus 3:5.' Ronald opened his eyes, stood up, and in the middle of class, he began to quote the verse out loud. Need I say more? We were all hysterical. He was so embarrassed when he realized what had happened. Then I felt bad for him. Mr. Johnson was kind enough to let it all slide."

Cathleen chimes in. "Today and yesterday must have been the days for pranks. When Mr. Brackmeyer was riding up the elevator, it stopped on the fourth floor. John Astor and Billy Kingston were standing outside the elevator waiting for some of the girls or guys they thought would be riding up. When the doors opened, they each took a bucket of water and aimed it right into the elevator, thinking they would get some of their friends. Little did they know it was Mr. Brackmeyer riding alone on the elevator! They ended up throwing water smack in his face and all over him. Can you imagine? I don't know what's going to happen to John and Billy, but I'm sure they were sent down to the dean."

"How did you hear about this?" I ask.

"Everyone in Church History was talking about it today. The whole thing is too funny!" replies Cathleen. "Those guys were crazy to do that, but I hope they don't get into too much trouble.

"You know what else I heard?" she continues. "John King was talking to his friend Troy after class, and I happened to be standing right near them. John told Troy that he was able to come to school here because of some rich Christian who donated money to keep as many of the guys out of the Vietnam War as possible. You know how college students are exempt from the draft, right? I thought that was pretty interesting. Don't you?"

I was a little surprised at that and nodded. I liked the funny stories better.

⁓

April 1974

"After all our hard work selling ads, I can hardly believe that we lost! I thought our skit was so much better than the one the guys did. I was sure we would win!" exclaims Christy.

"I know," Cathleen replies, "but I would suspect that the boys were sick of losing and were determined to get back at us for winning so many times in a row."

I add, "The day sure took on a new meaning for me when I found out that we had to be slaves to the guys."

"I couldn't believe how Doug made me sit for twenty-five minutes and fan him with a palm frond after I had fed him lunch," Christy complains.

"Well, did you see what Eric and Roger had me and Cathleen do? They made us dig huge holes in the sand and then get in them. They buried us side by side until only our necks and heads were showing," I say. "Then they took a walk and left both of us stuck there for at least fifteen minutes with the sun beating down on us."

Christy chimes in, "That doesn't sound like it was any fun. And Doug thought he was so funny when he made me wear that stupid-looking hat and the shirt that said, "'I am a happy slave of Doug's'! Well, at least it was all in the name of good, clean fun."

Now that Slave Day is over, I'm looking forward to the big spring concert in May. It's all everyone has been talking about. The winter one was definitely a highlight of the year here. I adore all the music that is so much a part of FBC. No matter what we do, there is always singing, which warms my heart. I heard that in addition to The Internationals, The Linen Sisters are going to perform. The other day when I walked by the laundry room where they work, they were harmonizing with their angelic voices.

$\sim$

May 1974

Our room is so empty tonight without Christy. Cathleen told me how lonely she is for her already.

"Didn't Christy look beautiful in her bridal gown?" Cathleen asks.

I grin as I think about Christy in her $125 gown that she splurged on and add, "She was a gorgeous bride. There's no doubt about that. I'm glad she talked us into buying the pastel-colored brides-maids' dresses and am so thankful that they were only thirty dollars each."

The wedding ended up being so pretty with me, Cathleen, Connie, and Betty Sue dressed in pink, yellow, lime green, and powder blue. And the way Mrs. Tilson arranged all our bouquets with matching flowers turned out to be perfect. I had no idea that she had been a florist before she became the wife of our dean.

I was happy that there was enough room for all of us to dress in the women's bathroom on the second floor. With its large sitting room, it is way more elegant than any bathroom I will most likely ever see in my life. It was probably where all the fancy ladies used to go to powder their noses in between dances.

Cathleen nods and goes on to rehash the details of the wedding. "Miss Marion did a wonderful job playing the organ. She's remarkable, isn't she? I've never heard someone put so much of her heart and soul into playing music like the way she does. The lady who served the punch told me that when Miss Marion was little, she learned to play piano by drawing a keyboard on her windowsill.

"Doug's father was pretty great himself when he sang 'Love Was When God Became a Man.' What a voice he has! He is the nicest man – like his son. They're a wonderful family. Thankfully, it looked like everyone from both sides got along nicely and seemed happy for Christy and Doug.

"I keep thinking about what happened when they knelt for their time of dedication, a time that should have been so serious. Roger was too much. What a prankster! I have no idea when he pulled off what did, but I still can't get over that he wrote 'Help Me' on masking tape and put it on the sole of Doug's shoe so that we could all see it when Doug knelt. I'm sure Christy and Doug were totally baffled and had no idea why everyone was laughing. What must they have thought? I tried not to laugh, but it was impossible to keep a straight face."

"At least you didn't giggle out loud like I did," I add. "There was no way I could hold in my laughter.

"I'm glad that Betty Sue caught the bouquet. Maybe Eric will soon ask her to marry him. There is no doubt in my mind that she's ready."

Now Christy and Doug are off to Disney World for two days, which is a perfect place for the two of them to spend their honeymoon. Doug has wanted to go there since it opened a few years ago, and Christy will be happy wherever she is as long as he's with her. Doug is such a kid at heart that, most likely, he is thoroughly enjoying his time in Orlando.

I didn't expect I was going to feel as lonely for Christy as I do. She and Doug will be back for their final exams, but she won't be living with us any longer. It won't be the same without her in our room. I know she's looking forward to moving over to the Towers. I'm pleased that she let me and Cathleen help them get their adorable apartment fixed up before the wedding.

Maybe one day soon Cathleen and I will be the brides. It seems like Roger might be starting to take a serious liking to Cathleen. I hope so for her sake. I'm still holding out for Gary. I hear he's thinking about asking me out. I would be so happy if he did, but he had better hurry before the semester is over.

ᶜᵛↄ

The school year is almost finished. When I reflect back on all that we've done and all that I've learned, I realize how wonderful it has been and how blessed I am to be here.

One of the best parts about FBC has been the fellowship among all of us students. I never dreamed that a college atmosphere could be one filled with such love, joy, and fun. It's like we are one big family. I've noticed how everyone takes care of one another. No matter what the situation, there is always someone by my side if I need company or a hug. We can always feel God's presence here.

Having Christy and Cathleen as roommates has been the biggest blessing for me. I learned what it's like to share a room with someone else and to have people I care about around me all the time. Just knowing that I could talk to them about anything has made such a difference in my life. I have a feeling that our friendship has been equally as important to them.

We're busy cleaning our room for inspection. Cathleen tackles our bathroom since she's a pro at that from her job at the Diplomat. I borrow a vacuum cleaner and sweep our blue shag carpet – something that we haven't done in a while. I realize now how badly it needed it. We pull open our beige and green drapes so the magnificent ocean is in full view. Cathleen takes everything off the top of our two dressers that the three of us shared. It's the first time they haven't been cluttered this whole year. We also make sure that our plant is watered and that there is nothing on our table by the window.

Once our room looks perfect, we are ready for the guys, who will be allowed on our floor for the first and only time this entire year. I heard through the grapevine that the administration lets them come upstairs so that we can show them what it means to keep a neat room. They are probably hoping that the guys will then go back downstairs and make sure that their rooms look as great as ours do.

We have the strictest of orders to ensure that our surroundings look spotless since the camp will be starting at the beginning of June, and they want the rooms in perfect condition. Our dear sweet Alfred, with his wonderful faith in the Lord and his constant singing as he cleans, can't do it all without our help. I am wild about that man!

Betty Sue told me that Eric and his roommates, Gary and Roger, are planning to come to our room first. Cathleen is making sure that everything looks exactly as it should. She wants to create a good impression, so maybe Roger will take a particular interest in her and will realize that she is a woman who will keep a clean and neat home. I've been humoring her because we know that of the three of us, Cathleen is the sloppiest. That's probably her way of rebelling since she cleans everyone else's rooms at the Diplomat.

Cathleen is going to be staying at FBC over the summer. She was fortunate enough to get a job with Alterman Trucking. They're going to pay her $2.10 an hour, which will be great. That way she can save some money and will be ahead of the game in the fall. It looks like she'll continue her ministry work with the homeless in downtown Miami. So far, it is her favorite thing to do. Cathleen feels so good about changing lives, and she would rather be anywhere than back with her family these days.

Unlike Cathleen, I can't wait to go home for the summer to be with my mom. From everything that she has said, my mother is lonely without me; I know she will be happy to have me there. We don't have too much planned, but it will be wonderful to work with her at the camp and also go to church together.

Mostly, I am grateful to Jesus that I have been able to experience this year and am hopeful that all of what I've learned will help me become a better person who will continue to spread the Word. FBC is exactly where I belong. I will look forward to being back in the fall for another year of learning and loving, but I'm going to miss Room 732 and the wonderful gifts it has given me.

HOTEL POSTCARDS AND PHOTOGRAPHS

Hollywood Beach Hotel

D. R. 1—Hollywood Beach Hotel, Hollywood, Fla.

D. H. 2— TROPICAL TREES AND FLOWERS ON LAWN OF HOLLYWOOD BEACH HOTEL

HOLLYWOOD, FLA.

U.S. NAVAL TRAINING SCHOOL
HOLLYWOOD BEACH, FLORIDA

M.E.BERRY
AERIAL
PHOTO
#205

FLORIDA BIBLE COLLEGE
HOLLYWOOD, FLORIDA

A NEW BEGINNING

HOLLYWOOD BEACH RESORT HOTEL
1988

The mellow music of Slic Friction's jazz ensemble by the pool would normally relax me in a way that little else does. Yet instead, at the moment, I am a bundle of nerves.

The wait until Amanda and Alex arrive at 3:30 p.m. feels like forever. I thought I would be wise to come in a day earlier than the two of them and familiarize myself with the hotel and its surroundings. In retrospect, it wasn't necessary and, in fact, being here alone has probably increased my anxiety.

I'm sure that Alex is looking forward to coming to Florida and spending time with me. Our relationship is solid. Amanda, however, is another story. This will be the first time I have seen her in over seven months. Unfortunately, she had made the choice to stay away from me during this time.

When I made reservations to stay at the Hollywood Beach Resort Hotel, I had no idea that this would be anything but a normal weekend. I first learned about the Grand Opening of Oceanwalk when I arrived yesterday and saw all the colorful banners and posters announcing the various celebratory events. It looks like we came on the perfect weekend.

Upon checking in, I asked a few questions of the receptionist and found out about the project. She told me that it cost over thirty-five million dollars and took two-and-a-half years to build Oceanwalk. An entire year was spent demolishing parts of the first and second floors and hauling away the debris. Now there are one hundred and ten stores, plus an area downstairs called Pushcart Alley, lined with street-cart style vendors selling a variety of items. On one of the carts, I noticed some t-shirts with funny sayings on them that Amanda and Alex might like.

Last night, I meandered around and watched the construction crew working as fast as they could to finish up before today's opening. It was complete mayhem. Carpenters were hammering brackets into the walls for the shelves. Painters were putting last minute touches on the woodwork. Electricians were installing fixtures. Building inspectors were going from one place to the next with their clipboards and two-way radios in hand. I didn't expect that they would ever finish up in time. Most likely none of them slept last night.

∽

We just arrived at the hotel from the airport. Amanda was quiet in the car on our way back. Alex didn't stop talking.

The kids are so excited about going out to the beach that they didn't pay any attention to the shops downstairs or even to the hordes of people milling around on the first floor. Coming from the cold weather and snow in Denver, all Alex and Amanda want to do is get into the warmth and sunshine and run into the ocean.

Within minutes, we have changed into our bathing suits and are ready to head to the elevator. I suggest putting on sunscreen, but both of them look at me like I am from an alien planet.

"Dad, we're only going to be in the water for a little while. We don't need it," Alex insists.

"But this is tropical sun, and you both have fair skin and are completely pale," I warn. "I wouldn't want either of you to go home sunburned."

Amanda rolls her eyes. I know enough to shut my mouth.

∽

Alex and I have always been okay. Maybe it is because he was only nine years old when Sharon and I separated, or maybe because he was just able to accept the reality in his own way. Alex is the only one in our family who can roll with the punches. Even three years ago when I told him I was moving to Orlando because of work, he was sad but understood and dealt with it in a healthy and loving manner.

Luckily, from the day I moved out of the house six years ago, he seemed at peace with the fact that we would only be together at pre-arranged times. Granted there were plenty of moments in which he would cry when I dropped him back off at his mother's. He would hold on tightly, not wanting to let me to go. But once he was inside the house and got distracted, Sharon informed me that he was okay. Of course, she would say anything to make sure I knew that our children were fine without me there. Even so, the gut-wrenching feelings I experienced after those incidents stayed with me for hours, sometimes days.

I'm grateful that Alex still jumps at every opportunity to talk to me and is much happier when he has a date for the next time we will see each other. He lets me know that he is unhappy that I can't attend his soccer and basketball games like I used to when I lived nearby. I make sure to find out the schedules. Now I call after each game, and Alex gives me play-by-play descriptions of what went on and how he and his teammates performed. We both love sports, so sharing that common interest creates a bond for us. And because he is accessible, I have found ways to remain close to him despite the distance and the fact that we see each other much too infrequently.

Unlike her brother, Amanda has been unforgiving since that awful night when Sharon and I told the children we were separating. We talked to both kids and explained as simply as possible why I was moving out of the house. Amanda, who was twelve at the time, got angry, ran into her room, and slammed the door. I went upstairs and tried to talk to her through her closed door. I did all I could to persuade her to answer me, but she refused and certainly wouldn't let me come in. I was devastated.

Ever since then, regardless of the attempts I've made, Amanda has acted as though she wants nothing to do with me and repeatedly gives me a cold reception. She almost always has a sullen look on her face when we are together, and from what I can gather, she still blames me for leaving.

∽

Back in our room, it's now ten o'clock in the evening. The three of us can hear the band playing down below. Room 732, where we're staying this weekend, is right above the hotel's outdoor bar. I notice Amanda swaying to the reggae music as she stands by the open window.

Our room is a little cramped with the cot that I ordered. We have a king-size bed where Alex and I are sleeping. But with the three suitcases the kids brought plus mine and the rafts I bought this morning for each of us, we don't have a lot of extra room to move around. No one seems to be complaining though.

"How about if we go down to the Broadwalk, take a walk, and get some ice cream?" I ask. "When I was exploring the beach earlier today, I happened to notice that there's a Haagen-Dazs about five blocks from here. Are either of you interested?"

Alex nods and Amanda smiles for the first time since she arrived. Chocolate chip ice cream was her favorite food when she was a little girl, and from the look on her face, that hasn't changed. Seeing her smile delights me.

When we get downstairs, the kids are amazed at how many people are out on the beach at this hour.

"Is it always like this here at night?" Alex asks.

"I have no idea, but I would imagine that most of the crowd is left over from the festivities of opening day. It looks like the people in uniforms are from the marching bands, and probably lots of others from the parade also decided to stay and enjoy this beautiful evening. There's a real celebration going on here.

"At lunch today, I heard someone say that they were expecting over 50,000 people at Oceanwalk this weekend. I'm not sure if that's good for us or not."

"As long as there's room for us to put our towels on the sand and sun ourselves, it'll be perfect," Amanda adds.

I'm pleased. It is her first direct comment to me since she arrived.

❦

From the day I moved out of the house and into my own apartment, I made a commitment to myself that I would stay involved in Alex's and Amanda's lives. Regardless of what was going on in my life, I knew it was what I wanted and needed to do. Sharon agreed with that initially, but after a year or so, she did nothing to encourage my relationship with our children. Ever since then, she has probably made things worse by what she has said to them. That hasn't stopped me. I have not and will not give up on Amanda – even as difficult as she makes it for me at times.

Right from the beginning, when I would take her and Alex out for an evening or a weekend, Amanda would barely talk to me. I tried hard to have a conversation with her, but she would inevitably reply with curt answers that bordered on being rude. I never tolerated that while I was still at home and decided I would have to be firm with Amanda and let her know that her behavior was unacceptable. As angry as she was, at least that stopped her from becoming downright nasty.

During that first year of persistent attempts to get our relationship back on track, her actions toward me became even worse, regardless of what I did or said. Amanda was soon to become a teenager and only cared about her friends. She began to make up every excuse she could to avoid spending time with me. Initially I was adamant about her coming with me. I gradually began to understand that my insisting on our being together was causing her to be more resentful.

Just as I had been doing with Alex, I continued to call Amanda frequently even if she refused to talk to me. At least once or twice a week, despite how she was acting toward me, I would mail her a card just to let her know I loved her. I accepted the fact that I was going to have to be patient and keep on trying. Amanda's rejection hurt, but I refused to give up.

It took about a-year-and-a-half for Amanda to slowly come around. After that for the next six months, once every second or third time I invited her to go out to dinner or to sleep over, she would say yes. She no longer acted lovingly to me like before the divorce, but at least she occasionally agreed to spend time together.

Then everything changed once again when I was forced to move to Orlando for work. My engineering company gave me no choice, and hard as I tried to find another job in Denver, there was none available. I needed the money and couldn't be without employment. Leaving Denver was not easy and certainly did not help my relationship with Amanda.

Since moving to Florida, she has refused to visit me. When I go back home, she usually agrees to spend at least a day or an evening with me as long as Alex is with us. Mostly she talks to him and manages to act polite but distant toward me. I am grateful for any time that I can be with Amanda, and I know it will take a lot more work to get our relationship back to how it used to be – if, in fact, that is even possible. While the whole situation is far from ideal, we have made some progress.

❧

Before going to sleep, I hand the kids the flyer listing the events for Oceanwalk's opening activities. "Why don't you check out what's happening here over the weekend and decide what you would like to do? It looks like there's so much going on that it might be hard to choose. Just so you know, I'm game to do whatever the two of you want."

Amanda studies the schedule carefully. She then looks over at Alex and says, "Hey, Alex, you ever hear of this? There's a place called Soleil St. Tropez where they spray on an even coat of tanning lotion. Any interest in doing that, so we make sure to get the best tan possible by the time we go home?"

Alex nods and says, "Sure!"

It's obvious that going back to Colorado with a suntan is top on Amanda's list. She probably wants all of her friends to know that she was in Florida in February while they were at home in freezing temperatures.

To no one in particular, she continues, "I'd also love to shop downstairs. It looks like they have some pretty neat stores from what I saw when we walked by them before. I'm hoping to get a few summer outfits, maybe even a new bathing suit or two. Florida's beachwear has got to be better than what they sell in Denver."

This weekend has suddenly become more expensive for me. The truth is that I would buy Amanda anything she wants just to make her happy.

Alex asks, "Hey, Dad, I see that there's a volleyball competition on Sunday afternoon. It starts around three o'clock. Will there be enough time to play before we have to leave for the airport?"

"We don't need to leave here until 6:30 p.m."

"Great. I really want to play. You in, Amanda, or are you afraid you'll break a nail?"

"Very funny, Alex. It's about the last thing I want to do. I'm hoping to lie in the sun as much as I can on Sunday. I'll be perfectly fine soaking up the rays at the pool." Amanda winks at Alex, and I sit on the bed grinning to myself. She acts so natural with him. Their bantering pleases me.

"I can't wait to go to the arcade," announces Alex. "I peeked in earlier today and saw that they have all kinds of great video games. I think I'll get lost in there for a while."

"That's okay with me," I answer. "By the way, since we're going to be on the beach tomorrow, there's a giant balloon release at one o'clock. I'm looking forward to seeing that."

"Sounds good to me," Alex replies. Amanda nods.

At least Amanda is agreeing with our plans. So far, so good.

༄

Because we stayed up late last night, I was not expecting to wake up this early. I'm not sure how I let Alex convince me to go to the midnight movie to see *Return of the Living Dead, Part 2*, a zombie, comedy film all wrapped up into one. The good news was that we didn't have to go far since it is playing right here at the new movie theatre. Alex and Amanda thought it was great. I couldn't wait for it to be over.

The kids are still asleep, of course. Since they're teenagers, both of them like to stay in bed whenever they get the chance.

168

I had agreed in advance to let them sleep in. So, I dress quietly and head down to the beach where I briskly walk along the ocean. The air is nippy and the water is chilly, but it feels just right on my toes.

I can't stop thinking about when I first saw Amanda at the airport yesterday. I was instantly struck by how beautiful she has become and how much she looks the way her mother did at that age. In fact, when we were in our senior year of high school, Sharon was the homecoming queen. Her looks were what first attracted me to her.

Amanda's silky, long blonde hair and her piercing powder blue eyes draw attention. I notice that the guys all stare at her when she walks by. Amanda is now all grown up, and I have lost so much that I will never get back. I remember when my little daddy's girl would throw her arms around me and give me the most wonderful, heartfelt hugs. Where has the time gone?

Instead of dwelling on that, I must be hopeful that perhaps this weekend might somehow lead to a closer bond between us. I want to be able to find a way for us to repair our relationship and begin anew. Through the years, I have been patient and steadfast. Yet, there is no question that I am sad. I yearn to have my daughter back.

If I am truthful with myself, I understand that I can't blame the problems that exist between me and Amanda solely on her. After all, I decided to leave Sharon, and when I did, I left Amanda and Alex as well. Granted I have made every effort to be with them, but my physical presence in their daily lives has been missing. Maybe it was selfish of me to desert my children.

Before Sharon and I separated, I suggested we go for marital counseling. Sharon wasn't keen on the idea, but eventually she agreed. We went for four sessions and didn't get anywhere. The therapist tried to encourage us to talk about our issues, but Sharon was resistant to work on our marriage. Instead, she blamed me for everything and took no responsibility for anything that was wrong with our relationship.

At our last appointment with the therapist, Sharon came right out and told me that she hasn't loved me since we got married. That was the moment I knew it was time for me to leave.

Since Sharon had always been good with Amanda and Alex, I felt sure that they would be fine remaining in the house where they were comfortable and with a mother who loved them. Besides, I assumed that I would get joint custody and never thought twice about any other options. That helped me to go because I was certain that I would be with the children for at least half of each week.

Sharon hired a cut-throat lawyer, thanks to her father who footed the bill, and the divorce proceedings began. Her shrewd attorney put up a real fight and did not make it easy for me. In the end, I was given two days and two nights each week and every other weekend with Alex and Amanda. It wasn't what I wanted, but thankfully, they were still in my life on a fairly regular basis.

I look up at the beautiful, aqua ocean and realize that I have been deep in thought for probably an hour already. Going back to that awful time in my life is difficult.

I pick up my pace and head back to the hotel. I'm surprised to find both kids awake when I walk into the room. They're sitting at the table looking out the window and are already dressed for the beach, waiting to go downstairs.

❧

"Dad, can we stop in the candy store and get some fudge?" Alex asks as we make our way through the crowds.

"Sure, you can have whatever you want, but I definitely am going to buy some chocolate chip cookies," I reply. "I can smell them baking from here."

"I want both!" Alex says with a big grin on his face.

"Not me," exclaims Amanda. "Since I had that huge blueberry muffin and a cheese omelet for breakfast, I'm stuffed. I probably shouldn't have anything else to eat until dinner. That is unless you'll swim laps with me, Alex. "Are you in?"

"I guess I can force myself to do that. Hey, how about if I challenge both you and Dad to a race – five laps in all? I remember when I could never beat either of you, but I have a feeling I might actually stand a chance now."

"Great," I reply. I like the idea of the three of us racing. We used to do that all the time when the kids were little – running, biking, skiing, and swimming races. I almost always let one of them win. Most likely now, they will beat me even if I try hard. I'm out of shape compared to the two of them.

"Okay, big shot," Amanda says to her brother. "Let's see who will win this time around."

As we walk closer to the cookie shop, Alex stops in front of the Gyrotron, a big, weightless flight simulator. When I first arrived, I had read about the wildly insane ride that was at Vancouver's Expo '86 two years ago. Even though it seems out of place here, someone was wise to bring it to the hotel. The line is already wrapped around part of the mall, and it's still early in the day.

"I'm getting in line so I can try this thing out. It looks so neat!" Alex declares.

I'm not surprised. He was always intrigued with anything that was related to space.

"While you're waiting in line, I'm going to Word-Worth bookstore over there. Okay, Dad?" Amanda asks.

Wow! It is the first time Amanda has called me Dad in five years. I'm thrilled and immediately realize how little it takes to make me happy when it comes to my daughter.

Alex looks surprised. "Don't you want to try out the flight simulator, Amanda? It's going to be so cool."

"Not really. I'd rather get a few magazines to read at the pool and maybe even a book for the plane ride home."

"Do you want me to come with you?" I ask, hoping that she'll say yes.

"No, thanks. You should stay with Alex. I have a feeling that you'll enjoy riding in the Gyrotron as much as he will."

∽

As Alex and I are walking out of the Gyrotron, Amanda greets us.

"I saw the neatest store over there," she says, pointing toward the direction of the restaurant area. "You have to come see this place."

Alex and I follow her as she takes us to The Last Wound Up, a unique store that sells only wind-up toys with prices ranging from one dollar to several thousand dollars. The three of us each get involved playing with the different toys that line the shelves. Alex seems fascinated with some space monster that, once it is wound up, walks up into a rocket ship.

I look over to where Amanda is standing and watch her staring longingly at a beautiful ballerina dressed in pink. As it twirls around to music, I begin thinking back to when Amanda was six or seven years old and took ballet lessons. She looked like an adorable ballerina in a frilly tutu, with a bun at the crown of her head.

Without giving it any thought, I walk up to Amanda and stand next to her. She looks up at me with a startled expression.

"Do you remember when you used to take dancing lessons?"

"I do. Dancing used to make me so happy. In fact, I still love to dance."

"Not just because you are my daughter, but I always thought you were the best little dancer in your class. Did you know that your teacher told your mother you had natural talent and could be a ballerina if you dedicated yourself to dancing?"

"I don't think I knew that. I do remember that Mom decided I should take gymnastics the next year because my friends, Shelly and Trina, were signing up for that instead of ballet. I kind of wish I had stayed with dance."

"Amanda, would you like me to buy you the twirling ballerina?"

A big smile lights up her face. "Daddy, would you really buy it for me?" she asks as she picks up the doll and holds it close to her chest.

I melt. This time she called me Daddy. I haven't heard that in years and feel myself glowing.

"Nothing would make me happier." I feel a sudden urge to put my arms around her. I don't, though, because I know I must take baby steps.

I buy the ballerina and am surprised that it costs seventy-nine dollars. Amanda thanks me and goes right up to our room to put it in a safe spot. She meets us back at the pool, and the three of us get set to race.

❧

Alex won two of the three races. Amanda was pleased that she won one. I didn't stand a chance next to the two of them. It didn't matter to me. I was just happy that we were having a good time together.

When we got out of the pool, the three of us rented bicycles and rode along the Broadwalk. We enjoyed going up to the northern end by Sheridan Street and getting away from the hubbub of Oceanwalk for a little while.

❦

The kids have chosen this restaurant, which definitely looks like one of the most expensive ones here at Oceanwalk. They probably liked the idea of picking out their own steaks and grilling them by themselves. After we decide on the kind of steaks and side dishes we want, the waiter leaves our table and comes back with freshly-baked bread. We each grab a piece before we head over to the grills with our steaks in hand.

On our way, I ask Amanda and Alex if they have any interest in hearing The Platters, who will be performing after the Beatlemania show tonight.

"No way!" Alex exclaims. "You're so old, Dad. That's your music, not ours. Personally, I'd rather go to sleep than sit through one of their concerts."

"Like your hair metal music with Def Leppard is so great, Alex?" Amanda adds. She looks at me and winks.

Amanda seems different tonight – softer, less tense, maybe.

"Okay, Alex. I get the message. I'm sure we'll find something to do later this evening. Now let's get some serious cooking going."

❦

After going to see Beatlemania, we find ourselves exploring more of the stores in Oceanwalk. Crowds are still everywhere, but at least we can get into the shops now. Before dinner, it was almost impossible to make our way past most of the doors to look inside at anything.

The stores are divided into sections of Yesterday, Today, and Tomorrow, with piped-in music that fits each era. We stop at Antique Boutique, and I buy Alex an army surplus jacket that he said he has been wanting. As we are walking out of the store, I see Amanda eyeing one of the jackets. I overhear her telling Alex that she wishes she could have one, too. How can I resist? Granted, I have already spent much more money than I ever expected this weekend, but I don't see her that often and this would make her so happy. So, I buy Amanda a jacket as well, and again, her face lights up.

From there we go into a store called the U.S. Socks Exchange. Not only do they have socks in every color and design, but across the top of the store there is a running tally of yesterday's stocks. Both kids find several pairs of socks that they want. Once more, we end up walking away from the stores with bags in hand.

೧

It is eight o'clock on Sunday morning, and this time Amanda and Alex have given me permission to wake them up. Since we leave later today, they both had decided that they wanted to take advantage of as much of the day as possible. The kids had agreed that they can always sleep on the plane ride home.

"There's going to be a sand sculpture contest at noon today out at the beach. Are either of you interested in participating in it?" I ask. "I was thinking that it might be fun for the three of us to work on creating something together."

"That sounds neat," Alex answers enthusiastically. "What kind of sand sculpture do you think we could make that might be different? All I can think of is the kind of castles that we used to build when we were little and went to visit Grandma and Grandpa in California. We always had so much fun there – especially when

Grandpa would cover our bodies up with sand, and we would have to struggle to get out."

Amanda, the creative one in our family, comes up with an idea. "How about if we make a big dragon? We could have it coming out from a cave, which we can make with a huge mound of sand."

"Great plan, Amanda," I reply. "We'll let you be the main designer since you already seem to have a picture in your mind of what it will look like. You give us the orders, and we'll follow whatever you say."

I can tell by the look on her face that she is pleased. The fact that she is going to be in charge is great for her. I am so glad I brought up the idea of the sand sculpture contest. When I first saw it on the schedule of events, I hesitated to mention it -- afraid that they might think it's only something for young kids to do.

Amanda and Alex get out of bed and start to get ready for the day ahead. Once they've brushed their teeth and are in their bathing suits, we leave our room and go downstairs for breakfast.

ೲ

"Okay, Amanda, you go get your death rays while Dad and I go jet skiing." Alex says.

"Say what you want, Alex. I'm going to be the one with a great tan. For sure, I'll look like I spent a weekend in Florida."

"We'll probably be gone about two hours, Amanda. Are you sure you don't want to come with us? I ask.

"No, thanks."

"Do you want anything before we go, then?"

"All I need is for the sun to keep on shining."

"Okay, then. Don't forget to use sunscreen, so you don't burn. We'll see you later," I say as Alex and I turn to go. I've got my arm around his shoulder; his arm is around my waist.

I look back at Amanda and unless I'm imagining something that isn't there, it looks like she has a sad expression on her face. My stomach drops wondering if I said or did anything to upset her. I feel uneasy and hope that she will be okay. I certainly don't want anything to be wrong after we have finally begun to make some headway this weekend.

As Alex and I walk away, he suddenly looks at me with a serious expression.

"Hey, Dad. Thanks for everything you've done for us this weekend. I'm really happy that we could be together – all three of us – far away from our everyday lives. When I come to Orlando to see you and we go to Disney World, it's always fun, but this is even better.

"Besides that, you're such a good dad. Two of my friends' parents are divorced, and they hardly ever even see their fathers. I listen to them complain all the time, and I know how lucky I am."

I'm taken aback. I never would have guessed that Alex would thank me as he has or acknowledge the kind of parent I have been to him. This is surely a moment to cherish.

I doubt that as a fifteen-year-old son, I ever gave my father a compliment and certainly never told him how I felt about him. Alex seems comfortable expressing himself in a loving way. He always has.

With that, I stop walking, grab hold of Alex, and give him a big hug. While there are situations when I would never do this in public because it would embarrass him, this time I can't resist. I'm touched when he hugs me back.

❧

After an hour-and-a-half of jet skiing, we head back to the hotel. As we are walking, Alex and I get into a conversation which comes as a bit of a surprise to me.

"I probably shouldn't tell you this, Dad, but there are times when Mom is mean to Amanda – and for no reason that I can tell. There is always tension in the house. Mom puts Amanda down for everything and never says anything nice to her. It seems like no matter what Amanda does, it's never good enough or right, according to Mom. It's really awful.

"Then when Amanda stands up for herself, Mom gets angry and either stops talking to her altogether or flies off into one of her screaming fits. That's when I get as far away as I can – usually I escape to my room.

"Mom never gives her any privacy either. She goes through Amanda's backpack without permission, and Amanda has even caught Mom reading her diary. It's almost as though she doesn't trust Amanda."

"How long has this been going on?" I ask.

"Well, from what I can remember, it seems like Mom hasn't been nice to Amanda since you left. Sometimes I think Mom doesn't even like her."

How can I have been so oblivious to this? How could it be that my own daughter could be suffering, and I didn't even know it?

From what Alex had mentioned to me from time to time, I had known that Sharon and Amanda have not gotten along particularly well with each other, but I had no idea just how bad it had become. I always chalked it up to Amanda being a teenager. And because of the way Amanda had acted toward me, I thought it might have been more of the same with Sharon. I didn't think it was anything out of the ordinary. I should have known!

Having lived with Sharon for sixteen years, I understand how she can be. When I think about it, there was never a time that I can remember when Sharon wasn't angry or finding fault with at least one person. Perhaps when I moved out and was not in her daily life, she transferred some of the anger she had toward me onto Amanda. I never expected that she would turn on one of our children as she has.

When we were married, things had to be done her way and if they weren't, she would be furious. She would stew over something throughout the night. Then the next morning, she would wake up and would begin the day by raging at me.

For whatever reason, I never stood up to her. Just when I thought I was ready to defend myself, I would chicken out. I was afraid of her anger. It reminded me of my father's, and that had always hit a nerve. Somehow as bad as Sharon's yelling was, it was easier for me to take the abuse than to confront her.

Sharon would humiliate me in front of our friends and neighbors. Once at an office party, she made a derogatory comment about me to my new boss. I was shocked that she would do that but probably not as surprised as he was. That was the last time I brought her to anything having to do with my work.

When she and I first started to date at the end of high school, she was sweet and attentive. But as the years went by, she was no longer the woman I had married. To me, Sharon had turned into a wretched, manipulative person. With each passing year, she made my life more miserable with her demands, her pathological lying, her need to control, and her excessive spending.

It was all about her and what she wanted and needed. She did anything she could to impress others and always felt entitled to the best. Everything she did was for show, including the kind of car she drove, the clothes she wore, and the neighborhood where she lived.

Her spending was totally out of control when we were married. There were many times when she was at the maximum limit on every credit card. No matter what I did and how much I threatened her, she wouldn't stop spending money. She didn't care about the consequences of her actions. She constantly lied to me about what she was doing. She would hide her purchases, find ways to take out new credit cards, throw away the monthly statements, and never think twice about any of this.

At the end of the month, if we were short of money to pay these huge bills, she would blame me. She had no trouble telling me that I wasn't earning enough. Of course, she never worked after Amanda was born, but I don't even want to think about that now.

It is so easy for my thoughts to go off on a tangent. This time, though, the real issue is realizing that my poor daughter has become the brunt of her mother's anger.

"Alex, how does Mom treat you? Do you have problems with her as Amanda does?"

"The strangest thing, Dad, is that Mom is always nice to me. It's almost as if she is like two different people with us. She does try to drag me in every once in a while. She'll say something bad about Amanda to me. I can tell she doesn't want me to like my sister. She is trying to divide us, but that isn't going to happen – despite what Mom does."

"This is so upsetting, Alex, but I'm glad you told me."

I'm now feeling all the more guilty for leaving the kids. Maybe if I had lived closer, things might have been better for Amanda. Maybe I should have just stayed in the marriage altogether and protected my children.

My stomach is turned upside down. My daughter must be so unhappy in her life. I have to find a way to talk to Amanda about all of this.

ᥱᥱᥣ

When we arrive back at the hotel, Amanda is still basking in the sun. She has headphones on and doesn't hear us when we approach. The pool is a mass of people, but she's in her own world.

When Alex taps her on her shoulder, she jumps up.

"How was it, Alex?" she asks.

"We had a totally amazing time. You wouldn't believe how much fun it is to ride the waves!"

"How about let's grab an early lunch so we can be ready for the contest?" I suggest. "I'm gearing up and am getting ready to win! I think our dragon will be a big hit with the judges."

ᔕᕓ

Right after we eat, I head back to the room to get more sunscreen for all of us, while Amanda and Alex claim their spot on the sand.

One thing I've observed this weekend is how organized Amanda is and how she always seems to have a plan. Amanda has kept her suitcase intact – no clothes out anywhere except for the new red and black striped bathing suit she bought and wore yesterday. I notice it hanging over the shower to dry.

Alex's mess is no surprise to me. It's pretty much the same way I kept my things when I was a teenager. As I look around the room, I see his clothes, shoes, and everything else he brought all over the place. What a disaster! It looks like someone dumped the contents of his suitcase on the floor. The only thing that is hanging up in the closet is his new army surplus jacket.

While I'm up here, I also put the valentines I brought for the kids on their beds, so they'll have them when we get back to our room. This is the first time in six years that we've been together on Valentine's Day, so I don't have to mail their cards to them. I wanted to get Amanda flowers, but I wasn't sure how she would react, and I didn't want to make her uncomfortable. Instead, I settled on getting them each a big bag of salt water taffy from downstairs. They could eat it on the plane ride home.

From the Broadwalk, I luckily spot Amanda and Alex in the mass of people on the beach. Amanda is in the process of smoothing out the area as I approach. Alex is beginning to gather piles of sand that we'll use for making our sand sculpture. All around us, I see others busy sculpting their creations.

We work for at least two hours. Amanda tells us what to do. Alex does most of the sand collecting. I'm in charge of fetching water from the ocean. Little by little, the three of us build a fearsome-looking dragon coming out from its cave. I am taken with Amanda's artistic touches. She pays attention to details and, in the most interesting way, has used stones, coral, and shells that she's found to decorate our sculpture. I'm impressed with her creativity and tell her. She seems pleased with the results.

In all, there must be at least sixty different groups or individuals who have entered the contest. When we finish, we walk around to check out the other entries, many of which are extraordinary.

Even though we don't win, we are happy with our results. Alex compliments Amanda on her artistic skills. "We should have won," he tells her and gives us both a high five.

I want to hug Amanda, but I hesitate once again – only because I don't know if she would want that or not. Instead, I smile at her and say, "Good job, Mandy."

I haven't called her that since she was thirteen years old. At that time, when Amanda was especially angry with me, she made it clear that she was no longer interested in hearing me address her with the endearing nickname we had given her when she was a baby.

Her smile has disappeared. She looks up at me and quietly says, "Thanks, Dad."

She turns away, picks up her towel, and tells us that she is heading back to the hotel.

Alex stays at the beach to play volleyball, but I've had enough activity. Also, I want to spend some time alone with Amanda.

As I walk through the hotel's lobby, in the distance I hear a rock band playing Elton John's "Sorry Seems to Be the Hardest Word." Suddenly, this song seems to have meaning for me.

On my way to Room 732, I find myself thinking about Amanda. I have been pleasantly surprised to see that she has been more comfortable with me this weekend, but I'm terribly concerned about what is going on at home with Sharon.

Lost in these thoughts as I turn the key to open the door, I hear a sobbing sound from inside the room. Sprawled across the big bed is Amanda, face down, with her shoulders trembling.

I rush over to her and sit down on the edge of the bed. "What's the matter, Amanda?"

She turns her head to look up at me and continues to cry.

Without giving it a thought, I move closer, bend down, and put my arm around her. As soon as I touch Amanda, her racking sobs get louder. She lifts herself up to move closer to me and puts her head down on my lap.

I gently stroke her hair with my fingers, just like I used to do when she was a little girl. We stay in this position – the closest we have been to each other in years. After a few minutes, I notice a shift in her breathing as she tries hard to stop herself from crying. Occasionally, she sniffles.

I look down at my daughter and see that her tears are still flowing. I am close enough to the Kleenex box to grab a few tissues without having to move. I place them in her hand. She sits up, wipes her eyes, and blows her nose.

"Do you want to talk, Mandy?"

"I do, but I'm not sure I can," she says through her gasping breaths.

Again we sit quietly. From my earlier conversation with Alex, I have my suspicions as to why she might be crying. I don't know what to say. I'm so afraid of ruining this moment.

She puts the tissues down on the bed and turns to look at me. Now face to face with her, I take both her hands. We sit staring into one another's eyes, and again her tears begin to flow.

I wait patiently and eventually, through her tears, she begins.

"This weekend has been great in so many ways," she says as she sighs deeply. "But I am feeling so sad."

"Can you tell me why, Mandy?"

"I have been watching you and Alex together, and the more I'm with both of you, the harder it is for me."

"Why is that?"

Amanda pulls one hand away to wipe the tears from her cheek. "Well, I see how close the two of you are. It seems like you and Alex can talk about anything. From the start when you moved out, I was stupid not to give you a chance. I have been so mean to you. I feel awful."

She pauses for a minute. "Alex was the smart one. He never was angry with you for leaving, which meant that he could always enjoy being with you. I watch how playful you are together and how much fun you have doing all kinds of things. I feel jealous.

"I just wish that I could have a relationship like that with you. I miss you and all the fun we used to have when I was little. Sometimes I sit and think about what my life was like before you left, and I find myself wishing I could go back and try again."

I am listening to every word and want to let Amanda know how glad I am that she is telling me all of this. Just as I am putting together my thoughts and thinking about the right words to say to her, she goes on.

"Part of why I treated you like I did when you left was because I thought I was the reason you and Mom got divorced. I used to lie in bed and think about all the things I must have done to make you angry enough to walk out on us. Now that I look back on it, I think I felt ashamed. I didn't know what to do with those feelings, so I blamed you instead.

"It took a long time for me to figure out that it wasn't my fault. In fact, I am only now just realizing what life must have been like for you being married to Mom. I know you probably aren't going to believe me, but for the past several years, she has been impossible with me. You used to be her scapegoat. Now I am."

I am stunned at what Amanda has just said. How on earth could she possibly understand all of this at her young age? Now that she has mentioned the issue with her mother, I want to ask her to tell me more about what has been going on at home. I can barely contain myself, but I must wait. I'll get my chance when she finishes.

Amanda keeps talking without taking a break. "I only figured it all out when I went to the counselor at school this year. Ms. Starkey, my all-time favorite teacher, suggested I see Mr. Gerwin. I didn't want to go at first because I didn't think I could ever talk to a man, but he was warm and welcoming and was the best listener. He helped me to understand more about Mom and why she was treating me so horribly. She keeps getting worse, and my relationship with her is miserable. Honestly, I can't wait to get out of there and go to college in the fall.

"And by the way, she's almost never mean or nasty to Alex. He is her golden child. Of course, he yeses her to death – something I can't and won't ever do. He plays the game in order to keep peace. He could win an Academy Award. Mom is clueless and just thinks he's the best."

Amanda shifts her position and takes her hand away to rub her eyes. I don't move nor do I say a word. My heart is breaking for my daughter.

"Don't get me wrong. I love Alex. He's such a good kid. He sometimes tries to stick up for me, but that only gets Mom angrier. I know he cares and does whatever he can to make peace in the house. Truthfully, I'm glad that he doesn't have to take her abuse like I do.

"But when I see how Alex and you are with each other, I want that, too." Amanda stops talking for a minute, and I hold my breath, waiting to hear what she is going to say next.

"The more I'm with you I see how kind you are. In all these years, you have never once stopped trying to have a relationship with me. Don't think I haven't noticed. Even today when I read your valentine, which is what started my crying, I realized that no matter how I've treated you, you have consistently done everything to show me that you have not given up on me.

"Mr. Gerwin talked to me about unconditional love and how there are some parents who show their children in every way possible that they are there for them. That's what you have given me, Daddy, even when I absolutely didn't deserve it."

I smile at Mandy and quietly mouth the words, "Thank you."

She continues, "The reason I came this weekend was that Mr. Gerwin said he felt that this would be an opportunity for us to heal. He thought it would be especially good because we weren't on my territory or yours. I think he was right."

As soon as she pauses for an instant, I jump in. "Mandy, I am so glad that you are here and that you are telling me all this."

There is much more I want and need to tell my daughter, but just as I am about to comment on her conversation with Mr. Gerwin, Amanda interrupts me.

"Daddy, please let me finish. I have to say all these things to you now while I'm finally doing it. I need to get it all out."

I nod and know that I am going to have to wait.

"Plus after all these months of talking to Mr. Gerwin, he felt I was ready to face up to the role I've played in causing the distance and pain between us. He made it clear to me that what I need to do is apologize to you. And so, Daddy, I hope you will believe me when I tell you I am sorry.

"I'm sorry for my anger toward you. I'm sorry that I have let all these years go by when we could have been together. I'm sorry that I never showed you that I appreciated your cards and calls and letters, and instead ignored you. I'm sorry that I have been such an awful daughter."

Amanda stops talking and scoots over so she is closer to my side. The moment I have been waiting for all these years is finally here. She throws her arms around me and gives me the biggest, most wonderful hug – the kind I have yearned for.

"Mandy," I softly utter as I cradle the top of her head. "Look at me."

She looks up into my face with tears once again streaming down her cheeks. "I want you to know that I have loved you since the day you were born. While I was sad that you chose to stay away from me, my love for you has never changed. It only made me long for this moment.

"For all these years, I have felt guilty for leaving you. I am sorry for that. And when I was really honest with myself, I could understand why you were angry with me.

"This is a new beginning. We don't have to look back. Those days are gone. Now we need to treasure every minute we have together from this day forward."

With that, I hear a key turning in our door. What timing.

Alex walks in, and immediately I see a shocked look on his face.

I smile and motion to him to come over to us. Alex sits down next to me, and I reach for his hand. As Amanda's tears subside, she takes my other hand. I have everything I could ever want at this moment in time.

GRANDMA'S LOVING LEGACY

HOLLYWOOD BEACH
OCEAN RESORT
1995

My plane landed in Ft. Lauderdale about a half hour ago, and now I'm hoping Esther's will be on time. Based on her flight information, I'll only have to wait another forty-five minutes, I hope.

We were together at Grandma's funeral two months ago, but being with Esther this time is going to be different. We won't have our mothers or anyone else from the family with us. I don't think we've ever been together for more than a day when there wasn't at least one other relative around.

The closest we've come to being alone with each other, aside from our mothers putting us in the same crib when we were infants, is when we went on the cruise with Grandma and Grandpa for our high school graduations. That was the best because they were terrific about giving us space to do as we pleased.

It helped that our grandparents wanted to participate in different activities than we did each night. They also understood that what appealed to them held no interest for us. Both Esther and I enjoyed the excursions with Grandma and Grandpa during the day because they sure knew how to have a great time and were such adventurous people. I doubt that my parents or Esther's would have been as willing to explore in the same way that Grandma and Grandpa did.

I haven't thought about that trip in a while. I imagine that being with Esther this next week is going to be filled with lots of special moments and memories.

I was bursting with excitement when I called to tell her my intriguing news and was disappointed when she wasn't home. So, instead, I left her an enticing message. "You need to call me right away. I'm still at my mom's and will be leaving here tomorrow. I found something for you and me from Grandma. Get back to me right away! Hurry! I can't stand having to wait to tell you about this."

It was a few days after Grandma's funeral, and Aunt Sylvia and Uncle Sidney had gone back to Chicago. Esther and Josh had already left for California. My sweet Gary had flown back to D.C. the night before for a big case the next day.

I had decided I would stay in Philly and help Mom clean out Grandma's dresser and closet. I knew it would be hard for her to do alone, and besides, I wanted to be with my mother. I figured she would need the company after Grandma's passing. It was all too close to my father's death.

Aunt Sylvia had helped my mom get rid of my father's wardrobe six months after he passed away. It had been difficult going through his clothes, with his scent still lingering on them.

My plan was to help complete this with Grandma's things before I headed home -- take Grandma's entire wardrobe to Goodwill and donate her books to the library. We discovered that Grandma had left a list of all her jewelry with the names of who should get each piece, so there were no questions and no arguments. It was easy to pass things out to everyone. Grandma had more than enough for our mothers, me, Esther, and all her nieces and great-nieces. She was a woman who loved jewelry. It didn't surprise me that she remembered everyone who mattered to her during her life.

In addition to being totally organized in every way, another thing I can say about Grandma is that she always looked immaculate. Her closets were filled with some of the most fashionable clothes one could imagine for an eighty-two-year-old woman. People would stop her on the street and in the grocery store and tell her how stunning she looked. Everything she wore matched, including her shoes, outfits, jewelry, and purses. She was like her own personal style show each day.

I always felt proud of her and bragged that she was my grandmother. She never looked her age. Sometimes people mistook her for my mom's sister, which Grandma delighted in and my mother hated!

When Grandma fell last year and broke her hip, Mom and Aunt Sylvia went down to Florida and closed up her apartment. Then they brought her to Philly and moved her into Mom's house. My mother let her bring her favorite, big red chair and the dresser that she loved and had had since she and Grandpa first got married. I think it helped her feel more like she was at home having those few things with her.

Grandma had a hard time getting rid of most of her "treasures," but she felt better when Mom and Aunt Sylvia agreed to take many of them. Then together the three of them sorted through Grandma's antiques and other cherished items and filled boxes of all kinds of goodies for me and Esther. For example, I got her sterling silverware, her Hibel plates, and her candlesticks. Esther was thrilled to receive Grandma's china, our great-grandmother's soup tureen, and hand-embroidered tablecloths.

One day after shiva when the rest of our family went back home, I told Mom I was going to get started cleaning out Grandma's stuff. My mother had some friends over, and it seemed like a good time to excuse myself and dig in. Aside from the usual things one would find in a dresser, like underwear and nightgowns, I came across all kinds of lovely items -- colorful, monogrammed hankies, a variety of decorative scarves, several small beaded coin purses, and leather wallets.

She had one drawer that was filled with eye shadow, lipstick, face powder, blush, and mascara. It was always important to Grandma that she put on her make-up and never missed a day, no matter how sick she was. I can't ever remember her leaving the house without wearing lipstick. To this day, I will never understand how it stayed on her lips. Mine sure doesn't.

Systematically I went through each drawer and only threw away a few things, since Grandma kept everything in such good condition. There were no overstuffed drawers as one would surely find in my dresser. It made me think about going home and getting myself a bit more organized.

When I came to the bottom drawer, I found several purses, two swimsuits, some old Playbills, certificates, birthday cards, and valentines. Tucked beneath everything else, I noticed a thick, manila envelope. I had no idea what it was until I took it out. On the cover was written in big black letters: TO BE OPENED BY MIRIAM AND ESTHER TOGETHER UPON MY DEATH. RUTH, DARLING, IF YOU FIND THIS, PLEASE GIVE IT TO MIRIAM AND HONOR MY WISHES TO LET HER AND ESTHER OPEN IT, AS THE CONTENTS OF THIS ENVELOPE ARE FOR THEIR EYES ONLY.

And so, here I am waiting patiently for my cousin to arrive so that we can finally open whatever jewel it is that Grandma left us. To ensure its safety up until now, I have kept the envelope in our safe deposit box. Yesterday I went to the bank and took it out.

‿◦

"Do you care which bed you sleep in, Miriam?" Esther asks, as she readies herself to plop down on the twin bed closest to the little kitchenette.

"I'm happy to have either one as long as I can look out at the sea," I answer.

With the time difference from California, the day has been a long one for Esther. She had to be at the Los Angeles airport at five o'clock this morning and had a long layover in Dallas. It's now almost six o'clock in the evening, and we are finally settling into Room 732 at the Hollywood Beach Ocean Resort.

"I'm exhausted," declares Esther. "I need to take a short nap before I do anything else. I understand that you can't wait to open the envelope, but I absolutely have to rest first."

While I can hardly stand another minute of waiting, I want the moment to be right for both of us. I must be patient. If Esther is that tired, the experience – whatever it is going to be – will not be right for her. With the two of us pregnant and both expecting within the next four months or so, we are often in need of a rest and seem to be much less energetic than usual.

I'm still not sure how it happened that we are having babies close together just as our mothers had the two of us within a month of each other. It has to be more than a coincidence. Without question, Esther is the closest person I have in my life. She is not only a first cousin but a friend as well. While I never was fortunate enough to have a sister, I doubt that any two sisters could be closer than we are. As we often joke, we can have it all without any of the sibling rivalry. It doesn't get better than that.

$$\infty$$

After about a half hour, Esther begins to stir. As soon as I see her eyes open, I practically pounce on her. "Okay, can we finally open the envelope?"

She immediately smiles and nods her head. "Thanks for being so patient. I'm sure that this was a stretch for you!"

"You don't know how agonizing this has been," I exclaim. "Whenever I receive anything in the mail, I always open it immediately. You're much different from me in that regard."

"That's only because my parents trained me. I was never allowed to open cards or gifts until my birthday. Since I've had to wait all my life, I guess it doesn't bother me like it does you."

"That's probably why Gary and I know we're having a girl," I say, "and you and Josh are waiting to find out the sex of your baby."

I make my way over to my briefcase and pull out the envelope from Grandma. I hand it to Esther with a huge smile on my face.

Esther holds it close to her heart, sniffs it, and exclaims, "It smells like Grandma's potpourri! Look at how perfect her lettering is. Her writing makes me think about her as a first grade teacher. I bet her students loved her."

I agree. "Grandma was pretty amazing in many ways – her printing included. No matter what she did, it was always done well."

"Now that you've held the envelope and seen it, what in the world do you think is in it? I showed it to my mother, and she thought that maybe Grandma saved some of our letters to her and old school papers for us to have when we got older. Or I'm wondering if it might be our mothers' things that Grandma has kept through the years."

Esther replies, "It could be just about anything, Miriam. You know how Grandma was – always sending us surprises. I'm sure she saved everything she received from both of us. I remember my mom once telling me that Grandma still had the invitation to her own high school and college graduations as well as those of both our mothers'. My guess is that she had ours as well. Maybe that's what's in the envelope.

"Can you believe that we're here at this hotel on the beach about to embark on this unknown adventure? Or at least I hope it will be once we open the envelope. I'm so glad that I suggested coming here right near where Grandma lived and at the beach where she always took us, rather than meeting at one of our houses. This makes it all the more fun and brings Grandma along with us in a special way."

"Yes, I'm so happy that we're here, but as they say at the Oscars, 'May I have the envelope, please?'"

Esther hands me the manila envelope, and I carefully open it. Inside are eight sealed, legal-sized white envelopes. On each one is written ESTHER AND MIRIAM with a different number from one to eight beneath our names.

"One last chance to guess what's in these envelopes," I offer as they cascade onto the bed.

"I have no idea, but I sure as hell can't wait to open them. Obviously there is some order to this – just like Grandma to have done it all perfectly."

At that point, I can wait no longer and grab the first envelope. I put the other seven back into the bigger envelope and hand the one to Esther. "Here, you open it."

Esther, in her teasing, adorable way, responds, "*Moi?*"

"Please do it already. The suspense is killing me," I plead. Esther excitedly opens the envelope and takes out a few pieces of pink stationery. As she unfolds them, she announces, "It's a letter to us. Shall I read it?"

"Go ahead," I urge.

And so, Esther begins.

January 7, 1995

Dear Miriam and Esther,

My time on earth is running out. Before I depart from this life as I know it, I want to share some thoughts I have with the two of you. First and foremost, please don't be sad. I beg of you to remember me with a smile and not with tears.

The most important thing to know is that life is not about how long we live. It's how we live that matters. Without question, I have led a fulfilled and wonderful life.

When you read these letters, you might ask yourselves why I didn't give each of them to you at the appropriate time in your lives. It's a good question, and one that I have given much thought to through the years. The truth is that if you reach back in your memory, you will realize that all I've written in here are things that I've talked to you about at one time

197

or another. Most likely there is little in any of these letters that will be new to you. The teacher in me never passed up the opportunities to teach right on the spot.

Instead, these letters are more or less something to ponder as you approach motherhood. I'm hopeful that you will use what I've written as a guide for raising your own children in much the same way that you were raised. My parting gift is to leave you with some thoughts and ideas which I hope will serve as a reminder of what I felt was important and which might make a difference in the way you live your lives from this day forward.

There were moments when I was about to weaken and send the letters, but something always stopped me. In retrospect, I'm not sorry now and wasn't then either. I figured that they would have meaning whenever you read them. At least that has always been my hope.

After I sealed each envelope, I never read the contents again. I can only trust that what I wrote will be of some importance for you. They were written from my heart, out of the deepest part of who I am to you as your grandmother.

Some of what is in the letters might seem like pure advice, which you can take or leave. If I sound preachy, ignore that as well. I have written what I did because it felt like the right thing to do at the time. Also, if any of what I wrote is outdated and/or inappropriate, then disregard it and consider the fact that I have written out of love for both of you. Even in my death, I guess I will continue to be somewhat of a controlling person – "the boss" as Grandpa called me.

Mostly I have written these letters to you to share what I have learned in my own life, what I have thought and felt, and what is important to me. I had a wonderful and special relationship with my grandmother and hope that in your lives, you will think of me and know that what we had between us was meaningful and lasting. The two of you, by being my granddaughters, have given me the greatest gift – that of being able to love you unconditionally.

Included in the seven other envelopes are letters which I wrote to both of you at five-year intervals from the time you were born. The first letters are individually written, and the rest are combined to the two of you. I always hoped and believed that you would remain close to each other and never considered doing this any other way.

Sometimes I would sit and fantasize about what the scene would be like when you would be together opening these envelopes. Always I felt sure it would be done in a loving atmosphere between you. I imagined various places you might be. I wondered how you would feel as you read my words – thus bringing my voice to you in some way.

I wrote the initial letter to you, Miriam, since you were born first. I knew that another granddaughter or grandson would soon follow, but I felt that it would be more significant if I wrote to you alone. Then a month later when you were born, Esther, I sat down and composed a letter to you as well.

With my physical health as it is and from what the doctor has said, I doubt that I will live to see either of you become mothers. However, I must say that knowing you are each bringing a child into this world leaves me feeling complete and happy. Hopefully, something of what you have gained from having me as your grandmother will live on within you and ultimately within your children. It is my wish that I will be remembered in that way.

Rejoice in the wonderful memories that we created together. When you look up and see the first twinkling star in the sky each night, know that I will be watching over you and will be smiling down on you. I will never be farther than a thought away. By staying alive in your memory, I will be living on forever.

My hope is that the two of you will continue to be wonderful daughters to your parents. My daughters, your mothers, are good women who love you very much. Always treat them with respect and kindness as you have all your lives.

In turn, also value the friendship you have with one another. You are truly blessed to have a cousin who treasures and cares about you in the way that you both do for each other.

Most of all, know that I considered the two of you as my most precious blessings. From the day I became a grandmother, my life changed in ways I could never describe to you.

Both of you have allowed me to trust in the present and have given me hope for the future. I love you more than you will ever know.

> *With love and gratitude*
> *for who you are in my life,*
> *Grandma*

I wipe the tears as they roll down my cheeks. Esther is doing the same inches away. Both of us are silent as Grandma's words sink in.

Neither of us is able to say anything at the moment. We sit on the bed lost in our own thoughts.

Some minutes later, Esther remarks, "How typical of Grandma it is for her to have written us a letter like that. I didn't have any idea what to expect, but surely I would not have dreamed that she would do something like this for us."

"I feel moved beyond words," I reply.

"I think that we should save the rest of the letters and each day read another one. How do you feel about that?" Esther asks.

"I like that idea," I respond. "That way we can savor them and have more than enough to think about throughout the day. Hey, how about if we read one letter every night before we go to bed? It'll be a meaningful way to end our days. I feel so close to Grandma now and just want to lie here and relish this special feeling."

After a while, we decide to get something to eat in one of the restaurants downstairs and then sit out at the beach. With Grandma's words still lingering in our thoughts, we enjoy the balmy breezes and the waves rushing onto the shore.

∾

I hear a muffled sound and a woman calling my name. I awake with a start. The hair on the back of my neck feels like it is standing up, and I begin to get uncontrollable chills. When I open my eyes, I immediately sit up and see an image of a woman in a flowing, white dressing gown floating to the edge of my bed. She appears bright and yet transparent, and within seconds, her voice fades and she is gone.

I quickly lie down and my mind drifts back to the dream I had moments before I woke up. In it, a woman walked into this room late at night. In bed, a man still dressed in his military uniform was crying. The lady made her way over to comfort him. He kept talking about the awful nightmare he had in which he killed several innocent children who were victims of a grenade he threw during a war.

She calmed him down with her sweet voice and pleasant manner. The woman began to undress the man and before long, she started to make love to him. While he was enjoying all that she was doing to arouse him, he suddenly sat up and said, "Is this you, Mary Beth?"

"No, sweetheart, it's Ashlyn." That was when I woke up and saw that image before me.

Was it a ghost? Am I going crazy? Did I really see something? Esther will think I'm out of my mind if I tell her. What do I do with this? For now, I'll try to ignore the fact that this happened and do my best to go back to sleep. The clock reads 12:12. There are many more hours until daybreak.

∽

My first thoughts as I hear Esther in the bathroom are about what took place when she was asleep. While I hesitate to tell her what I experienced in the middle of the night, I doubt that I can hold it in and not to talk to her about it. On the other hand, I'm not sure it was real.

As I lie here waiting to brush my teeth and take a shower, I realize how grateful I am for what my grandmother has done for us and also how she has inspired me. Before I fell asleep last night, I was thinking about when I become a mother. I decided that, similar to what she did, I would like to write my child a letter on each of her birthdays.

∽

Esther and I have had a full and wonderful day and are both happy to be in one another's company. The two of us always have so much to say to each other. I thought that while we sat down by the water, we might end up reading the books we each brought, but that never happened. We were way too busy talking. I never did tell her about what I saw last night, though. Somehow the words wouldn't come out.

We walked down to Nicky's and had pizza for dinner. Both of us are being careful about what we eat because we want to give our babies the best nourishment. However, once in a while, we need to splurge. Besides, we agreed that tomatoes and cheese are healthy, so having a few slices of pizza was just fine.

It's great to have this time to relax and enjoy being together. Esther is easy in every way and is often quite funny. Josh must appreciate her great sense of humor. I sure do enjoy laughing with her.

We are back in Room 732 and ready to open up envelope number two. The anticipation mounts. According to Grandma's letter yesterday, this is the one that has a letter for me and one for Esther, so we have decided that we will each read our own silently and then switch and read the other's.

June 14, 1965

Dear Miriam,

Welcome to the world! According to what your father told me on the phone, you look like your mother did in her baby pictures. The genes in our family are good and strong ones.

It's going to be difficult to wait six days before I can come and see you. All I keep thinking about is what it will be like to hold you, but until then, I will fill my time imagining and dreaming about you and what you look like.

Grandpa and I have been waiting anxiously for you to be born. Today was an especially long day since we knew your mother was in labor, and we had no way of getting in touch with her or your father. In fact, we hadn't asked what hospital they were at, so we were at a loss.

Each time the phone rang at Grandpa's office, he was sure it was news of your birth. I was in my classroom all day and could barely concentrate. I doubt that my students learned anything. With it being the end of the school year, it really doesn't matter. I'm not doing all that much teaching anyway – mostly closing up the books for the semester.

Grandpa left the office early, and both of us were home by 3:45 p.m. waiting to hear from your dad. Finally, at around 4:30 p.m., he called to tell us that you had been born. When we heard that you were a girl, we had huge smiles on our faces. Then when he told us that your name was Miriam Sarah, I melted as it touched a soft spot in my heart. It is one of the most beautiful names I've ever heard.

You are named for my mother, Malka Sora. She was a brave and kind woman. She left Kiev with two small children and her mother and came to the United States by boat in 1910 to meet my father who had arrived a few years before. They settled in Philadelphia, and I was born three years later.

Great-Grandma Malka had five children. She sewed all our clothes, cooked delicious meals, kept an immaculate home, and worked hard at assimilating into the American culture. She did not want to be one of those foreigners who never learned the language or the ways of her new country. That made my life much easier because she was not an old-fashioned kind of woman like so many others who came from Europe.

Throughout my life, she stressed the importance of an education. That's why my sisters and I went to college, while none of our other girlfriends did. It was almost unheard of in my day – but not with my mother in charge.

One of the things I appreciated most about her was her generous spirit. She always made room at the table for anyone who was alone and needed a meal. My father would bring home people whom he met and liked through shul or work in the tailor shop. My mother never complained.

She was a good soul who had a heart of gold, loved people, and was cherished by everyone. Great-Grandma Malka was a warm and affectionate person – one who always went out of her way for others. Your mother has a lot of these qualities, as you will learn when you get older.

My mother has one living sibling left, her sister Leah, who will soon be eighty-eight years old. When we called her tonight to tell her about your birth and who you were named after, she said, "Malka knows." She adored her sister, so it means the world to her that someone has been named after her.

I got chills listening to your father describe how absolutely beautiful you are. He told us that you have a full head of dark brown hair. He also explained how he got to carry you to the nursery and how he is already in love with you. He sounded wonderfully joyous, as are we.

About an hour ago, we were able to speak to your mother. She described how you were lying by her side and how peaceful and precious you were. I could hear in her voice that she is thrilled to have a daughter. She mentioned that you have olive skin like your father and that you already have a pink bow in your hair.

I close my eyes and imagine your soft skin, tiny fingers and toes, and bright eyes. Soon you will be cuddled in my arms.

My wish for you is that you will live your life fully – learning for yourself and finding your way. In doing so, my hope is that you will feed your soul with goodness and love and will kindle your spark within as you experience all that is available to you.

You have given me a dream come true. I now am a grand-mother and hope I can become the same kind of wonderful grandmother that my mother was to your mother.

> *With love always,*
> *Grandma*

I am left speechless. I look over at Esther who is lost in her own world as she reads the letter Grandma wrote to her.

July 12, 1965

Dear Esther,

Early this morning before Grandpa left for work, we got a call from your father telling us that you had been born. I am ecstatic at the thought of having another granddaughter. The first thing that occurred to me was how special it will be for you to have a girl cousin the same age as you. One day you will understand what I mean by that. I love the idea of having two granddaughters.

Your name is a beautiful one – Esther Lynn. The fact that you are named for my father, Edward Louis, is thrilling to me. He was a gentle soul whom everyone loved. Your great-grand-father had an abundance of friends, was a fair and honest man, went to great lengths to let each of his grandchildren and nieces and nephews know that he or she was important to him, and always had a kind word for everyone he met.

When your great-grandfather left Russia, he came here without knowing a single person. He landed at Ellis Island and quickly learned that he was truly a foreigner in this new country. When he gave his name upon arrival, within minutes he discovered that he already had been given a new Americanized name.

He was able to find work in a clothing factory and soon after, he moved to Philadelphia with one of the men from his hometown, someone whom he had met up with on the street in New York City. A few years later after he had saved enough money, he sent for your great-grandmother and their two children. They reunited and three years later, I was born.

Great-Grandpa Edward was a proud man. He would have been delighted at the idea of having a great-grandchild named after him. Generally girls are named after women in our Jewish tradition, but in this case, I don't think it much matters. How meaningful it is that your parents chose to honor someone who was as special as my father. You have a wonderful legacy to live up to for the rest of your life.

I'm glad that your father still has two grandparents. They are the lucky ones to experience having a great-grandchild and you, in turn, will be fortunate to have them in your life.

I can't wait to hold you in my arms. I know that I am going to fall in love with you the minute I lay eyes on you. Just thinking about that brings a huge smile to my face. Luckily, because I'm on vacation, I'm not going to have to wait more than a few days to be in Chicago with you.

Your mother called us a little while ago, and it sounds like she had an uneventful labor and delivery. It took about ten hours from start to finish for you to come into this world. She appears to be absolutely thrilled about your birth.

You are a little one — only five pounds, twelve ounces and eighteen inches long. Your dad said that your eyes are like big blue saucers. I wonder if they will stay that color. We aren't used to anything but brown eyes in our family, but your dad's side has a few relatives with hazel eyes. Maybe you will break the mold for both families.

The way your mother described you, I can picture you all swaddled in a pink striped blanket with your fair white skin and rosy cheeks. She said that you have a little pink cap on your head and tiny mittens on your hands. You sound like one adorable bundle of joy.

From what I hear, your lungs are working fine. I under-stand that you came out crying. Maybe you weren't ready to leave the comfort of your mother's womb, but believe me when I tell you that you are going to be one lucky child to have your wonderful parents. They will provide you with everything you need to lead a contented and fulfilled life.

My hope for you is that you will always experience a life-time filled with adventure, love, and happiness. Let your inner flame be your guiding light as you make your way into this world and embrace each moment as it presents itself to you.

With love always,
Grandma

We look at each other with tears in our eyes. We exchange letters, read them, and know that we are the ones who have been given a tremendous gift.

◦∽◦

"This has been another fabulous day, but I'm ready to put my feet up and relax," Esther declares.

"Let's not waste any time getting to the next letter. I'm so curious to see what Grandma wrote to us when we were five years old. What on earth could she possibly have said to two little girls?" I wonder aloud.

Esther opens the envelope and begins.

September 10, 1970

Dear Miriam and Esther,

Tomorrow is a big day for you as you begin kindergarten. These five years have passed quickly.

It's an exciting time for me personally, since the first day of school each year is always my favorite. My students come dressed in their finest clothes and shiny shoes, armed with sharpened pencils and brand-new boxes of crayons, and sporting eager attitudes and best behaviors – ready for whatever I can teach them.

In addition to thinking of the boys and girls in my first grade class, my thoughts turn to the two of you and how it will be when you kiss your mommies goodbye, walk into your classrooms, and begin your lives as students. You will be foremost in my mind as I anxiously await word on how you did on your first day of kindergarten.

Grandpa and I just hung up from talking to both of you. Esther, you told us you can't wait to meet your teacher, but you don't want to stay in school. My guess is that once you have spent the day there tomorrow, you will be fine. Often we fear those things that we don't know. Perhaps in life if you can face your fears by tackling them head on, you will be much better off in the long-run. That's usually the way it works best.

Miriam, you seemed a little more enthusiastic about embarking on this new experience. It probably helped going to school last week for orientation. Unlike Esther, you know what your classroom looks like, who your teacher is, and how you will be spending your day. That makes a huge difference. You are the lucky one in all of this. I'm surprised that Esther's school didn't invite the kindergarteners to visit for at least an hour to prepare the students for what is to come.

Going to school is the start of growing up. Within these next five years, you will discover many things which will become the basis of your lives. Aside from the normal studies like learning to read, understanding numbers, becoming aware of the world around you through science and social studies, much of what you will be exposed to will serve as a guide to who you will be later in your lives. While academics are important, what matters most to me is the development of your character.

Some of that will come by way of play. It is during kindergarten and the early elementary school grades that you will learn what it means to cooperate and share with others. There may be times when you are going to want to be the one to make the rules or will want to play with a certain toy. I hope you will also step back and give others a turn. Being the line leader feels important and special, but we can't always run the show. Sometimes we learn more from taking orders than from giving them.

One of the most important things you will experience during these years is learning to be a good friend. I hope you will always be nice to others. If you show that you care about them, it will make a difference in their lives. If you see a classmate by herself on the playground, please make an effort to include her in whatever you're doing. Helping someone when you see she needs a little kindness is the right thing to do. Also, if you get into a fight with a friend and in your heart you know you were wrong, learn to say you are sorry. Asking for forgiveness goes a long way; so does forgiving someone else.

When I remember back on my elementary school years, some things were a little different for me. My parents were learning

English, so they weren't able to communicate with my teachers the way yours can. Yet, my mother always encouraged me to do my best, to come right home from school and do my homework before I did anything else, to follow the rules and listen to my teachers, and to be as independent as possible. She exposed me to exploring my world – always interested in what could be learned in my own backyard. I feel sure that your parents will make every effort to support you in much the same way my mother did.

During these next few years, you are going to learn how to read and will master that skill. At some point, you will begin to understand that reading is a path to learning. The world is open to you. There is so much that you can gain from books. I hope you find a comfortable spot in your school library and visit it often.

My wish for both of you today and for the rest of your lives is that you take learning seriously and realize that there is always something new to explore. Embrace your education and stay open to every experience and opportunity that comes your way.

With love always,
Grandma

We look at each other and realize that what Grandma has written holds many important truths. While we would not have understood this as kindergarteners, we know in our hearts that her advice will be a guide for us as we raise our children. I have a feeling that Grandma was aware of this and wrote the letters with that in mind – knowing that she might not be alive these many years later. Her plan to save these letters, like so many other things in her life, was carefully thought out.

❧

Even though we knew we were risking indigestion from spicy Italian food, we chose to have a delicious meal of eggplant parmesan at Angelo's on the Broadwalk. Now we are slowly meandering back to our hotel. It's probably a good mile each way, so we are doubling our exercise for the day. Each morning we are taking wonderful walks along the shore.

We have done little else but talk, walk, and rest. Neither of us is used to this kind of relaxation between work and all that we have going on in our lives. We also know that soon everything will be drastically different and that a week like this will be a luxury.

At the end of each day, our only focus is reading Grandma's letters. We open envelope four.

December 18, 1975

Dear Esther and Miriam,

Now that you are almost halfway through fifth grade, your lives are beginning to take shape. You both have celebrated your first double-digit birthdays and are officially pre-teens. You soon will be making the transition from elementary school to junior high school. I don't want to rush the time away, but it is on the horizon.

The greatest thing about this part in your life is that you can still enjoy being a child at times and yet, at other times, you want nothing more than to be all grown up. I noticed that when we were together for Rosh Hashanah this past September, you were both much more interested in sitting with the adults than in going off to play with your younger cousins. It used to be that you couldn't wait to be excused from the table.

Believe me, I'm not complaining. It is wonderful to have you joining in on our conversations. You definitely are showing signs of more mature thinking. The only difference is that as hard as you try to act like adults, you don't have the experience and judgment that comes with years of living. That will happen in time, but it is fascinating to watch the process beginning.

I also notice that your friends are becoming your main interest. No longer is your world identified by family alone. It won't be long before what they say will matter much more to you than what your parents tell you. You are going to want to be accepted by your friends, and as a result, I imagine that you will be doing whatever you can to be like them. You might want to dress exactly like your peers, so that you all look the same. Embrace your own special traits and never lose sight of your individual uniqueness. Please don't forget that you have opinions and thoughts that are yours alone. Don't follow the crowd in order to be accepted. Make sure to find friends who will value you because of who you are and how you think and not those who only want you to agree with them.

During these next few years, you will become more aware of how people treat one another. I hope I can count on you to be respectful of everyone you meet. If you see that someone is not being kind to another person, please make a point to let him or her know that there is another way to be – whether through words or deeds. Doing a random act of kindness is a mitzvah, which feels good for both you and the person who benefits.

When I was exactly your age, I learned an important life lesson. My Uncle Sam, my mother's brother, was an old man by then and lived in another city far from us. He would visit once a year. It was important to me that he knew how much I adored him. I decided that I needed to tell him, so I wrote him a letter. Each day I would ask my father if Uncle Sam had received my letter. From that time forth, I made up my mind never to wait to tell anyone how I felt about him or her. As a result, I began to live my life differently. I didn't hold back my feelings and made sure to let people know that they mattered to me. Even at that young age, I knew that I never wanted to live with regrets of unspoken words.

When we were last together in Florida, the three of us spent a lot of time outdoors. I hold dear the memories of our walks along the ocean searching for shells and then going back to my place and looking through all the shell books to identify what we found.

I noticed that you both also seemed more aware of the physical beauty that surrounded you. You commented on the weather, the skies, the palm trees, and the birds overhead. I hope you will always respect and appreciate our environment. Take the time to pick up a piece of paper that is littering the sidewalk. Plant a tree or a garden. Make an effort to leave this a better world.

One of the things that helps get me through the tough times in my life is having a sense of humor. If I can laugh at myself and/or a particularly difficult situation, I am always better off. I've watched both of you and see that you also enjoy a good laugh. You are each clever and know how to have fun. Keep smiling and joking around so that you can enjoy your days in a special way. Remember, though, that your jokes should never be at the expense of someone else. Know that ethnic jokes or those that poke fun of anyone are not okay.

I hope that when you read this, you will better understand what has guided me through my life. I'm writing these letters to you as not only a grandmother and a teacher but as some- one who loves you both dearly and wants to share with you what I have learned.

With love always,
Grandma

214

"Miriam, wake up! Do you see what I see?"

Opening my eyes from a deep sleep, I look over to the flowing curtains covering the window and wonder if she's referring to the way they are moving in the ocean breeze. I have no idea what she means until I look at her face. Then I quickly am reminded of what I saw on my first night here – that *thing* I tried to forget about because I didn't want to believe it was true.

"Miriam, I could swear there was a woman or maybe a ghost standing at the edge of your bed. Am I seeing things? What in the world was that?"

"I didn't see anything *this time*," I reply calmly. "However, a few days ago I had a dream about a woman and woke up to find someone standing over me for a brief moment. I was afraid to say anything to you because I thought you might think I had lost my mind talking about ghosts and all, but I haven't stopped thinking about it."

"Do you think this place is haunted? Was that really a ghost?" Esther asks.

"I honestly don't know, and I'm not sure I want to know. Can we keep this as our own little secret?" I plead. "Maybe if we don't talk about it outside of this room, it will vanish from reality."

"I'm fine with keeping this between us," she says. "But was what you saw ethereal looking – beautiful in an almost transparent way?"

"Yes," I exclaim, "but I had a dream along with my sighting."

After I describe the details of the dream, Esther says, "The whole thing is too freaky, Miriam. Let's close the window and trust that she left and won't come back."

I nod my head in agreement. "I'm good with that idea. I hope you aren't too scared. I sure as hell am spooked out myself."

Esther climbs into bed with me, and the two of us begin to talk about Grandma and her letters to us.

"You don't think the ghost is Grandma, do you?" Esther asks.

"Not according to my dream," I reply, "although I feel that her spirit is definitely with us. All that she said is coming alive as we read what she wrote. Even though she had told us so much of this while we were growing up, seeing everything in her handwriting, especially after her death, makes it that much more profound. I'm overwhelmed that she took the time to leave all of this with us in the way that she has."

Esther says, "I don't think too many grandchildren are as fortunate as we are to be given something like this from a grandmother. I always knew that Grandma was special, although I never stopped to think of all that she taught us. I realize now that she continues to do so even after she's gone."

November 16, 1980

Dear Miriam and Esther,

As I write this letter and think ahead to the next five years, I feel certain that your lives are going to change drastically. This is the time period in which you will greatly mature and will make decisions that will have an effect on you for the rest of your lives.

These next few years of high school will be important ones in many ways. You are going to experience a wide range of choices including the subjects you take in school, the friendships you develop, the extracurricular activities you get involved in, and eventually the career paths you decide to follow.

During these last years as teenagers, you will also begin to experience independence on a much grander scale than ever before. In another year, you'll be driving, which in itself will give you a feeling of freedom. While that will be wonderful, your real autonomy will come when you leave for college. That is when you will understand what it means to be making decisions on your own – to be living without your parents helping you with every new step you take.

One of the biggest freedoms you will be granted when you turn eighteen is the right to vote; it is your responsibility as a citizen of the United States. Whether you realize it or not, one person can and must stand up, speak out, and make a difference. While it may not seem plausible, your single vote can decide the outcome of an election. Please remember this always and exercise your civic duty. We must be grateful for those who served in the armed forces – many of whom lost their lives while fighting for our freedom. Voting is one way to show our gratitude to them. It is a sacred obligation.

I am hopeful that as you go through high school and then on to college, you will understand the value of your education. If you study for the sake of learning and not just for tests, you will be all the wiser. Too often these days, schools seem more interested in your standardized scores than in how you are doing in your day-to-day courses. That is not what learning is all about.

When I was young, for those of us few women who went to college and then decided to work, we had limited choices. Things are different today for women than they were in my time. The world is open to you. What you decide to do with your lives depends completely on you. Remember that you are both capable and can be whatever you want. Don't let anyone tell you differently.

One day many years ago, I was with a friend of mine who was the president of a huge company with hundreds of employees. He took me on a tour of the facility so I could better understand what went on there. What struck me was how he stopped to talk to people. He started friendly conversations not only with the heads of departments and other "important" individuals, but also with the janitor who was sweeping the floor and the woman who was operating the elevator. He spoke to each person equally – their rank and position meant nothing to him. I left there having learned an important lesson about respecting everyone regardless of whether he is rich or poor, famous or unknown. We are all alike in so many ways.

As you go out into the world, please be aware of the importance of diversity and always celebrate it. Too often, we tend to stay close to those whose skin color looks like ours or whose religion and ethnicity are the same as ours. Sometimes we fear others because of their appearance and never allow them a chance to show us who they are. I beg of you to look beyond one's exterior and get to know others who may be different. Remember that when we are cut, we each bleed the same red blood.

In all of this, you will make mistakes. We all do. Some mistakes will be bigger than others. Some we will accept easily and others we might beat ourselves up over. Be forgiving of yourselves as well as those in your life who make mistakes that affect you. One of the most important things to know and understand is that our mistakes and misfortunes can become the jumping off point for our future successes. There is much to learn from the mistakes and failures we experience in our lives. If we look to them as our teachers, we can then grow and benefit in ways we never imagined possible. From negatives come positives. Look for them.

Each time I sit down to write to the two of you, I ask myself how you will receive all that I have written. I can't help but wonder about that, although I will never know. There is a part of me that feels these letters are the way we can stay connected when I no longer am alive to talk to you. Please take them in the spirit in which they are meant. I want to tell the two of you – my special granddaughters - as much as I can. I pray that they will hold meaning for you and that you will find something within them that helps to make your life a little better.

With love always,
Grandma

Esther speaks first. "How could Grandma have any doubts at all about how we would feel about these letters? The fact that she has imparted her wisdom is meaningful. Don't you think?"

"I agree. What she's telling us is invaluable. I wonder if our mothers learned as much from her as we're learning. Do you think she ever wrote anything like this to either of them?"

"Most likely in some way," Esther replies, "she gave them all that we're getting. My guess is that she did it in their day-to-day lives growing up."

"These letters would not have meant much had she given them to us when we were younger. I'm glad she decided to wait, although I sure would love to be able to thank her."

❧

"I can hardly believe that we only have two more days here in paradise," says Esther while fluffing up a pillow before bed. "I've been so happy in our little hideaway just around the corner from where Grandma used to live. It definitely brings back memories of our visits with her down here, doesn't it?"

I listen to her words as she recalls the time spent with Grandma. "I used to love coming to Hollywood Beach with her, and especially when we would play in the sand and walk along the Broadwalk.

"Do you remember the time when those college students from Florida Bible College came up to the three of us? We must have been about twelve years old then. Grandma was helping us create that amazing mermaid sand sculpture when those two guys stopped to talk. I can still hear Grandma doing her best to be polite but telling them she had her own faith and was perfectly content to believe as she did."

Esther's words bring that memory back for me as if it were yesterday. "Do you remember the conversation we had after that?"

She looks at me with a serious look on her face and remarks, "Yep. Grandma went on to tell us how, as we approached our B'not Mitzvah, we needed to think about what it meant to be a Jew and how lucky we were for all the wonderful traditions our faith held. She tried to explain to us how there are so many different religions and how some people believe that they have the one and only answer and must let others know.

"I can hear her words now. 'We must always be respectful of others. Those boys who stopped here were enthusiastic and wanted to pass along to us what they know to be true for them. I hope you understood that their intentions were honorable. Regardless, it didn't mean that we had to believe in what they said or that we had to listen if it wasn't of interest to us. But it's important that we were courteous to them.'"

"She was something else," she says with a smile. "I realize now that no matter what Grandma did or said, there was always a lesson for us to learn.

"Let's get to letter number six!" I exclaim. "I can't wait to see what Grandma wrote to us as we approached another milestone year."

May 30, 1985

Dear Esther and Miriam,

You are both about to enter into a new decade in your lives – twenty years old with so much to look forward to, so much to think about.

When we were on the cruise during spring break for your high school graduations, I remember watching the two of you and thinking that you are now young ladies. I saw how the men on the ship were looking you up and down as you walked by. I noticed how the chemistry changed each time you entered a room and young men were around.

There is much to consider when you start looking for a man to marry. In fact, my mother gave me the best advice about this that I have ever heard. When I started to date your grandfather, my mother told me that I should pay attention to how he treats his mother. If he is good to her – listens to what she says and shows respect for her – then he will be good to me. Luckily, your grandfather was a wonderful son and has been a loving and devoted husband. I wish the same for the two of you.

You need to know, though, that men and women speak a different language, even if we think we're all speaking English. Our brains do not work in the same ways. Most women I know want to talk and when we have a problem, we want to be listened to and have a place to vent. Men want to solve the problem. They seem to be more solution-oriented and only able to focus on trying to fix the issue. It's rare that Grandpa ever has the patience to hear me out without trying to give me his opinions and advice. No matter how much I let him know what I want and need, he does not seem to get it.

In addition, there is something to be said for the old prehistoric caveman theory that men are the hunters and women are the gatherers. There is some physical basis to all of that with men generally being stronger than women. While men went off to hunt, women were home with the children collecting berries. Unfortunately, some of that doesn't appear to have changed all that much thousands of centuries later.

My hope is that in your time, there will be a greater coming together of the sexes and things will be more equal. I believe that women are as capable as men. We need to figure out a way to let the world know that. Maybe your generation will make more progress than mine has made. I hope so and want that for you and for your children – my great-grandchildren.

As far as your careers, you appear to have decided what you want to do with your lives. I am tremendously proud of both of you. Esther, you will be a wonderful teacher. Having been one all my life and without seeming self-serving, I do believe it is truly a noble profession. You will change lives and learn while you're doing it. And you, Miriam, will be a great lawyer. I always thought you held your own in any argument you were in. It is no surprise to any of us that you have chosen to make this your life work.

You each seemed to have easily slid into deciding what your careers will be. In many cases, you might find that some decisions will not come as easily or be as natural as these were for you. Know that there are very few times in life that you have to decide on something immediately. Also, down the road, you might come to realize that there is something else you would rather be doing. Don't look to your career choice as forever. You are not tied to your decision should it suddenly not feel right for you. Be flexible if your desire to do something different arises.

Most important of all is that you love what you are doing. In addition to that thought, and equally as significant, was what my father used to always tell me. To quote him, "Any job worth doing is worth doing well." I grew up on those words. They guided me throughout my life.

The bottom line in all of this is that no matter whom you marry or what you decide to do, you will both be successful and will live happy lives. It's who you both are.

With love always,
Grandma

❧

After a long and delightful day at the beach, Esther has souvlaki and I have a gyro at Oasis by the Sea. When we finish dinner, we slowly make our way back to the hotel. As we walk, we talk a little about our experience with the "ghost" and decide that it probably didn't happen. It makes us feel better that way. After all, who believes in ghosts anyway?

We sit out in the back of the hotel for a while and watch people pass on the Broadwalk until both of us are ready to call it a night.

Now that we are upstairs, Esther sits on my bed and pulls out the seventh letter. We've been dreading this one because, even before reading it, we assume that there will be some sadness in Grandma's letter to us.

November 1, 1990

Dear Miriam and Esther,

My life has changed drastically as a result of Grandpa's death a year ago. Having both of you and the rest of the family surrounding me during that time made a tremendous difference. I don't think I could have gotten through that first week had it not been for the distractions you all provided.

I was grateful that your parents let the two of you stay with me instead of insisting that you join them at the hotel. Your being in my apartment was a tremendous comfort. Both of you were extremely vigilant, and never once did I feel as alone as I might have if you weren't there each morning when I opened my bedroom door.

Getting through the week of shiva with everyone here was somewhat surreal. While I acted strong on the outside, inside my heart was breaking. Grandpa and I had been together for fifty-four years, so his death shook my core in a way that nothing ever had before. I understood that I would need to get through it and to the other side in my own way, but I welcomed having you all with me.

Once everyone went back to their respective homes, I had my friends who were there for me, but the nights were terribly lonely. I cried myself to sleep for weeks after we buried Grandpa.

At some point, something changed for me. Perhaps it was the support group that I joined at the Jewish Community Center. Meeting and talking to others who had lost their spouses was definitely helpful.

My friend Frances gave me some wise advice along the way. She told me to accept help from others because people need a chance to give. She said that if I'm open to letting people do for me, then I will be doing a mitzvah for someone else at the same time. Being as independent as I am, this was not at all easy for me, but it made sense. I listened to her advice.

Anita, another wonderful friend, gave me an important gift when she told me about angels that inhabited her world. She talked about how she speaks to all the people whom she had loved and lost and whom she now considers her angels. She explained how, during quiet moments, she communicates with them, and because of that she never feels alone. I listened and considered it, and you know what? I started to "talk" to my departed loved ones, and things shifted for me. It probably sounds bizarre, but this has become part of my life and brings me a sense of having someone by my side at all times.

I have a constant conversation with Grandpa going on in my head. He doesn't answer back, but I feel a sense of connection that gets me through the days. I tell him everything – probably more than when he was alive.

Another thing that made a difference for me was something my mother had told me years ago and that I never forgot. She suggested that when I'm hurting, the best thing I can do is to help someone else who is less fortunate than I am. I remember when I was in junior high school, and my father lost his job. We were living on very little money, so everything was scarce. My parents had gone through difficult times before that and somehow had managed; they were determined to do so again. My mom took me and my siblings to the Jewish orphanage in town to play with the babies and young children. Something about doing that felt good for all of us. Then during the Depression, we found different ways to help others and to cope with our own problems.

Once Grandpa died, I knew that I was going to need to do something for someone else in order to feel better myself. That probably sounds strange, but I get more from volunteering my services than I give. So, I found a group that volunteered at a soup kitchen in Broward County. I now go there once a week and feed the homeless. I also started to give some hours each week at the Miami Jewish Home for the Aged where I work in their library and read to residents who have lost their eyesight. Both these things seemed to have helped pull me up from the depths of the despair I was experiencing.

I know you have seen my favorite poem which I have framed on my dresser. I have read it over and over again, and it has given me the courage to go on whenever I feel depressed and alone. I'm including it here because it is something I want you each to have.

> *When you walk to the edge of all the light you have*
> *and take that first step into the darkness of the unknown,*
> *you must believe that one of two things will happen:*
>
> *There will be something solid for you to stand upon,*
> *or, you will be taught how to fly*
> *By Patrick Overton*

That fortifies me during difficult times and reminds me to have faith.

There has been a lot of joy in these past years as well as the sadness I have written about. Most exciting of all has been your engagements and forthcoming marriages. You have each chosen wonderful men.

Esther, Josh was a winner from the start when he sat right down and talked to me, asking all kinds of questions. That is unusual for a young man – for most people, in fact. So few take the time to ask about others and instead seem only interested in talking about their own lives. The minute I learned Josh was an English teacher who is continuing his studies so that he can become a college professor, he had my vote. He is a dear in every way, and it's obvious how much in love you are. His parents seem like wonderful people, too, which is a great sign as well.

Miriam, I think Gary is perfect for you. The fact that you met in law school, that both of you have passed your law boards already, and that you each have jobs in prestigious firms in D.C. leads me to believe you are well-suited for each other. Gary charmed me the instant I met him. His outgoing personality and loving ways have endeared him to everyone in the family. He worships the ground you walk on and vice versa. It's a perfect combination.

I am tremendously happy for both of you. In a little while, you will each be married women. There's so much I want to say to you about that. I'm going to talk to you personally about my views on marriage before your weddings. It's too important to wait until after you get married. Instead, I'll write a few thoughts as a reminder so that when you read this, you can think about how your marriages have been for you and if you are doing everything you can to be happily married.

Here's my short list:

Revere your vows and treasure them

Know that the more you give to your loved one, the more you will receive

Be realistic in your expectations of one another and discuss them

Put the other before your parents, careers, or children

Be a team but maintain your identity

Praise one another

Listen

Learn

Communicate

Share

Care

Be nice to each other

Trust

Play

Kiss

Consider

Spend less time worrying about who is right and more time with what is right

Respect each other

Well, how are you doing as you reflect on this list and think about your marriage? On that note, I will end this letter.

The next five years are going to bring you a whole new, wonderful life. I can't wait to be part of what is yet to come.

With love always,
Grandma

"It amazes me how open Grandma was with us in these letters," I comment. "It's interesting that she never let on about how sad she was when we were with her. She always seemed so brave."

Esther replies, "I remember being surprised that we never saw her cry during the week after Grandpa died. I knew she loved him so much, and yet, she handled his passing with such strength and courage. Now we know that she kept from us what she was really feeling."

I'll never forget the day Grandma sat me down before I got married and made sure to tell me everything that she possibly could about marriage. I think if my mom had done that, I never would have been as receptive to it, but somehow I always appreciated when Grandma talked to me about what she knew to be true.

"Did she tell you all of this before you and Gary got married?" Esther asks, interrupting my thoughts.

"I was just thinking about that. For the most part, yes, she did. In fact, after my conversation with her, I remember calling Gary and talking with him about everything she had told me. I wished he had been with us for that talk, but I don't think Grandma felt she knew him well enough to speak as freely with him as she did with you and me."

Esther then tells me what a difference Grandma's advice made for her and Josh. "One of the biggest things that surfaces for us in our marriage is how sometimes we aren't nice enough to each other. Each time that happens, either Josh or I make sure to remind the other that there is a better way to say what the other has said. It's something we probably wouldn't have been aware of had she not mentioned it to me. It has made a big difference in our marriage."

"Gary and I have focused on the one about expectations. Somehow it has taken me an especially long time to get that he cannot meet my every need. He becomes frustrated when he feels I'm putting too much pressure on him to give me something that he isn't capable of giving – like communicating on a deep level. He does the best he can, and I have to remember that. Without Grandma's great advice before we got married, I might not have understood this.

"All I can think about is how fortunate we are to have had Grandma as a guide throughout our lives. She has made an impact on us in ways that no one else ever has. We are blessed."

⚬〰⚬

"Since we are leaving later today, I think we should read the last letter now, before we head down to the beach for our walk," Esther suggests.

"I'm fine with that," I answer, "although I'm sad coming to the end of these letters. They have framed our week in such an unexpected way."

I get out the last envelope and hand it to Esther, as has been our routine this week.

December 6, 1994

Dear Miriam and Esther,

In a few weeks a new year begins – one that will bring you into a world which you can't imagine yet. Being a mother is like nothing else you have ever experienced. Don't spend time wondering or worrying about how it will be. Soon enough, you will know. Eventually you will create your routine, and everything will fall into place.

Where have the years gone? How is it that my two daughters will be grandmothers and that I will be a great-grandmother? I can still remember when they became mothers. Here I am experiencing the cycle of life as it continues on. My dream is to hold your babies in my arms and rock them to sleep with the same lullabies I sang to you. I pray it will happen, but I am aware that it might not considering what the doctor has told me about the severity of my condition.

There are so many things I could tell you about being a parent. Part of me feels I should let you find out for yourselves. However, it wouldn't be like me to do that – not after all these years of passing along my unsolicited advice. I'll do my best to limit my thoughts to a minimum.

If I were to choose the most important thing I could tell you, it would be that above everything else, you must always remember to keep your relationships with your husbands in the forefront. Too many new mothers become so consumed with their babies that they forget that there is someone else who needs them and wants their attention. The mistake they make is to devote all their energies to their child and neglect the person who will be there long after their baby has grown up and left the nest.

I remember how it was when your mom was born, Miriam. Grandpa would come home and would expect his meal on the table. He was not happy if I didn't make time for him. In fact, there were moments when he was jealous of the attention I was giving to Ruth. He would end up pouting and eventually, it led to a huge argument. Fortunately, he knew enough to communicate his feelings.

It didn't take me long to rethink my actions. From that day forth, I found a way to give him what he needed. Granted it was a balancing act for me, but in the end it was worth it. I learned that a couple-centered rather than a child-centered home was a much happier place to be.

In the same vein, figure out a way to engage your husbands in the process of parenting. Times are different than they were in my day. Daddies need to be involved. Encourage them to change diapers, help with feedings, and stay home with the baby some time each week, so you can have a little freedom. Sharing in the responsibilities fifty – fifty would be wonderful, but it's probably asking way too much. I'd settle for sixty-five – thirty-five. In my day, it was 100% the mother doing it all.

To me the bottom line in raising children is that if there is love, your child will grow up to be secure and happy. Since both of you are capable of giving huge amounts of love, this is never going to be an issue for either of you.

As a mother and a teacher, I believe that after love, it is most important to be consistent. Nothing else you do will have as great an effect as this. If the child knows what the boundaries and rules are as you consistently set limits, he or she will be well-behaved and will function well in the world. I know this with all my heart, and through my years of teaching, I have seen how magically it works.

All the rest will come to you naturally. Of course, there are little pieces of advice that might be helpful to know. For example, make sure to sleep when your baby is sleeping. Take care of yourself as best you can. Find time to shower each day and put on make-up.

Babies will sometimes cry for no reason. It's okay to let them cry if they have been fed and diapered. It isn't anything you've done wrong. Don't take it personally as so many new parents tend to do.

Trust your instincts. Well before there were books on parenting, parents raised children, and they grew up to be fine citizens. You are both smart and caring women. You and your husbands will be wonderful parents. Your children will be lucky to be born to you.

I love you both very much and feel like the luckiest woman alive to have you in my life. You are such wonderful grand-daughters who always take the time to think about me. Thank you for that and for who you are in my life.

With love always,
Grandma

Grandma is not going to be here to see our babies grow up. I need to believe that she will be watching over us and our children. That is the only way I can find comfort in her passing.

"How can it be that Grandma will never see us as mothers?" Esther asks softly.

"From the moment I got married and thought about having a baby, I always imagined Grandma being part of my child's life. The thought that she won't be fills me with profound sadness."

Esther continues on, "Since we'll both be naming our children after her, we're going to need to find names that we like and that won't be the same.

"I'm sure we can do that," I say. "By the way, I was thinking that besides naming our children after her, maybe we can commit to doing something special in her memory. How about if every five years, the two of us meet here and spend some time together just like we did this week?"

"That's a wonderful idea, Miriam. Let's do that – only you and me -- no one else. Not our babies. Not our mothers. Not even

Gary or Josh. Our husbands can join us at other times as they have when we've all been away together with the family.

"That way we can start our own tradition in honor of and in memory of Grandma. Now that we have a plan, I feel a lot better," I add.

This time with my cousin turned into a week spent with my beloved grandmother. She was here with us in every moment and will forever be in our lives.

JOURNEY OF AWAKENING
RAMADA HOLLYWOOD BEACH RESORT
2001

August 2, 2001

Dear Wendy,

I thought I would fill you in on where I'm at and what my plan is for the week. You always seem happiest when you can picture me in my surroundings.

I arrived at the hotel today a little before check-in. The person at the desk was kind enough to let me register early since summer is off-season in Florida, and the hotel is not as full as in the winter. My room is right on the ocean, which was the only requirement I had when I made my reservation.

The Ramada Hollywood Beach Resort, where I'm staying, was built in the mid-1920s. From the picture that I had seen of it on the Internet and then seeing it in person, I never would have guessed that this salmon-colored hotel is seventy-five years old. It has a grandiose presence on the beach.

While some of the areas are closed off and completely vacant, other sections are updated and quite lovely. I took a walk around just to familiarize myself. The main area of the second floor is a little spooky because it's a huge, wide-open space with nothing there. In another section nearby are a bunch of empty rooms and offices. I am trying to imagine how it used to be long ago when the hotel was thriving.

I found a few small shops on the first floor – mostly kiosks where I can pick up sandwiches and coffee. Tonight I'm planning to have dinner at O'Malley's, the restaurant bar downstairs by the pool. From what I understand, there are lots of places to eat along the Broadwalk parallel to the ocean, so I won't have to leave the beach while I'm here.

Not only that, but my room has everything I'm going to need. The bed, with four big, fluffy pillows, is positioned so when I sit on it, I can see out the window. It is great having a kitchenette with a refrigerator, small stove, and microwave, although I doubt that I'll be making any meals for myself, except maybe breakfast. On the dresser sits a television which, as you can probably guess, I will never turn on. Right now, I'm sitting on the powder blue, yellow, and white plaid lounge chair and matching ottoman where I plan to read before I go to sleep every night. My most favorite spot in the room is at the table which faces the ocean. I'll be spending a lot of time in Room 732, so I'm glad that it's a bright, cheery place to be with pale yellow walls and a cream-colored tile floor.

All I really care about is the view. One of the best things is that I can be downstairs walking along the shore with the water kissing my toes within a matter of minutes.

As I was exploring earlier, I thought about how I would like my week to be. I intend to get up every morning before dawn and be outside before the sun rises. I don't want to miss a minute of it, since that's my favorite time of day. You probably never even notice sunrise when you're up at that hour. After all, you have other, slightly more important things on your mind then.

I've decided that I'm going to treat my time here as a personal retreat. I don't plan to make any calls, won't be reading the newspaper or watching any news on TV, and most likely won't even talk to anyone the entire week. I've always dreamed of one day doing this and experiencing silence in this way. I wonder if I can pull it off. It will be strange to be so out of touch with everyone in my life, except you, of course. However, I want to experience the quiet within and not be bothered with interruptions from the outside.

Granted, I'm by myself and have been since your father left me five years ago, but my life is full. I never feel alone. In fact, I'm hardly ever without something going on and someone by my side; of course, there's always my cuddly Buffy, who, by the way, is staying with Aunt Sue this week.

Since retiring from teaching in June, I feel as though I've been on a merry-go-round. Because I went right from school to your wedding and then on to see Andrew in Utah where I helped him set up his office, the past six weeks have flown by. I'm glad Ken came with me. I loved being together with both of your brothers.

It's a gift to have this time to figure out what I want to accomplish in the months ahead. My main goal this week is to prepare myself to begin the painting I've been thinking about for a long time.

I've brought with me the five volumes of my journals that I kept from 1979 until 1984 when I went back to working in special education. Since then, I've often regretted not continuing with my journal writing, although it seemed impossible back then when I had a full-time job, had the three of you who were into all kinds of activities, and didn't have any help from your father. There was no time for myself.

My plan is to read through these journals before I do anything else. I want to see where I was in those days – to reflect on my life as a wife and a mother. Perhaps it will even give me a better perspective on my marriage to your father and why it ended up the way it did.

You're always on my mind. We'll catch up by phone next week when I get home. I'll want to hear everything about your week. I'm going to miss talking to you since we're used to speaking almost every day.

However, these letters will be a way for me to continue to feel connected to you. I'm happy to be able to share my time here with you in this way. It will probably be the only contact I have with anyone from my life while I'm at the beach.

You are tremendously important to me. I'm grateful that we have the kind of loving mother-daughter relationship that we do. There isn't anyone else whom I speak to as often or would ever consider writing to while I'm away.

In a way, it's a lot like Grandma and me. She always enjoyed writing although, unfortunately for most of her life, she didn't follow her dream and do anything about it. One day when she was about sixty years old, I received a letter from her in the mail telling me that she was going to start sharing her life with me through letters. I was thrilled. In those days, long distance phone calls were costly and your father didn't like to spend the money (even though we had it), so we didn't talk more than once a month. My mother and I then began to write to each other several times a week. I cherish those letters. In fact, they're in a big Office Depot file box in my closet at home. I just might take them out and read them when I get back.

What I learned from that wonderful writing exchange with my mother was how close a relationship can become through communicating in this way. Of course, I understand that you have almost no time to call your own. Believe me, Wendy, I don't expect you to answer me. Just writing to you is going to be meaningful for me.

With your schedule, you're lucky if you have time enough to be with your sweet husband David, who also leads a hectic life. I don't know how you two do it. Those calls in the middle of the night letting you know that yet another baby is on the way surely keep you more than busy – not to mention David's life as an emergency room physician.

I admire the two of you and know that you are doing what you were meant to do. I'm sure that your patients are grateful to have such a caring and competent doctor helping them bring their babies into the world. I'm so proud of you for choosing this field of medicine and for achieving all that you have. I bet that the attending doctors are going to miss you when you complete your fellowship.

I'm going to take a walk down by the water now. When I come back up to my room, I plan to begin reading my journals. I wonder what it'll be like. Talk about taking a walk – that's what I'll be doing, walking back in time.

I love you,
Mom

ᏇᎧ

When I came back to my room, I picked up my first journal. After reading for over an hour, I am beginning to notice a theme. Interspersed among the issues of raising a family and the mundane day-to-day happenings, it seems as if I was preoccupied with the women's movement. I had forgotten what a tremendous source of frustration the struggle for equal rights was for me. Somehow I seemed much more concerned about it than most of the women that I knew at the time. As I sit here going through these passages, it is bringing back the memories of how I used to feel.

March 23, 1979

I will never understand how it is that after Congress gave our country seven years to pass the Equal Rights Amendment, the deadline yesterday came and went with only 35 of the needed 38 states ratifying it. It was proposed in 1923 to affirm that men and women have equal rights under the law. How is it possible that women in this day and age still do not have equal rights? What am I missing? Why is this okay with our society?

What concerns me more than anything is the idea that this is obviously acceptable to the majority in our country. Even more upsetting to me is that if our government doesn't accept us women as equals, then how can we expect our husbands to?

I'm sure that Phyllis Schlafly, who organized people against the ERA passage, must be celebrating tonight. What is she thinking? Does she truly believe that the ERA would deny a woman's rights to be supported by her husband, that privacy rights would be overturned, and that women would be sent into combat? I don't believe that any of these things would happen with the ratification of the amendment.

I would like to meet Mrs. Schlafly one day and let her know how I feel about the campaign she ran. But the reality is that I can't even imagine what it would be like to have a discussion with a woman like her. Actually, the more I think about it, I doubt that I could even be civil. People like her infuriate me. I don't know that I would be able to stay in control of myself.

May 22, 1979

I just finished reading __A Total Woman__, a book by Maribel Morgan. She is definitely an anti-feminist who thinks wives should be doing more for their husbands to keep them happy. She suggested that we dress up in Saran Wrap with nothing on underneath and greet our husbands at the door. Her philosophy is to cater to one's man whether it is through sex, food, or sports. I am outraged and vow that it will be the last of her books I will ever read.

Of course, when I read a few of the ridiculous passages to Elliott, he thought they were terrific and agreed with Maribel that women should do whatever they can to please their husbands. He thinks she is onto something pretty wonderful. I hope Elliott got the message that as much he would like it, those things won't be happening in our home.

December 12, 1979

Years ago, we weren't made aware of the possibilities of women's roles outside of the home. Things were not discussed as openly as they are now. Few women were fighting for their rights, but in the last ten years, the battle has escalated as more women have become aware of their limited choices.

I knew at a young age that I would go to college, graduate as a teacher, get married, and have children. That had been ingrained in me since I was a young girl. I began creating this reality with my dolls when I was three years old.

In fact, in my sophomore year of college, I decided that I wanted to switch my major and become a psychologist. I remember calling home and telling my parents of my decision. My father adamantly told me it would be a huge mistake – that I would always have a job as a teacher and that being a psychologist was more of a man's job. Being an obedient daughter, I listened to my father and stayed in education.

It took me a long time to understand how important it is to stand up for myself. I still have a long way to go in doing that, but I imagine that I will always remember this example of when I didn't consider fighting for what I wanted – but only did what my father insisted on.

◦◦◦

August 3, 2001

Dear Wendy,

After reading some of the excerpts in my journals last night, I feel compelled to share with you some of what I'm uncovering. I realize now that of all the conversations we have had about anything and everything, I somehow never specifically spoke to you about the issues that women in my generation and those before me faced. I would imagine that you picked up on some of it just by observing the things I did and said.

When I went to college, it was expected that my friends and I become either teachers or nurses. Nobody I knew ended up in nursing school, though. We all went right into education and came out with our degrees in teaching. While I never regretted becoming a teacher, I do wish that I had been aware that there were other options. No one ever spoke to me about what jobs I might have been suited for or been interested in after I graduated from college.

Fortunately, for your generation and the ones to follow, things are, and will continue to be, different. I remember when your father and I began to talk to you about college. You were determined to become a doctor. The question of the medical profession being unsuitable for a woman was never discussed. You knew that you wanted to go to an Ivy League school, get a solid education, and have a better chance of getting into a top medical school. I felt sure that you would succeed and was glad that you were focused on what you wanted to accomplish.

In my day, I doubt that there would have been any way I could have made a decision like that. I can still remember my feelings of frustration – mostly because I knew that I couldn't go against what either of my parents said – but also because there seemed to be almost no alternatives then. We did what society expected of us.

I'm not even sure you know about the Equal Rights Amendment that never passed in our country. It was on the ballot for seven years during the '70s and yet, there were those (including other females) who felt that women should not be given equal rights. That probably is hard to imagine since things are different today. Although maybe not. Perhaps you experience a bit of this inequality in some way at the hospital. We've never talked about it, but now I wonder if female doctors are treated with the same respect as your male counterparts. I would be interested in hearing your take on that.

When I was reading my journal last night about all the issues that women endured, I found myself starting to get agitated all over again. All of what I've committed to paper took place so long ago, yet it stirred some feelings in me that had become dormant over the years. Although I'm grateful that things have changed, I know they are still far from perfect. We have a long way to go to have fifty-fifty relationships in every respect.

On a different subject, I am happy to be at the beach. I took two walks yesterday – one on the sand in the early morning during low tide and the other on the Broadwalk. It's steamy outside. August is not an ideal time to be in South Florida, but despite the heat and humidity, I'm glad I'm here.

I did a little shopping at a few of the stores on the Broadwalk. There are several beachwear shops that have great-looking bathing suits and cover-ups. I bought two of each plus a beach chair and an umbrella, so I can sit down by the water.

Hopefully, you and David are having a good week. I'm wondering if you've heard from Ken. He is supposed to be on his way to California to interview for a job. He said he would send me an email when he gets there, but I don't have access to the Internet while I'm here. Even though I wanted solitude, it is strange to be so out of touch.

I love you,
Mom

ᘕ

May 4, 1980

More recently, there appears to be a revolt simmering in the women's movement. It hasn't yet translated to my own community where so many men I know think women should be one step behind or beneath them.

I am starting to get vibes from a few of my friends' husbands that I'm a rebel and am causing trouble because I'm raising the consciousness of their wives. I prefer to think that this is an awakening for these women as they journey into a new way of being. Some of these men have informed me that they don't like what I'm doing. I am not at all happy about what they are saying.

One of the husbands was upset because I encouraged his wife to get her own credit card. As it happens, some of the department stores are finally allowing women to get cards in their own names and not their husbands'. According to a few of the men I know, this is giving too much freedom to women.

September 15, 1980

Since taking a full-time teaching job, I am overwhelmed, overloaded, and have so much to do both at home and at work. I have become more aware than ever of all my responsibilities around the house. No matter how much Elliott talks a good game about women's lib and equal rights, I end up being the one who does all the work. I feel resentful.

All I'm asking is that he shares in some of the household responsibilities. I would be satisfied if he picked up after himself. When he gets something to eat, he never cleans up. He leaves his dishes and silverware in the sink. I better stop or I'll be writing in here all day. At this point, Elliott barely does anything around the house – taking out the garbage is about it!

When I mention anything to him about how much I have to do, Elliott says he has more to do and less free time. We got into a fight last night about that. I asked him for a list of what exactly he does aside from going to the office, playing golf and tennis, and meeting the guys once a week for a card game. He couldn't come up with much, which is no surprise.

He has yet to drive the boys to any of their baseball or football practices and hardly attends any of their games. I think during the entire school year, he saw Wendy play in one volleyball game. So not only does he not do anything around the house, but he also does little with the kids.

My resentments have begun to bubble from within. I feel so put upon. Will the time ever come when the scorecard is evened up?

November 14, 1981

Some men in the neighborhood seem threatened by me. Maybe I come on too strong for them. All I want is fair and balanced recognition and equality. These days, so many women struggle for that. We've been held back in our society, and I'm not too sure that it is changing.

A scary thing happened at the party we went to last week. Two of my friends' husbands came up to me and told me not to be surprised if I get kidnapped when I'm jogging in the neighborhood. They point-blank said that I am causing way too much upheaval in their homes because I have begun to talk to their wives about becoming more independent – simple things like standing up for themselves. I realize that they wouldn't really kidnap me, but what they told me came through loud and clear and said everything about how they feel.

May 9, 1982

The Equal Rights Amendment has once again become a subject more people are talking about. What has happened is that the pro-ERA groups, like the League of Women Voters, have appealed to Congress and were able to get an extension of the time-limit for ratification until June 30, 1982. As that date draws near for the final vote, there is more discussion about it on the news and in the newspapers. I can only hope that this amendment finally becomes a reality after fifty-nine years of trying.

From what I am observing with the majority of men I know, they preferred the way things used to be when they could get away with doing little and having no hassles. Who wouldn't?

July 1, 1982

The Equal Rights Amendment failed to receive the required number of ratifications yesterday before its final deadline which was mandated by Congress. Therefore, it was not adopted. Are we living in prehistoric times? It feels that way.

August 4, 2001

Dear Wendy,

My time here at the beach has been wonderful. I'm getting a lot of exercise and am doing a good deal of reading, writing, and thinking about my painting. I am in a rhythm and love the solitude. I should have done this long ago.

I remember reading <u>A Gift from the Sea</u> by Anne Morrow Lindbergh, who left home for two weeks to live a simple existence at the beach. I'm sure that in some way, what she did gave me the idea to come here and do what I'm doing this week. Everyone should probably experience this at least once in their lives.

I find it interesting to see what surfaces in my silence. I'm not sure why, but I have been thinking about Jacob, a student who has been at the school for the last several years. He was one of those children who warmed my heart as soon as I met him. Jacob was born with cerebral palsy and, unfortunately, had a father who rejected him from the start because of his disability. The man was a difficult and unloving father and had little to do with his son's care. Jacob's mother had a slew of physical problems and did the best she could.

When Jacob was in first grade, the school helped his family get him a service dog. From the beginning, Shadow has been there for him in a way that no one else is. In some ways, it reminds me of my faithful and loving companion Buffy.

This probably sounds awful, but remembering Jacob and his father makes me think of your father - a narcissist in the truest sense. He cares only about himself and does little for anyone else. I understand that I shouldn't be bad-mouthing him to you, but after having read my journal entries last night, he is foremost on my mind. Of course, you know your father and how he is, so nothing I say should be a surprise to you.

In my journals in 1980, I had written about how he professed to believe in equal rights for women, but there was never a thing he did while we were married that proved he meant it. Personally, I believe it was all show. I would hear him tell others how he was a proponent for passing the ERA bill, but his life never reflected these values.

As a result, you, the boys, and I were the ones who suffered. When he announced that he was leaving, I don't suppose any of us were all that surprised. The shock was when he called you and your brothers and wanted you to meet his girlfriend, Mindy, who is barely older than you are. Well, he has his trophy wife now. He can walk into a room with that breast-enhanced, made-up, anorexic-looking model of his and men will stare - drawing attention to him, which is exactly what he likes best.

In the five years since your father left, I have come to realize how selfish he was in every way. I'm not sure if I was living an illusion. I believe he loved me in the beginning of our marriage. But when I look back, his love didn't last very long, and fairly early on, he began to show his true colors. I definitely am better off without him in my life. I do not need a man to make me happy.

How did I ever get off on this tangent? I probably shouldn't even mail this. In fact, as I write, I am deciding that I'm not going to send you this letter. My talking badly about your father to you isn't in your best interest. And so, as I learned in a writing class I participated in many years ago, it's great to express angry feelings or work through issues in a letter to someone but never mail it.

My journals used to serve that purpose for me. After reading a few volumes over the past three days, I am pretty clear that that's why I wrote in them in those earlier years. It was an excellent place to vent feelings I had kept to myself.

I obviously still feel anger toward Elliott and all that happened. After about ten years of marriage, he was anything but a good husband. To have lived with him for twenty-eight years before he left the house was probably about eighteen years too long. In fact, while this is a horrible thing to say, there were times when I felt that it would have been easier for me if he had died than to have lived with all the misery he put me through.

When I think about what he did when he left the house for good — how he cleared out all our bank accounts so he made sure none of those assets showed up, I become enraged all over again. Luckily, I had a sharp attorney who was able to help me get my fair share of the rest of what we had, although I never did see any of that money from our accounts.

I don't even want to think about this any longer. It's time to stop here and put this letter in my file of uncensored and unsent letters – of which I have written many to Elliott in the past five years. It has always been such good therapy for me.

In the meantime, I'm going to read more from my journals.

July 20, 1982

Today I had a final interview with the principal of the private school. I left there feeling unnerved. After he offered me the job and I accepted it, he had the balls to tell me that he hopes ERA never passes. Don't men get it? Do they truly believe they are superior? I often feel that they do.

We discussed my role as a woman coming into this school as the ombudsman between the faculty and the parents of students who have special needs. While I am delighted about the position, I'm also concerned that the principal's attitude may affect my work. I realize that I am walking into this situation in the working world where women still have to know their place, accept it, and endure it. Maybe I was better off staying in the classroom.

It is upsetting and frustrating. While I hate to view men as my enemies, in some ways when I listen to what they say, I almost feel as if they are. Some men become belligerent when I state my views. Elliott gets defensive.

I don't like that I always have to fight for my rights. As a woman, it's my plight. I want a more equal, balanced system for people. I dream of a world that is just and peaceful. In doing my part for equality, I'm working on erasing my own prejudices and viewing mankind in a much more accepting way.

August 7, 1982

The other night, Elliot and I watched "20/20" on television. They featured something called premenstrual syndrome – PMS for short. Finally, there is a name for the outrageously horrendous feelings I get before my period. I believe women are going to be pleased to hear that this has been studied scientifically by men.

This news is bigger than men are making of it. For all these years, women have had to endure the physical and emotional side effects of being premenstrual, and now it is being recognized as a valid medical condition. I couldn't be happier. It's time for women all over the world to celebrate.

October 3, 1982

I woke up and within seconds, I had a screaming match with Wendy. I got upset because she waited until the last minute to do her homework. After that rampage, I walked into her room and went nuts over the mess. I became totally wild – like a lunatic!

I am definitely experiencing PMS (so glad it has a name) and am a total bitch to be around. I need to understand when to make myself scarce and get out of everyone's way.

It feels like these moods are out of my control. I am usually fairly cool, but near the onset of my period, I start feeling like I'm crawling on the inside and want to get out of my own skin. At times like this, I'm better off by myself. Thus, I am in my car at the park waiting out a major rainstorm. I see a lone woman jogging – maybe she is as desperate and crazed as I am!

August 6, 2001

Dear Wendy,

A few days have passed. I've been consumed with reflecting on my life and thoroughly enjoying my time here at the beach. It is everything I hoped it would be. I haven't talked to a soul except for the few words I've spoken to waiters at the restaurants on the Broadwalk, the cleaning women in the hotel, the saleswomen in the shops, and an occasional passerby when I'm sitting down by the water.

Reading my old journals has been absolutely fascinating. Last night I came across an entry that I had completely forgotten about. Do you believe that until July of 1982, the condition of premenstrual syndrome had gone without a medical diagnosis and did not have a name? To your generation, the term PMS is standard. Yet, there were all those centuries when women suffered, and men thought we were just complaining about nothing.

On the night that your father and I saw a "20/20" show announcing PMS, I remember how grateful I was and how all I wanted to do was celebrate with my female friends. The next day at school, we talked about it among ourselves during our breaks. At my book club the following week, we barely discussed the book and mostly just talked about PMS. It felt like women had taken a giant step ahead. Finally something unique to us and our bodies was being acknowledged. It was as if men were becoming aware in a new, scientifically-based way. While it was long overdue, at least it happened.

I also read in my journals about the time when I left my job at the public school and went to work at the special private school for disabled students. I should have known from the start that it would not be a pleasant atmosphere for me. The fact that I lasted there only seven months and quit in the middle of a school year says it all. You know me and how faithful I am. I'm jumping ahead of myself, but reading about the beginning there reminded me of the end.

Do you remember when I quit that job? I was so concerned about telling you and your brothers – afraid of the message it would give you about quitting in the middle of something.

I did my best to put a positive spin on it. I remember that we had a long talk about how sometimes it's important to know when enough is enough and especially when something isn't working. I wanted you each to understand that while it's generally not a good idea to be a quitter, there are times when it is the best option.

Ken's and your reactions were touching and a bit funny. At first, you were extremely sensitive and felt sorry for me because I was so miserable at the school that I decided to quit. Then a little later, you told me you were wondering how I felt being unemployed and if I was sad. You suggested I become a cleaning lady like the woman in the book you were reading. Ken told me to start reading the want ads in the newspaper.

Your father didn't care one way or another. He just wanted to come home to a smiling, subservient wife. He didn't like when I was in a bad mood and surely let me know it. He was only happy if I had his dinner waiting for him. He never let me forget that feeding a husband's stomach was what wives were supposed to do. Enough of that!

My stay at the hotel is half over. I should have made it longer, but I feel sure that I'll come back here. Maybe one of these days you and I can take a little vacation with each other. You probably won't get much time off in the next few years, and with what time you do have, you'll most likely want to spend it with David. Perhaps down the road, we can figure something out. It would be special to be together in a wonderful place like this.

I can't wait to read on in my journals. I am amazed to see what I've committed to paper. Reading all of this makes me want to start writing in a journal again.

I love you,
Mom

November 29, 1982

I ate lunch at the Hunter's Run on Friday with my closest friends from high school. I sat watching the heavy, wet snow while we talked for hours. I'm not used to snow now that I live in California.

We've all come home for our twentieth year high school reunion. The last time we were together like this was when we were in college. All of us but Pam are working, and each is juggling schedules trying to find the perfect balance. It's no surprise that we're all teachers or educational administrators of one type or another because it's the only thing we have ever known.

Our discussions went from general to specific – leading to some intimate revelations. First, we caught up on one another's lives. When we discussed how we are as mothers, some talked about how they take out their frustrations and moods on their children. It was interesting to hear what they had to say. I felt a lot better knowing that I'm not the only one who yells at her kids.

In that same vein, we also shared something none of us had ever talked about before. I'm not sure who brought up the subject, but we began to relate how bored and unfulfilled we had felt being stuck at home raising babies and toddlers. There isn't a single one of us who doesn't love our children. That wasn't the issue at all.

At that time when our kids were little, it would have seemed like we were complaining about being mothers if we talked about how we felt. We craved adult conversation of any kind. But to go out of the home and into the working sector was unheard of at the time – at least in our corner of the world.

I must admit that it was a tremendous relief and felt good to say those things out loud. I remember how I used to feel as though I would go out of my mind without anyone over six years old around. I would practically accost Elliot when he walked through the door. I was starving for stimulation.

The only thing that got me through that time in my life was getting involved in creative endeavors – learning to do macramé, refinishing furniture, painting wall graphics, and sculpting. They all saved my sanity while I was stuck at home with young kids. That's also when I began to write poetry as well as paint landscapes. Oil painting became my lasting, creative outlet. The rest were just hobbies to keep me going.

Sitting around the table, it felt liberating to be able to talk so honestly. I also walked away with validation for feelings I had kept inside for so many years.

There is nothing like another woman to talk to when I need to be heard. My female friends understand me like no man ever can. Thank goodness for them. I don't know what I would do without women in my life.

We began discussing our fantasies and the excitement of an affair – some more than others longing for someone else for variety. Fortunately, each seems happily married, except for Pam who appears pretty miserable with her husband – and for good reason. He is impossible. Of course, I could be a lot happier, but I didn't say much about that. I decided that I wasn't ready to let the whole group know how difficult Elliott can be.

I did talk to Pam later when we were alone. We compared notes, and it looks like her marriage isn't a whole lot different from mine. It makes me wonder what will happen down the road if things don't improve.

July 19, 1983

I feel edgy and moody. I'm sending off, "Don't come near me – don't touch me" vibes. At pre-menstrual times like this, I'm impossible and can't stand being with myself. I feel unbalanced. My hormones are wreaking havoc with my emotions. I don't feel like I can subject other human beings to who I am right now. No wonder Elliott said I looked like I had fire coming out of my eyes when he walked through the door.

August 31, 1983

Tonight in our writing group, we discussed our roles as mothers and housewives. Now that I'm home and not officially working at a paying job any longer, life is different for me.

We got into a whole conversation on the way others view those women who stay at home and, according to them, do nothing. One of my friends read us an article from <u>Vogue</u>

about women at home versus those who go off to a job outside of the house. The terminology and how we look at this is something we need to rethink.

I am at home painting and learning additional techniques to improve my art. It amazes me how people don't seem to think this is considered work. Since I haven't brought in any money, no one believes that there is any validity to this. Elliott is first in line to make it known that painting is not work. He never was all that supportive, so I shouldn't be surprised about this.

No wonder there were so few women artists in days gone by. I imagine that it's different if it's a man who is an artist. At least they get some recognition, but women sure as hell don't seem valued when it comes to being an artist.

One of the things I'm finding now that I'm home is that it is impossible to paint when anyone is around. That being the case, I often stay up late into the night so that I can have the solitude I need. Elliot keeps telling me to come to bed. The kids aren't too happy when I lock myself in the spare room (that I am gradually turning into a studio) and paint. It feels like it's a no-win situation trying to be an artist, but I can't give up. It is what I need to do.

There's always so much to get done around here. I find that no one helps keep the house neat. I'm constantly cleaning the kitchen, washing the floors, and picking up stuff. Not to mention that I am expected to run all the errands since I have "nothing else" to do! Oh, the plight of the housewife! I wish people would understand that I am a painter as well.

I just drove my first car pool of the season. The good news is that I have managed to fit it into my schedule. The bad news is that I probably have about two hundred more trips to make this school year.

August 7, 2001

Dear Wendy,

Things have certainly changed since you were a child! When I read my journal entries last night, I was reminded of how different life was when I was at home with you and then later with your brothers. At the time, it was the responsibility of the mother to be there. I didn't know anyone who worked outside of the home while raising young children. Instead, what was expected of us was to take care of the house and bring up the children – 24/7.

Unfortunately, your father didn't do well with little kids so even when he was home, he wasn't any too interested in paying attention to the three of you. Never once did he participate in parenting responsibilities like bathing you, feeding you, reading stories to you, or anything else for that matter. For sure, he never helped me out by doing anything around the house either.

I used to be frustrated because there was no assistance from anywhere. Worst of all, though, was how bored I felt. Yet, I could never admit that to anyone. Sure I was happy raising you and your brothers, but I needed more in my life in order to feel complete. Wendy, don't get me wrong. I loved having you kids. You were my world and still are. Don't ever forget that.

It wasn't until I was around thirty-seven or so that I first admitted any of this out loud to anyone. My high school friends and I were together for our reunion, and one of them was brave enough to say something which completely opened up the floodgates for all of us.

The good news is that your generation will have every possible option. You can stay at home, work part-time or full-time, and whatever you choose to do will be acceptable. Thankfully, we have come that far, but unfortunately women still have a long way to go to be equal in the eyes of men.

I hope that when the time comes, being a mother will be a different experience for you and your friends than it was for me and mine. My wish is that you will find a better balance and will exercise your options to work out of the house if that's what you choose.

Sometimes I wonder if women of your generation have any idea how much those before you had to fight to get where we are today. It's funny because I remember how my mother would talk to me about the very same thing. She told me that she was born soon after women were granted the right to vote in the United States. After all, the women's suffrage movement only took place two generations before you. It's such a basic privilege, but it just shows how women have had to struggle to be heard and recognized in our society.

One of the other issues I read about last night was how I felt when I left teaching for a while and began to paint. I was working on my first painting. Your father and every other man I knew gave my role as an artist no credence because I wasn't earning money. I felt discouraged and furious because I was hard at work, but to them it didn't count at all.

This reminds me of what my mother told me years ago about what she did as a volunteer and how it was received by the men in her life. Grandma was the president of a wonderful organization that helped the Vietnam vets get back into their lives when they returned from the war. She also organized the food drive at the community center. In addition to that, she spent one day a week at the library working with individuals who had never learned to read. I remember her telling me once that none of the men she knew validated her work because it wasn't a paid position. On the other hand, the women she knew understood the significance of her efforts on behalf of others.

Despite it all, my mother never gave up on men. She was always trying to teach them the importance of a woman's role in their lives and to help them see how women should be treated. She told me that my father was one of the few men who understood, but it took him a long time to come on board.

In the end, it is a relief for me to know that while your generation has many struggles of its own, some of those that Grandma and I dealt with are in the past. I am hopeful that with each passing year, life will get easier for you and the women of today.

I love you,
Mom

September 20, 1983

I was at a breakfast this morning where Gloria Steinem spoke. Before she started to talk, the woman next to me told me that the best of life is yet to come. She said that when one reaches her sixties, wisdom emerges in a special way.

Gloria said that it's the system that's crazy, not us. She told us that we need to come together and continue to be hopeful and hold onto our dreams. Change is coming. A sign of progress is that we have new names for experiences and that we are trying to make language accurate. "Imagine," she said, "if a man graduated with a spinster's of arts degree or had to work as a sistership instead of a fellowship."

Some of the other things she said were equally as important and interesting to me. For example:

"A pedestal is as much a prison as any other small space."

"If women could raise themselves to wealth and power, as "they" (men) say they do, there would be more of us there."

"Working women – a phrase that is a curse. Feminists prefer words like working in the home and working out of the home."

"When we speak of human rights (like Soviet Jewry), we aren't speaking of women's rights. What about women all over the world who are trapped by their husbands and need to acquire their permission to do anything? We must fight for all people to be free."

"When a woman feels she's missing a man, she may just be missing the rest of herself."

Gloria Steinem is powerful in that she has given women the confidence and security of knowing that others feel the same way. She left us with the following. "Do one outrageous act. Make an impact. Make someone aware."

Since hearing the lecture today and realizing that Gloria is not married, I've given lots of thought to what it would be like to be a single person without the responsibilities of raising children. I would guess that without having to divide oneself in various directions and being able to devote all one's energy into a single focus, one could become rather accomplished in a particular area of concentration. With a family and its many obligations, I am like a hub of a wheel and am scattered in many directions.

One thing that was apparent today was how much further we women must go in this struggle – fellow sisters – abused people in the world with no country of our own – a different breed than any other minority.

What I most liked about Gloria Steinem was her sophisticated approach and her inspiring words to keep up the fight for what's deservedly coming to us and nothing more. She left me with a lot of food for thought.

October 8, 1983

Tonight I met some of the teachers from my old school. One of them told us about a lecture she heard on how to defend oneself from rape. I found it fascinating when she described how to pull out the rapist's eyes or slowly slip a hand under him and turn his testicles.

It led to a discussion on rape and how women are so often blamed. I've heard many nightmare stories about how police often treat women who come to them after having been raped. Some act as if the woman did something to lead the man on. It was unnerving to talk about this and to think that we aren't necessarily safe or believed even by the authorities in charge. How can that be? What woman in her right mind would want to be raped? Something about this must change along with so much else.

February 5, 1984

In one corner at the party last night, five women sat discussing Danielle Steele's most recent book and then changed the subject and talked about their children's after-school activities. I quickly vacated my spot because it was pretty boring and moved over to the bar where one of the men was refilling his glass of wine. He had had too much to drink and while talking to me, he reached over and grabbed my breast, which totally shocked me. What right did he have to touch me? What an uncomfortable moment. It isn't the first time he's come on to me, but this time he was far more blatant than ever before. I pushed his hand off me and walked away.

If his wife knew, I am sure that she would be hurt and furious. Most likely, I'm not the only woman he has done this to and will probably not be the last either.

April 10, 1984

This morning, my friends and I sat in my kitchen and talked. I sensed the strength of the collective power of women. It's difficult to describe, but I feel like there is so much that can be accomplished when we join together for a common cause.

We discussed how stifled females have been through the ages. The three of us decided that it will take a lot for our society to alter how it views women, but we also agreed that we can at least start the process by making changes in our own homes. If we teach our sons to look at females in a more equal way, we will at least be making a difference for the women in their lives.

The comfort of close friends and talking with them on an intimate level adds an important dimension to my life. I've been blessed with women who have been there for me, who have helped me along the path, who have understood me, and who have listened to me when I've needed to be heard. Somehow, we translate our lives and better understand who we are through our sharing.

April 15, 1984

A family of five requires a major time commitment on the part of the mother. Demands pull me in every direction

– driving car pools, shopping, cleaning, cooking, planning, coping, listening, nurturing, loving, and balancing. My roles today consisted of being a maid, a laundress, a chauffeur, a gardener, a cook, and a sympathetic listener. Truthfully, I'd rather be painting.

Karen and I have discussed how we need to find the time and space for our creativity. It isn't easy and often means that I paint and she sculpts in the middle of the night. At least it is quiet then, and we can work without interruptions.

May 10, 1984

Tonight I took Wendy to the mall, and we shopped for a while. She was happy that I bought her a pair of heels – her very first ones. Although her ankles keep turning in, she's parading around the house in them. This brings her one step closer to growing up and being a woman.

July 19, 1984

The Democratic Convention ends tonight. I am delighted with the idea of Geraldine Ferraro being the first woman vice-presidential candidate – a sign of the times and a hope for the future. What a boost for the women's movement!

August 8, 2001

Dear Wendy,

When I read the last of my journal entries, I was left thinking about when you were beginning to mature. The day you got your first pair of heels was not only a big moment for you but for me as well.

I remember watching as you slowly began to make the transition from a pre-teen to a teenager. While prior to that you didn't much care about what you wore or how you looked, all of a sudden you insisted on buying a certain brand of jeans and a particular kind of sneakers. You would settle for nothing less. It was especially strange for me when you looked in my closet to borrow clothes of mine. No longer were you my little girl. I knew it was the start of a different kind of relationship for us as you began to separate and become more independent in every way.

I have been thinking about the feelings I had after hearing Gloria Steinem speak in 1983. She is such a dynamic woman who, still today, continues to be a galvanizer for the women's movement with her powerful messages.

One of the thoughts that I was left with back then had nothing to do with what she said. It was more about her life in comparison to mine. She didn't have children – hadn't been married, in fact. After listening to all she was accomplishing, I thought a lot about what it meant to have a family. I love you and your brothers and would never have traded my life for hers or anyone else's. Yet I couldn't help but be aware of the tremendous responsibility, as well as the time and energy, it took to be a parent of young children.

Of course in those days, most women stayed home and raised their children. The majority of men expected it to be that way. In fact, many would have felt humiliated if their wives went out into the world to earn money or accomplish anything significant. And as young mothers, we were sacrificing our own needs and desires for the future happiness and well-being of our children. I remember working to keep my priorities *straight and telling myself that my time would come when I had the freedom to do as I pleased.*

In all of this, what makes me happiest is that times have changed. If a woman chooses to stay at home, her life does not have to be isolated as it was when you and your brothers were toddlers. Women today have a variety of alternatives – play dates, Mommy and Me classes, even part-time daycare or nannies. It's a different world, thankfully. I am glad that when you and David have children, you will have a variety of choices.

Now that I've finished reading my journals, I am surprised by how frustrated I was back then. I felt a great deal of anger over the lack of women's rights in general and your father's behavior in particular.

I had joined National Organization for Women and had begun to go to their meetings in the hopes that maybe I could help the cause in some way. That lasted a brief time. While I wasn't happy with the way things were and wanted change, their approach seemed a little too drastic for me. In retrospect, I probably should have stuck with them. They've helped institute a multitude of important changes for women.

After that, in my own way, I tried to awaken my friends to the journey we were on and the battle we faced. When I look back, I realize that many of us were struggling to survive and were dealing with husbands who were unwilling to change. Being out in the working world wasn't a whole lot different either, so progress was slow all around and has continued to be in many ways.

Having a woman run as a vice-presidential candidate in 1984 was a great victory for the women's movement. Unfortunately, Walter Mondale didn't win. Nonetheless, it was a step in the right direction - a first for our country to have a female on the ballot. My wish is that I live to see the day when a woman will be elected as President of the United States.

I feel confident that your generation will make great strides in ensuring equality for all. I'm proud that you were chosen as chief resident and that you are leading the way for other women. Your relationship with David and how the two of you share in all responsibilities gives me great hope.

I love you,
Mom

FULL CIRCLE

HOLLYWOOD BEACH RESORT
CRUISE PORT
2010

I've been dreading my father's visit knowing that it will be the first time in all these years that he'll be here without my mother. Thirty years ago when Russell and I moved to South Florida, my parents began coming down at the end of each March to celebrate their anniversary by vacationing at the Hollywood Beach Hotel. In their sixty-one years of marriage, of all the places they visited and the many trips they took to far-off lands, this was their favorite place.

Their routine was to stay at our house for the first week or so. Then they checked into the hotel for the remainder of their vacation. If we wanted to see them after that, we had to go to the beach and visit them there. Sometimes we would end up having dinner with my mother and father at one of the restaurants on the Broadwalk. My dad has always delighted in having us and his grandsons together enjoying a wonderful meal.

On occasion, they would invite our boys to sleep over at the beach. Shane and Bradley would bring their sleeping bags and would sleep on the floor next to my parents. Mom and Dad, who never liked to sleep apart, always pushed the twin beds together as soon as they arrived at the hotel.

Many years later, Bradley and Shane told us how my mother and father would think that the boys were asleep when, in fact, they were wide awake but faking sleep. With the way the television was situated, the two of them would watch the reflection of the TV on the mirrored wall until my parents turned it off. Bradley and Shane thought they were getting away with something – especially when Mom and Dad were watching a program that we never would have approved of our sons seeing. Of course, the grandparents would have been horrified had they known. They were pretty strict about bedtime, television watching, and things like that — even with their grandchildren.

My siblings and I knew better than to plan any family event during the last week in March and the first week in April. Coming to Hollywood Beach had become my parents' sacred tradition. For the most part, Russell and I left them alone, particularly on March 28th — their special day. As long as they were together in Room 732, it was a celebration.

This year won't be the same. When my father called to announce his plans, I tried to convince him to stay at our home instead of the hotel. I thought it might be easier for him.

"Lily, I'm sure that this is what I want to do. My staying at the hotel isn't up for discussion or debate."

"But, Dad, you're going to be so alone there." The truth poured out of me. I didn't know how to soften it.

"Do you think I'm not alone wherever I am? I miss your mother from the minute I wake up in the morning until the second I go to sleep. No matter how I feel, right now the only place I want to be is at the beach."

With that, our conversation ended.

My mother had been better at winning an argument than I was. Most of the time, she had gotten her way with Dad. His favorite reply, or at least the one that I best remember hearing him say to her throughout the years was, "Yes, dear!" He was probably wise to stick with that since she liked having the control.

My brothers Gregory and Anthony agreed with each other and were sure that my father would be fine. They didn't think that staying at the hotel alone would be a problem for our dad -- maybe because my brothers aren't as tuned into feelings (theirs or anyone else's) as I am. Only my sister Cynthia agreed with me. She and I look at things differently than they do. The bottom line is that it doesn't matter what we think. Dad is going to do what he wants regardless of what any of us says.

࿇

After Russell and I picked up my father at the airport, he agreed to come to our house for dinner and at least sleep over the first night. I was taken aback when I saw him. The last time we had been together was in December when we were at Anthony's son's wedding in New York. Then Dad's face had looked drawn and more wrinkled than ever. He had lost some weight, but now he looked even thinner. His pants hung on him. His shirt was at least a size too large. My father had always been a meticulous dresser. Now he didn't seem to care much about how he looked. In fact, he didn't wear a suit on the plane – something he had always done in the past.

This has been such a difficult year for Dad. He most likely isn't eating right. Mom watched over him, making sure his every need was met. He never was one to cook, so he is probably grabbing whatever he can and not giving much thought to what's good for him. From what he says, he has little appetite. He claims that food doesn't taste the same.

I can tell that it's a struggle for my father to be in social settings. He looked miserable at the wedding even though I know he was happy about his grandson getting married. He tries hard but without my mother by his side, his sadness is apparent. He avoids being with people, which is not at all like my father. He always loved a big party with family and friends surrounding him.

I invited Shane, Bradley, my daughter-in-law Holly, and their two children over tonight for dinner. I hope being with them will ease my dad's sorrow a little and maybe even cheer him up. He loves nothing more than his grandchildren and great-grandchildren. As a former pediatrician, and because of his out-going and fun-loving ways, he enjoys being with children of any age.

I felt lucky growing up because Mom and Dad always enjoyed having our friends around and took an interest in them. Sometimes my parents would sit and talk with us and would shower my friends with the kind of attention that they never got from their own parents. It's probably why our house was always filled with young people.

Russell and I appreciated how my dad played with our sons when they were little. He found ways to turn learning into games. He played Bingo with his grandchildren as soon as they were old enough, and it was through that game that they learned how to read double-digit numbers. He spent hours with Shane and Bradley in the backyard helping them build a tree house, and once they completed it, he climbed up with the boys and read them their favorite stories. Now he's just as wonderful with his great-grandsons, Kyle and Tyler, who adore being around him.

Watching everyone together tonight delights me. Shane and Bradley are thrilled to see their grandfather. Shane hasn't seen him since my mother's funeral, so their reunion is the most special and heartfelt of all. I know that Shane misses his grandmother; he loved her dearly. He was a favorite of hers and hard as she tried to hide her partiality, it didn't always work. He knew how she felt about him.

Dad sits down at the table next to Shane. He turns to him as soon as we are all seated and says, "Shane, your grandmother would be so proud of you. From the time you were little, she used to tell me that you were going to grow up to be someone important. Once you decided to follow your heart and become a doctor, she would constantly tell me that she was sure your patients were going to love you. Grandma was convinced that you would be the best pediatrician around."

Dad puts his arm around Shane's shoulder and gives him a big smile. "The day of your medical school graduation was one of the happiest in her life."

I look over at Shane and am not all that surprised to see his eyes brimming with tears. Shane, the sensitive one of my two sons, cherished the attention my mother gave him as well as the pride she showed in him, her beloved grandson.

"Your dad told me that you are going into practice with a great group of pediatricians in Hollywood and that you'll be working at Joe DiMaggio Children's Hospital. Maybe after dinner, we can have a chat and compare notes. I'm looking forward to hearing how things have changed in the field. I sure do miss it, but I'm happy you're carrying on the tradition. I always knew you had it in you."

"Hey, Dad, will you pass the ice cream?" Kyle interrupts.

"Where's the *please*?" Bradley asks.

"Sorry. Please pass the ice cream."

"Do you want some apple pie first?" I ask.

"Grandma, you know I don't like pie – only cake!"

As Bradley hands the half-gallon container of vanilla ice cream to Kyle, my father chimes in. "Lily, I am touched that you made my favorite pie. It's exactly like your mother's. I never thought I would taste a pie as delicious as hers again. I miss everything about her, especially her cooking."

With that, my father cups his hand around his mouth, leans his elbow on the table, and asks, "Did she give you her recipe?"

"Remember Mom made me and Cynthia those beautifully bound copies of her recipes? She was serious about our learning how to cook."

"Truthfully, Lily, all I have are memories."

He bends his head down and sits quietly for a minute. With his right hand, he begins to slowly tap on the table almost as if lost in another world. No one else says a word. We all share his pain. After a few minutes, my father continues. Everyone's eyes are on him.

"There are so many times when my thoughts take me back to life with Grandma and all our children. I feel as though they're happening now. It's the strangest thing. I find myself sitting for hours at a time just reflecting back."

Dad turns to his left and looks directly at me. "The other day I was thinking about when you kids were little and how you would all fight to ride in the front seat with me and your mother.

"That led me to remembering the first brand-new car Mom and I ever bought. I think it was around 1950 – two years after we were married and a year after you were born, Lily.

"Your mother was so thrilled to have a shiny black car – a Ford sedan. Her family was pretty poor, so they never had a car of their own. They used to take the streetcar wherever they went."

"What's a streetcar?" asks Tyler.

I am pleased that he is paying attention. Tyler seems curious about everything and always wants to learn as much as he can.

"It was similar to a trolley car you might see at Disney World today. It ran on tracks and was public transportation that people would take to get from one place to the next – the way some use buses today. Anyway, Grandma and I acted like two little kids because we were so excited to have this new car."

"Was that before you went into the Navy, Grandpa?" Tyler again questions.

"No, Tyler, I was in the Navy from 1943 until 1945. I wasn't married then. In fact, I hadn't even met Grandma yet. I went into the service immediately after I graduated from high school. My original plan was to go right to college, but with the war being fought all over the world, I felt it was my obligation to join the armed forces."

Kyle suddenly perks up and becomes interested in the conversation. He puts his spoon down and looks at my father. "Grandpa, did you go on a big ship?"

"Yes, but initially I was stationed at the United States Naval Training Center at Great Lakes in Illinois for a few months, Kyle. They had to teach us how to be sailors. After all, none of us had ever been on a ship before.

"We not only learned how to navigate the ship but also how to fight in a war. From there, I crossed the Atlantic Ocean on the LST-325 and went to Europe where part of the war was taking place. I was over there for a year-and-a-half and came home once World War II ended."

I still have trouble imagining my father fighting in a war. He had never talked about it to any of us kids. In fact, in all my years growing up, I can't remember him ever mentioning that he had gone to war. My mother told me long ago that she and my father didn't discuss his stint in the Navy.

I therefore found it rather fascinating that, through the years, my dad discussed his two years in the service with Bradley, Shane, and his other grandchildren. From the time the kids were about ten years old, Dad would tell them all kinds of stories – but never in front of me or my siblings.

It's hard to understand why that was. Mother thought it was probably because he didn't want to share his suffering with his children and, in fact, maybe he wanted to protect us from his pain.

What he did tell the kids was most likely only a small part of what he had experienced. Maybe the fact that they were one generation removed had something to do with it. I've heard that grandparents can talk to their grandchildren about things that they can't speak about to their own children.

He saw way too much for a young man of eighteen. Much of the anguish he endured is probably buried inside him forever.

Holly interrupts my thoughts with a question for my dad. "So when did you go to medical school, Grandpa?"

I notice my father adjusts his hearing aid before he answers her. "I first had to go to college, since I hadn't had the opportunity to do that as I had originally planned. I was home by the end of 1945 and began school at the University of Illinois in 1946. I didn't start medical school there until 1950.

"Luckily, in 1944, the government passed an act known as the GI Bill. It allowed me and others from the service to go to college without having to pay full tuition. Once I was in college, I knew I wanted to become a doctor."

"And what about Grandma?" Shane asks.

My dad takes a deep breath. I can tell that the mention of my mother catches him off-guard.

"Well, Grandma lived in Chicago with her family. She was the sister of one of my buddies in the Navy, who later went to college with me. You might remember Uncle Teddy. He fixed us up on our first date. We went to a dance, and Grandma and I liked each other from the start. She was a wonderful dancer and a beautiful girl with a great figure. All eyes were on her when she was out there on the dance floor.

"We dated for almost a year and then got married. Soon after, your mom was born. Grandma spent the next twenty years or so raising kids, since we had four little ones right in a row.

"I'm not sure how we managed financially because I was in school for so many years. Somehow, though, we did it. Maybe it was because I was born and grew up during the Great Depression. My parents were frugal, and I learned how to live on very little. Then later when I was in medical school, my father got involved in a lucrative scrap metal business and made some money. Once they could afford it, my parents were generous and helped us out when we needed it."

After he says that, I can tell that my father once again is getting lost in his thoughts. I feel as though we had pushed him enough tonight with our questions and conversation. Yet, I am glad that he is speaking openly about my mother. This is good for my dad. It surely is better than him going off to be in a hotel room by himself – especially one that holds so many years of memories with my mother.

I am also sure that after a long day of travel, he is exhausted. I get up to clear the table, and Shane and my dad go into the den to exchange stories about being a pediatrician.

ᘒᘓ

My father requests a few days alone at the hotel, which I give him. I insist that we speak at least once a day, and he is amenable to that. He doesn't want company, though.

Whenever we speak, I hear sadness in his voice. It sounds like he isn't doing much of anything, but I know that being back in Room 732 is filled with a slew of memories for him. He needs the time to reflect and remember in his own way. I respect that.

He finally agrees to walk with me at sunrise. We're meeting down in front of O'Malley's at 6:30 a.m. It will be the first time that I have been alone with him since Mom passed away. Always either a sibling or Russell or one of his grandchildren has been with us. This will be a special time for my father and me.

∽

"Lily, did you know that Mom and I used to get up every morning when we were here and go downstairs for sunrise? We would time it so we would be walking north just as the sun was coming up over the horizon. Sometimes we would go down by the water's edge and stand there watching the sun rise without anyone else around. It was our favorite way to start each day.

"If a lot of clouds dotted the sky, there was a good chance that they would turn a multitude of colors, and the sky would be ablaze with oranges, reds, pinks, and yellows. Or if there wasn't a thick cloud cover on the horizon, which there sometimes was in the early morning, we would know that the sun was going to be completely visible as it rose over the ocean. Those sunrises were always an incredibly beautiful sight.

"No matter how sad I am and how your mother's dying may feel like the end of the world to me, I know that no matter what, the sun will come up over the ocean each morning signaling a new day. The cycle continues day after day, week after week, and year after year. It reminds me that regardless of what is going on in our own personal lives, there is a much bigger picture. We aren't the ones in charge of so many things that happen."

As he says that, I link my arm through my dad's. He pulls me close and looks at me. Everything reminds him of my mother.

There is no escaping it. Yet, I can tell that being out in nature is good for him.

"Dad, tell me more."

He smiles at me. "The most breathtaking sunsets we ever saw were in Hawaii. Mom and I used to stroll along the beaches there just like here and never tired of the scenery. Still, we both always agreed that there is something about this beach and being here that beats anywhere else we've ever been. Maybe it's because you're here, and everything is better with children and grandchildren around."

I smile back at him. I hold his words tightly inside my heart because I understand that he means them.

"Since you were our first child, you were the one who helped us understand the meaning of being a parent. I remember the first time we were up all night with you. Your fever had spiked to 104.5 degrees. I saw the fear in your mother's eyes. That was the moment when I knew how much I loved you and how important it was for me to protect you.

"Having you and your siblings made me a better pediatrician. When mothers came in petrified that something was seriously wrong with their children, I could understand their fears. I don't think I would've had the same empathy if I hadn't been a parent myself."

My father's willingness to talk about his feelings fills me with joy. I am the lucky one. After all, so many fathers never talk about things like this with their children. My brothers obviously didn't learn from him. They are much more closed off and rarely show emotion – more like my mother, I suppose.

Dad and I walk in silence for a while, each engrossed in our own thoughts. After a bit, my father mentions how lovely the bricks are on the Broadwalk. He likes the recent additions to the beach. A little girl with her father by her side is walking on the new cement wall that parallels the bicycle path.

"She reminds me of you, Lily. When you kids were little, you would try to balance yourselves on rocks or on any short wall you would pass. Do you remember the time you all got into trouble because Mr. Bushman had just painted the ledge surrounding his garden, and the four of you decided to walk on it? He was furious!"

I like when my father brings up old memories from when we were young. He never seems to forget any of our childhood. He relishes those moments. I am pleased to see the smile on his face -- something he hasn't done that often lately.

"When I came home from work that night, your mother was not at all happy. In fact, as soon as I walked in, I could hear her yelling. You know how she would get with you kids every once in a while." He winks and goes on.

"Mr. Bushman had come over himself to report you, and to begin with, Mom never liked him. I think that having to deal with him was what enraged her more than anything else. After all, aside from the ledge being freshly painted, what you did wasn't all that terrible. Meanwhile, you were all in your rooms hiding from her."

Since I had been the ringleader on that excursion, I hadn't forgotten the incident. As usual, my mother's temper was much worse than my father's. He rarely yelled at us.

Dad once again becomes quiet. I look over at him and see that his smile has vanished. I notice how he fades in and out – going into his own world of sorrow and grief.

"There are times when I think about Mom, and my heart feels too heavy to bear. I can't even describe it adequately, Lily, but it grabs me when I least expect it. In those moments of pain, all I want to do is withdraw to my room, pull down the window shades, and never come out.

"Even though I'd known your mother was sick for the last year and I understood that she was going to die, nothing prepared me for the feelings that have surfaced now that she's gone. I have days when I stay in bed and don't do anything.

"Sometimes I feel so completely alone and lost. It's strange because I'm still the same person I always was, but without my Nancy by my side, I feel less than half of who I used to be.

"At our wedding, the minister described love in a way that I will never forget."

"Dad, you don't have to do this." He was having a difficult time with the memories. Yet, I knew my father needed to revisit them, to be close to my mother.

He takes a deep breath and says in a whisper, "From every person there rises a light that reaches straight to Heaven. When two souls are destined to be together, their streams of light flow together, and a single brighter light goes forth from their united being.'" His eyes are flooding over.

"That light has been extinguished forever."

"Oh Dad, this is so hard for you, and I'm sorry." I stop walking and reach up to give him my outstretched arms. I can't ease his pain, but I try.

He holds me tightly, and the tears roll down our cheeks. There we stand in the middle of the Broadwalk, hugging each other and sharing our grief as the rising sun shines down on us.

⁓

The next day when I call my father on the phone, I can tell he is once again on the verge of tears. It is hard to hear him sounding so depressed. It's about nine o'clock in the morning, and I'm sure he has been up for hours.

"I had a dream about Mom last night. It's the first time I saw her in my sleep since she passed away."

"Will you tell me about it?"

"I dreamed it was many years back when the two of us were about sixty years old. We were on a cruise in the Mediterranean between ports. We had this lovely, large cabin with a balcony. I was sitting out there and staring at the sea – just as I used to do on the naval ship. I had gotten dressed for dinner and was patiently waiting for your mother.

"When she finished dressing, she came out to where I was. Earlier in the day, she had purchased a new amethyst necklace and matching earrings we had found while on an excursion in Istanbul. She was wearing the exquisite, new jewelry and a lovely, flowing white evening gown. In your mother's usual style, she looked stunning. Behind her, the setting sun appeared as a radiant ring of light surrounding her – a magnificent sight to see. She reminded me of an angel.

"I got up and put my arms around her and as we hugged, she slowly began to melt away – as though she were a candle burning down. Within minutes, my arms were empty except for her white dress which slowly fell to the ground. In my hand was the necklace with the purple jewels glimmering in the rays of the sun."

My father can barely get these words out. Suddenly, he begins to sob. There is nothing I can say or do. I sit listening to him cry. My heart is aching for him. Finally, he mutters, "Lily, I'll call you later." The phone is silenced.

∾

I often find myself thinking about my mother's last days before she died and wonder if my dad is doing the same. My siblings and I arrived several days before she passed away; however, by the time we reached the house, she was already in a coma.

We gathered in her room and surrounded the bed. Ours was a loving family, so being together at a time like that was filled with a special warmth and closeness. There were plenty of tears, but we also talked and shared good memories as we sat with each other hour after hour. Sometimes we even laughed at something someone said, which surprisingly felt okay to do.

My father never left my mother's side except to go to the bathroom. We tried to get him to take a nap or go outside for some fresh air, but he refused. I watched as he stroked her arm, kissed her forehead, or simply sat and stared at her. Periodically, he begged her to wake up. He was desperate to keep her with him.

At night, we would take turns staying with my mother. None of us were sleeping much anyway, so there were times that we would all gather in the middle of the night and sit vigil together. Not only were we there for my mother but also for my father. While no one could bring him comfort, it probably helped for him to have us by his side.

On the morning of the day she died, he seemed to sense that the end was drawing near. He asked us all to leave the room. He said he needed some time alone with Mom. Of course, we understood. We didn't go far from the room, but we did give him the privacy he requested. We could hear him talking to her non-stop. When he called us back into the room, I saw that his eyes were red-rimmed and damp.

During the next several hours, each of us and the few grandchildren who had arrived said our goodbyes to my mother, some caressed her, while others bent down and gave her a gentle kiss. Cynthia sat on one side of the bed and held her hand for hours on end. My father kept saying, "I love you, Nancy. Please don't leave me."

We understood that it was important to let her go – as difficult as it was to do. It is hard to lose the mother whom we loved so much. Yet, in the end, this is all a natural part of life.

For around a half hour or so, I was watching a vein in my mother's neck which kept visibly beating. Her breathing had slowed down and was becoming more labored. At one point, as I looked down at my hands, I heard a strange sound coming from my mother's throat. When I picked up my head, I noticed that the vein was no longer pulsating. Mom had taken her last breath. My first thought was how I hoped that her soul would easily transcend to Heaven where she would live for eternity.

What took place after that is pretty much a blur to me. I remember immediately rushing to my father's side. My brothers were crying – something I hadn't seen either of them do since they were little boys. Cynthia ended up being the strongest of all of us. She took charge and placed the call to the funeral home. My brothers and my father stayed in the room with my mother's body, but I walked into the living room and sat with my nieces and nephews. I didn't have the strength or wherewithal to do anything else.

√

My father has agreed to spend time with me and Russell this evening. We're on our way to the beach to have dinner together. He is meeting us at Las Brisas, our favorite Argentinian restaurant a few blocks from the hotel. He told me specifically not to come to his room. I get the feeling that he doesn't want anyone to intrude on his space.

Two days from now is March 28th – my parents' anniversary. I tried to convince my father to be with us on that day, but he has absolutely refused. He told me he wants to be alone after tonight, and I shouldn't bring it up to him again. I'll honor his wishes, but it's definitely hard for me to do. It'll be such an agonizing time for him. Surely having company would be better.

At the restaurant, Dad surprised me. "I wasn't even going to mention this to you, Lily, and I hope you won't be upset," said my father after deciding what he wanted to eat and closing his menu.

I couldn't imagine what he was going to tell me.

"The women in my condo are driving me crazy. They started about a week after your mother died. All of a sudden, it was like they were coming out of the woodwork. There are usually at least three or four of them each week who insist on bringing me dinner.

I have had enough tuna noodle casseroles and chicken pot pies to last me a lifetime. It's not that I have a great appetite anyway, plus I detest casseroles of any kind. Your mother knew that, but these ladies have no idea."

I listen and can just picture these women swarming in and preying on the vulnerable widower.

"Do they drop in or at least call first?" Russell asks.

"A little of both. Sometimes I'll open my door and a container filled with turkey tetrazzini or shepherd's pie will be sitting on the floor all wrapped up with a note from one of the ladies. Other times, one of them will call and without even giving me a chance to say anything, will tell me that she's bringing me dinner that night. The worst part is when they come and won't leave. Not only do I have to pretend to like what they cooked for me, but I also have to sit and listen to them babble on and on. I have no interest in what any of them talk about.

"As if that isn't enough, one woman invited me to go on a cruise -- her treat! A few have asked me to go out to dinner, again with them offering to pay. One called and told me she had tickets to a play and wanted to take me as her guest.

"It's not as if I'm a young Adonis or anything. After all, I'm up there in years and can't imagine that I would appeal to anyone. But then again, none of them are exactly beauty queens either."

I notice a slight grin on his face. It's almost as if he is acting a little playful -- the way he always used to be. For however long it lasts, I'm thrilled to see him like this.

"Dad, it's amazing to me that these women would be that bold – especially since I'm sure you've made it obvious you aren't interested."

My father shifts in his seat, picks up his napkin, and places it on his lap. Before he says anything, he takes a sip of his water and then puts his glass down on the table.

"No one will ever replace your mother. There isn't any way that I would even think about getting involved with a woman now. First of all, who needs some old lady's health problems, and besides, I can't ever imagine myself with anyone but Mom. I have no desire to even consider it."

"Sometimes I sit and think about all we had together and can hardly believe it's over – that your mother is gone forever. I find myself getting lost in memories. It's the only way I can cope with the loss. I miss her terribly."

"I'm sure it's difficult for you, Dad, to live without Mom. After you retired, you were together all the time, so being alone now has to be all the harder for you. I don't know anyone else whose marriage is as perfect as yours and Mom's was."

"Hey, wait a minute!" Russell exclaims. "I thought ours was the best marriage around!"

I figured that would get a rise out of Russell. It's no secret that we had our share of problems early on. After about twelve years of a somewhat rocky marriage, I knew that things weren't going to get any better unless we took serious steps to change our behaviors. Several of our friends had gotten divorced. I didn't want that to happen to us.

I understood we needed better tools for communicating with each other. Russell didn't seem to notice. He had walked into our relationship having no idea what constituted a good marriage. Russell came from a broken home with an abusive father and a beaten-down mother. His parents were separated by the time he was fourteen years old, and after that, his father was pretty much out of his life. He had no siblings and no one to teach him how to be in a healthy relationship.

On the other hand, my parents had set a wonderful example for me and my siblings. After meeting Russell, they warned me that it was better to marry someone who comes from an intact family and has a good relationship with his parents. Russell certainly didn't. Yet, I was in love and nothing was going to change my mind – hard as my parents tried.

I knew that Russell and I were in serious trouble when our fighting escalated with each passing year. I tried hard to convince him to go to marriage counseling with me, but at first he wanted no part of it. After much persuasion, he finally agreed. It turned out to be the best thing we ever did for our marriage. Still it isn't perfect. We both slide back into earlier patterns on occasion, but fortunately we are aware enough to get ourselves back on track. It has taken years and a lot of hard work to reach the point where we are now.

"Russell, you know I love you, but you've got to admit that we have had more than our share of ups and downs. I don't think my parents ever had those kinds of peaks and valleys in their marriage."

"Well, I can tell you for sure that my parents never even had one year of a decent marriage," Russell admits. "They were such a pitiful pair. Neither one of them was fit to be married, let alone have a child. So my frame of reference is a lot different from yours."

I can see my father listening intently to both of us as we speak. He has never heard us discuss our relationship before, although he has talked to me about it more than once.

He and my mom were concerned about us early on and let me know it from the start. Dad was gentle and kind about it and tried to help me figure out ways to make things better. Mom, in her typical style, was forceful and relentlessly talked to me about how Russell had to change – as if I had any control over that.

I am not expecting what my father says next. "Don't be so sure that our marriage was all that perfect. I don't think there is such a thing. Mom and I didn't always have it easy. Many times throughout the years, your mother would be furious with me over one thing or another."

What a shock to hear my father talking like this. He has never before said anything to me that wasn't a positive about my mother and their marriage. At this time when he is deeply mourning her, it surprises me even more. In keeping with how my father normally is, I would have thought that if anything, he would be putting her on a pedestal as most people do after someone they love dies. Since he seemed to have done that from the time I was old enough to remember, what I'm hearing is hard to believe.

"Early on, she resented when I would work long hours and make my office a priority over her -- or at least that's how she saw it. For whatever reason, she didn't seem to understand that while she was home raising all of you little ones, I was out there struggling to make a living so that I could put food on our table.

"True, I loved my work, but given the choice, home was where I wanted to be. I don't think your mother ever completely believed that. She gave me a difficult time about it through the years and never came to terms with the fact that I had no alternative but to work hard to support a big family like we had."

I can hear by the tone in his voice that my father is right back there remembering how this had been an issue for such a long time in their lives together. As he talks, I'm wondering how I didn't know any of this.

The waiter interrupts our conversation to serve the antipasto. We stop talking for a minute and wait until he leaves the table. My father picks up where he left off.

"Believe me, if I could have been home more, I would have been. Nothing made me happier than to be around all of you. I would walk into the house, and the four of you would run to greet me, grab onto my legs, and beg for piggyback rides. It was a delight to come home to my own children and not have to be with someone else's. There would be times during each day at the office when a child came in and reminded me of one of you. I'd get this pang of missing you, which lasted for a minute or so, and then I would go back and focus on my work.

"Some nights I ended up at the hospital or at someone else's home with a sick child and wouldn't even see any of you until the next morning. Those were the times when your mother would be the most upset. I'm sure some of it had to do with the fact that she had four children to care for by herself with no help from anyone else. It couldn't have been easy for her. I have to admit that not only was she a wonderful wife, but you couldn't find a better mother. And I know because I saw all kinds of mothers in my practice."

I listen to Dad talk and am amazed at what he is saying. I had no idea that this had been an issue for my parents. Now I'm curious about whether there were other things like this that I never knew about in their marriage. They had presented such a united front and never once had I heard them argue.

I've always been aware that my mother was the controlling one and that my father often had little power over what went on in our home. When I got older, I would watch their dynamics and wonder how he could tolerate her bossiness. He seemed to take it in stride, but I feel certain that I couldn't have stood having a spouse who took complete charge of everything and left me with little to say about anything. It didn't appear to bother my dad.

"You know, it's funny how things work out. It took years for me to understand it all. I was pretty naïve when we first got married. Your mother would demand a lot from me and later from all of you kids. There were times early on when she made it clear that whatever the situation might be, it had better be done her way.

My dad explains how at times he would feel defenseless. He says it took him many years, but eventually he began to understand that he needed to do something to change how things were. He tells us how that led him to stand up to her and so he did. He explains how that would turn into an argument which lasted well into the night, but my mother didn't always win.

"All of that aside, I began to understand that there were some things worth arguing about and others that didn't matter. I would seriously consider how important something was to me. If I could let it go, then that's what I did. If I felt that I needed to have a say in it, then I would stand my ground and fight to be heard. But as the years went on, we learned the magic of compromise." His voice dances when he says these words.

"As we got older, basically what changed was that the person whose needs were the greatest around a particular issue was the one who won. We would battle it out and finally come to an agreement. We knew enough to understand that it was important to respect the needs of each other."

"Did Mom get angry when you stood up to her?"

"You'd better believe it! She would rant and rave and sometimes even stomp her feet like a little kid if she wanted to get her way, and I was preventing that from happening. We had some pretty heated arguments in our marriage as a result of this.

"But how is it that I never heard you fight, Dad? How did you hide that from all of us?"

My father looks at me thoughtfully and tells me something I had never known before. "My mother and father fought all the time when I was a boy. I remember cowering in my bed, shaking at the sound of their anger. Sometimes my mother would even turn her anger toward me. As a result of that, at an early age, I knew that this was one way I did not want to be. I was determined that my children would *never* hear me yelling and screaming.

"When Mom and I had our first fight after you were born, I got up enough nerve to let her know that we were not going to continue the fight until you had fallen asleep and we were in our room behind closed doors. That started a pattern between us which continued throughout our married life. We made a conscious effort to avoid all arguments whenever anyone was around. It wasn't always easy to hold it in."

Here I had thought my father and mother didn't argue. Believing that had colored the way I saw marriage and led me to think that my parents had this perfect marriage. After all, aside from my mother yelling at us kids, I never experienced anything but a peaceful home growing up. So, I assumed that Mom and Dad never fought. Now at this point in my life, I am learning something new about them.

I think about what my father is saying and wonder whether or not it is a good thing to shield one's children from their parents' fighting. I'm not sure which way is better. I suppose it could be helpful to children if they saw their parents arguing and, as a result, learned how to deal with conflict.

From what our therapist taught us, there are ways to fight that are completely healthy. She explained how those fights which address the issue – regardless if one is talking or yelling about them – are the fights that take the couple to the place they need to be. As long as the problem is the focus and the two individuals are listening to each other, the issue can be resolved constructively.

It sounded to me as if my parents had found a way to do just that. Russell and I have worked to do the same. Perhaps had I seen my parents actually disagreeing and trying to resolve those disputes, I might have been better equipped to handle them in my own marriage.

This makes me think about what Shane and Bradley saw and learned from us. Bradley and Holly seem to have a solid marriage. My guess is there is a lot, both positive and negative, that he brought with him into their relationship. That's the way those things happen. One way or another, good or bad, messages get passed along to our children. It's the legacy we leave behind.

The waiter once again interrupts us as he serves our dinners. I can tell that Russell is hungry by the way he digs right in. The shrimp fra diavolo he ordered smells as good as it looks. My father glances at his skirt steak and creamy mashed potatoes, picks up his fork, and then puts it right back down. He doesn't seem to be interested in the meal. As it is, he has only eaten a few forkfuls of olives and roasted peppers from the antipasto. He looks up at me.

"Is it awful that I'm telling you this? Your mother wouldn't be happy if she knew I had."

"Dad, I'm glad you shared this with us. I must admit that it's surprising since I never saw anything but love and happiness between you and Mom. I'm still not sure how it was possible to shelter us from your fights. I certainly didn't do the same with my children."

"You know, Lily, the truth is that it wouldn't have been normal if we didn't have arguments. There are no two people on earth who can be together all the time without having occasional disagreements. It was more about how we managed them that led to a good relationship for the two of us. We were always able to say what was on our minds. That was what was most important. It's part of what makes up love between two people."

I'm amazed that my father is going on about all of this. He appears to want to have this conversation. Perhaps it's helpful for him to look back on how things were with my mother. He glances over at Russell and me and gives us one of his loving smiles.

"Let's face it. Your mother and I were in love from the start. After sixty-one years, many different factors led to our successful marriage. The basis of it all was that we were good friends. We loved being together. We had fun and laughed a lot.

"When Mom and I got married, one of my uncles told me that the key to his good marriage was that he and my aunt made a concerted effort to be nice to each other. I liked that, told it to your mother, and did my best to follow his simple but wise advice."

With that, the expression on his face changes once again. I can tell that all this talk about my mother and their marriage is taking him to places that are bringing back a lot of memories. Once again, I think it's good for him, even if it is painful at times. The fact that he can talk like this rather than keep it bottled up inside is important.

"When I look back on all the years that we spent together, there are times I want nothing more than to join her."

Tears well up in my father's eyes and one rolls down his cheek. I put my fork down and reach over and place my hand over his. He grabs his napkin to wipe away the tear. He sits quietly, deep in thought.

❧

I respected my father's wishes and didn't call or visit him on what would have been my parents' anniversary. It is the first time since my mother passed away that a day went by when I didn't speak to my dad. It was unsettling and yet, I needed to comply with his wishes.

Today, however, is a different story. It is seven o'clock and since I know that my father is an early riser, I decide to call him. He doesn't answer, so I assume he must have gone for his usual sunrise walk.

I wait for another hour and try again. Still no answer. I call two more times. My father does not pick up the phone.

At this point, I am crazed. I'm on my way over now to see if I can find him.

ᥱᥱ

I have finally arrived at the hotel and am quickly making my way upstairs to Room 732. With my heart palpitating, I knock on the door, but there is no answer.

"Dad, Dad, are you in there?" I call to my father hoping that he's wearing his hearing aids and that he will hear me through the door.

When he doesn't answer, I pound on the door. Again there is no response.

"Dad, please open the door."

No response.

Surely he is in the room. After his walk each day, he comes back here and spends his morning watching television.

Where is he? Why isn't he answering?

I knock again.

I spot a housekeeper down the hall and race over to her. I quickly explain that I need her to open my father's door, and we both rush down the hall to Room 732. My hands begin to tremble as she reaches in her pocket for the master key. I take a deep breath. She opens the door and moves to the side to let me in. My knees are shaking. I'm starting to feel dizzy as I make my way past her and walk into the room.

There sits my father at the table, facing the ocean. I walk up behind him and startle him as I put my hand on his shoulder. He jumps up from his seat, turns around, and looks at me.

"Lily, what on earth are you doing here?"

I wrap my arms around him and hug him tightly. "Oh Dad, I was so worried about you."

After a minute, I glance up at my father and see a look of peace on his face.

"I've said my goodbyes and yet, I know your mom will always be with me. I am okay."

Relief floods through me. My father is ready to go on living.

AUTHOR'S NOTES

Below is a composite of excerpts adapted from my journals about the Hollywood Beach Hotel and *Room 732*. In essence, the following is the story about the story.

DAY ONE

Sunday, April 22, 2012   7:00 p.m.

I checked into the hotel at noon today. I'll be here for ten days and during that time, my plan is to finish the first draft of Room 732*.*

Upon arrival, I felt my excitement mounting the moment I saw "732" encircled on a plaque on the door. Of course, I had to laugh when I first got off the elevator because, just as in chapter three when Janet and Donald weren't paying attention and got off at the sixth floor instead of the seventh, I did almost the exact same thing – except that I got off at the fifth floor. Something about arriving at Room 532 instead of 732 felt a bit like dèja vu.

Room 732 is bright, newly-renovated, and modern with white walls, white tile floors, and a seascape hanging on the wall near the queen-size bed. In a far corner across from the kitchenette sits a powder blue chair and a matching ottoman. The wall opposite the bed is completely mirrored, and in front of it is the television. Like the woman in chapter seven, I won't ever turn it on. I already know that the place I will spend most of my time is at the small, round table in front of the window overlooking the sea.

There are no traces of days long ago – no echoes of the past – at least not yet.

10:45 p.m. As soon as I close my eyes, my characters come alive. They float through my mind like billowing clouds drifting in the sky. They are real to me. Every one of them has been created through my words and imagination. I feel as if I am a four-year-old with an imaginary friend who accompanies her wherever she goes. There is no way of convincing that child that her friend does not exist in real life. Together they live in their own little world.

At this moment, no one could possibly persuade me to believe that the characters in my book didn't stay in this very same room. Each had a life here as do I in the present moment. My characters feel like ghosts from years gone by. How did this happen?

ॐ

DAY TWO

Monday, April 23, 2012 8:30 a.m.

While staying at the hotel, my goal is to journey back along the path I have traveled from the first time I ever mentioned the Hollywood Beach Hotel in my journals to the present as I complete the writing of this book. And so, I begin....

December 24, 1982

Tom, my new friend whom I met here at the beach a few weeks ago, gave me a present today. He handed me a card to Hollywood Beach Hotel's facilities, which is good for two years. It's all free – sauna, exercise room, and pool. I expect that I will use it often.

November 4, 1984

Today I decided that my next book will take place right here on Hollywood Beach. I might even use the Hollywood Beach Hotel as the backdrop. It would be an excellent way to attract attention to the hotel and maybe get another free membership to the health club, since mine is about to expire. What a good feeling to know that as I'm finishing up one book, I have planted the first seed for the next.

December 2, 1984

Each person I talk to could possibly become a character who might stay at the Hollywood Beach Hotel. One thing I'm learning is that anyone and everyone is potential material for a book.

That reminds me of the time many years ago when I was at a party. One of my friends introduced me to someone and warned, "Be careful. She's a writer. Watch what you tell her, or you might find yourself and what you said in her book." Perhaps he wasn't all wrong.

December 12, 1984

When Ed, a regular here at the beach was walking along the shore a little while ago, he stopped by my chair to chat. I told him that I'm contemplating writing a book which will take place at the Hollywood Beach Hotel. He suggested that I trace it back to the days when it was a bible college.

I'm remembering when Daryl (my husband) and I spent days at the beach with Rebecca and Michael (our children). Inevitably, students from the school would stop at our blanket and try to convince us to embrace Jesus so that we would go to Heaven. It never fit for me. I just wanted them to move on and let us enjoy our day without interruption.

As I was writing that last paragraph, I had a thought for a chapter in the book. One of the students who attended the college in the '70s would come back to stay at the hotel years later and would reminisce about the great times at Florida Bible College. That might work.

December 14, 1984

I can imagine how this weekend could very well be included in the book I hope to write someday about the Hollywood Beach Hotel. I'm glad that Daryl decided that this is where he wanted to bring me to celebrate my fortieth birthday and the completion of my book, <u>A Slice of Life</u>.

We are staying in a beautiful room overlooking the ocean. From the moment we checked in, I have been enjoying the adventure of exploring every corner of this historic landmark. I am taking notes and am tucking them away for that time someday when I write about this magnificent hotel.

I would be much happier if the management would leave us alone. Since they have turned the hotel into a timeshare, they keep pestering us to schedule an appointment to meet with them. They have called us three times already. Apparently, they're trying to get people to purchase timeshare units. We just want to be left alone to enjoy the weekend with each other.

At breakfast today, I heard a woman telling the man she was sitting with about how this was the place where they filmed parts of "Porky's II" two years ago. We never saw the movie, although I did see them filming it on the Broadwalk.

DAY THREE

Tuesday, April 24, 2012 5:45 a.m.

Last night I went for a walk and met up with my friend's aunt. When I told her about the book I was writing, she shared a memory from when she was six years old.

Eddie Cantor was performing at the Hollywood Beach Hotel in February 1936. Her father brought her to see the show, but he wasn't happy since Jews were not permitted to stay there. It's interesting that they would let them perform but not vacation at the hotel.

♒

March 1, 1985

I met Jeff Newsome, project manager of the Hollywood Beach Hotel, this morning. He told me about the history and described the beauty of this hotel in its early years.

Until I had spoken to Jeff, I thought I would write as if the Hollywood Beach Hotel were like any other hotel on the beach. However, now that I've got real history to work with, everything changes.

He took me on a tour. I saw the dining room and huge ballroom, both of which are now closed to the public. While walking around the building, he pointed out windows, floors, and wall fixtures from the early beginnings in the mid-1920s.

June 9, 1985

Strange as it seems, the Anne Frank exhibition, Anne Frank in the World: 1929 – 1945, that I'll be bringing to Miami in December has become an inspiration for my Hollywood Beach Hotel book. Being consumed in thought by Anne's diary has led me to think about writing the book in a journal format.

I'm not sure that I'll be able to write much for a while, though, since planning and then overseeing the exhibit is going to take up most of my time for the next seven months. If nothing else, I can let the ideas germinate until I'm ready for my next project.

February 28, 1986

They're tearing out part of the interior of the Hollywood Beach Hotel. I heard they are converting it from timeshares to condos and are also building some kind of a mall. Thus begins yet another phase in the hotel's history.

My ultimate fantasy becomes clearer. I envision a fairy tale ending – Daryl and I buy a condo on the seventh floor of the hotel; I become a full-time writer, and we live at the beach.

Since I will be beginning my new job at the South Florida Holocaust Memorial Center tomorrow, writing is out of the question. For now, all of this is nothing but a mere dream.

May 12, 1986

Last week, I sent a letter to Ben Tobin telling him I'm planning to write a book about the Hollywood Beach Hotel. Since he was the developer and owned the hotel between the time the Navy moved out and the Florida Bible College moved in, I wanted to meet him and get some facts verified. Instead, I'm meeting with Barbara Gompers, who worked with him. As long as I get the information, I'll be happy.

February 12, 1988

Today is the opening of Oceanwalk in the Hollywood Beach Hotel. It's going to be terrific to have a mall at the beach. I'll be able to take care of many of my errands right here in one spot. The only negative is that it is now going to be unbelievably crowded. Certainly, I will need to move either south or north if I want quiet.

I haven't given up on the idea of writing the book about the hotel someday, but so far, I haven't been moved to do so. No muses have come visiting to help me along.

∽

Sunday, January 1, 2011

Now that I am beginning to look at my retirement from the Center by next year at this time, I've decided that my first project out the door will be to write the Hollywood Beach Hotel story that I had dreamed of doing way back in the mid-1980s. The idea continues to intrigue me and, once again after all these many years, calls to me.

Friday, January 27, 2011

As I work on my journal project of culling excerpts, I am reading back in February '86 about wanting to write the

Hollywood Beach Hotel book. Since it's my life and my reality, I know the end result. I did not write the book then. The research I had done remains buried in a folder in my writing cabinet. There is something about this now that feels as if it is finally coming full circle.

Sunday, May 13, 2011

For now, I am content to think about starting to write the book on January 1, 2012. It has given me the focus I need as I officially announced my retirement from the Holocaust Documentation and Education Center this week.

Sunday, July 8, 2011

Today when I was with Jane (my college roommate), we were remembering our days at Ohio State University when we were elementary education majors. We talked about where we were then and where we are now. Being a successful painter, she could relate to my plans to write full-time. She liked the idea of the book but understood why this is not the time for me to get started on it. Before I do anything else, I must tie things up at the Center, which will take me the next six months. Saying goodbye after twenty-six years will not be an easy thing to do. First things first.

Thursday, December 29, 2011

Today was my last day at the Center. I am now ready for the next step along the path. Tonight I went to my cupboard of writing folders and pulled out the one with all of the research on the Hollywood Beach Hotel that I had collected years ago. Some of the paper has already begun to yellow. The good news is that historical facts don't change.

Monday, January 1, 2012

Tomorrow I plan to begin working on the book. I have my writing gear all ready to go -- pens, legal pads, my laptop, folders, and most of all, my enthusiasm to begin my life as a full-time writer. It has been a long countdown from all those years ago when I first envisioned making this possibility become a reality. Somehow I got sidetracked, but I am back on the path and eager to begin. This is a time of endings and beginnings.

Tuesday, January 2, 2012

I got a call early this morning with the unfortunate news that my mother fell and is being rushed to the hospital by ambulance. I'm taking a plane up to Cleveland tomorrow – the first flight I could get. I'll bring my laptop with me and hopefully will be able to begin writing my book during the long hours sitting at the hospital.

Friday, January 20, 2012

I spent these past two weeks mourning my mother and coming to terms with the fact that she has died. Sadness permeates my soul.

The timing of her death was significant. Days before, I had closed the doors on my life at the Holocaust Center and was just beginning to open the gates to a new world of writing and teaching. Throughout my mother's life, she had embraced the value of education and had instilled in me the joy of reading and writing.

When I was a young child, my mother told me something that her grandmother, whom I'm named after, had told her when she was about six years old. "Whenever you see a rainbow, make a wish and keep it tucked inside your heart." Since then, rainbows have symbolized hope for me.

And like the spectrum of a rainbow, my mother completed her journey from life to death and reached her pot of gold through her rich, golden spirit. She left me her legacy – to share the gift of knowledge and wisdom. Now it is my turn to carry the banner of educating and enriching others through my writing and the sharing of my life experiences.

Today when I look at a rainbow, I am reminded of my mother's unconditional encouragement and support and am grateful for her love, life, and legacy.

Monday, January 23, 2012

This morning as I walked at the beach, I began to "talk" to both my parents. I opened myself up and called on them to help me create my characters and formulate the stories for my book. My mother and father are the angels who will guide me along on this journey. I have no idea where my muse will come from and if there even is one, but it was my parents who gave me life, and so I am counting on them to be by my side as I write my way through this book.

I let my mind wander and by the time I completed my walk and went to sit in the lifeguard stand to meditate, I came up with an idea for chapter one.

4:30 p.m. Page one of chapter one is written. I have done some research on life in the 1930s - the kinds of clothes they wore, the businesses that flourished during the Great Depression so that some people could afford to go to Florida on vacation, the popular names of people during that era.

I'm amazed at how easy it is to do research with the Internet. Twenty-eight years ago when I was writing a book,

I went to the library day after day and searched through microfiche to get information. Today, I googled a few words and immediately got my answers. I'm almost positive that my granddaughters will never use an encyclopedia, let alone ever go to a library to do research.

Thursday, January 26, 2012

At one point yesterday, I felt like my writing was going no place at all. I couldn't imagine that I would be able to write a full chapter and, for sure, not a complete book. I put it down and found something else to occupy my time. At around eleven o'clock last night, I decided to read the seven pages I had written, and all of a sudden, I was busy at work writing again. I'm not sure how that happened.

This morning, I met with Silverio Lantigua, the general manager of Hollywood Beach Ocean Resort, who talked to me about the history of the hotel. It was reassuring that all the research I had done long ago was accurate and that I had the facts pretty well down-pat.

He took me on a tour of the building, where I chose Room 732 as the one where my characters will stay. I was especially interested when he told me that several people have reported that they've seen a ghost in the hotel – talked to her, in fact. Her name is Ashlee or something close to that. He said some-one had recorded her talking. I will definitely find a way to incorporate the ghost into the book.

After our tour, he left me on my own to roam the halls. Fabulous old photographs line the walls in the hotel. In so many of the pictures from the early years, people are dressed in formal wear. It is obvious that this was an opulent hotel when it first opened. Even the wait staff and bell boys wore fancy uniforms. The pictures from the naval training center showed men lined up in perfect precision – exactly as one might expect from the military.

The pool used to be in the front of the building where the garage is located. Pictures of the cabanas and the lush, flower-filled gardens that surrounded the entrance portray scenes of how it used to be. Some of the details of the hotel in the '20s and '30s, like the gargoyles, beautiful urns, statues on the tallest tower, and bells across the top front, are all gone now. The beauty and elegance of the olden times has disappeared.

Thursday, February 2, 2012

Today I finished the first draft of chapter one, which definitely is not light reading. I am still not sure how I got from one paragraph to another and why it went in the direction that it did. However, it's done.

I started to contemplate the next chapter and have absolutely no idea what to write. It most likely will take place in 1942 or 1943 at the naval center, but that's all I know. When I began to write chapter one, I didn't have much more information than the year it would take place and the fact that it was an elegant hotel, so there is hope for what is yet to come.

Sunday, February 5, 2012

I have decided that I am not going to let anyone read my book until it's completed. About thirty years ago in the writing group I participated in, Marianne, the facilitator, told us never to talk about what we're writing during the process because it dissipates the creative energy. That means I must live in a world which only I inhabit – strange and difficult for me who openly shares with others what is happening in my life.

Thursday, February 9, 2012

All night long, I had dreams about the book. In so many ways, it is consuming my thoughts. I was writing sentences and was plotting the remaining chapters that I have yet to write. Unfortunately I didn't get out of bed to put any of it down, so I remember none of it!

Monday, February 13, 2012

On my way to the beach this morning, I had a thought that in no time mushroomed into a connector for my book. "Motherhood" in some form will be included in each chapter. It will be a way to honor my own mother, will keep her close in my thoughts as I write, and will help me along with the mourning process.

I looked up the Florida Bible College alumni website on Facebook and sent messages to several people asking whether they would be willing to speak with me about their experiences at the college. So far, Pat Wesolowski, who attended FBC, has responded and said she would be happy to help.

I asked my friend Tom (a former priest) to look up the college in order to find out the sect and/or religion of the students who attended Florida Bible College. It turns out that they are born-again, which is completely foreign to me. From what he has told me so far, being born-again is associated with Salvation and with one having a personal relationship with Jesus. This chapter is going to be the greatest challenge of all for me.

Wednesday, February 15, 2012

Yesterday I spoke to a man named Steve Ohlrogge, a friend of my cousin Donna's. He lives in Wisconsin and served in the Navy in Vietnam. He answered all my general questions and verified the naval terms. He told me that enlisted men had a completely different experience from those who became commissioned officers.

It will be impossible to locate anyone who was stationed at the hotel in the 1940s because those men would all be much too old by now, if in fact any are still living. The youngest one would be at least ninety-three since all the officers went to college first and would have been approximately twenty-two years old when they arrived at the training center.

What I reaffirmed from my conversation with Steve is that nothing compares to getting information from a primary source. Of course, I already knew that from working with the Holocaust survivors, but this hit home more than ever.

I am in the midst of creating, and that's always tremendously fulfilling for me. In some ways, I feel like my new life is the only one I've had. That's how immersed I am in this writing. The Center and all my years there feel like long ago and far away. However, I draw from my reserve of experiences and life knowledge and am reminded of what a privilege it was to do the work that I did.

Monday, February 20, 2012

For one of the chapters, I had planned to write about two Holocaust survivors who came to the beach and stayed at the hotel. The more I've thought about it, the more I'm sure that I won't. I don't think I could do them justice or speak in their voice. Most importantly, I would not be comfortable fictionalizing anything about the Holocaust – even if the facts were completely accurate. I need to save my Holocaust writing for another time down the road. Through the years, survivors shared many incredible stories with me which I will one day want to pass down to the next generation in order to educate them about the dangers of prejudice. This is not the time and place for that.

The piece I've just written in chapter three about the non-Jewish woman who was in the Holocaust is adapted from a true story taken from Beach Life *that I wrote in the early '80s. I included it now because it seemed like it would fit into the story. The woman I wrote about did stop me at the beach and had talked to me about her Holocaust experiences even before I became involved with the Anne Frank exhibition and later the Holocaust Center. At that time, I knew little about the Holocaust and, for sure, never knew that non-Jews were taken to concentration camps.*

I have to skip chapter four for now. I am going to need to talk to people from the bible college before I dip my feet in the water and then submerge my entire being.

I spoke to Steve again because I wanted to make sure that I have my facts straight now that I rewrote part of the chapter on the Navy. He explained what it was like to be at a port rather than in a war or out at sea. Most of the guys, his father included, would do their jobs in whatever time it took to complete them, would get liberty, and then would go out to a bar and get completely drunk.

He told me that Post Traumatic Stress Disorder (PTSD) was called battle fatigue during World War II. He explained that those men who suffered from battle fatigue (or PTSD) often treated those under them horribly. Some were downright cruel to their subordinates. There was no treatment for this during that time in our history. Only more recently is our country becoming sensitive to those who come back from war suffering from PTSD.

One of the things he described was how the men often felt when they were in battle. The sailors would hear the bombing right by their ship and would never know if they were going to get killed the next minute. He claimed that what ended up happening for many was that they got to the point where they didn't care if they lived or died. They were numb and shut-down, and to them that was the only way to get through it.

Steve went into great detail about some of his experiences during Vietnam. At one point, he explained what it was like to come home from the war and be treated so terribly by the people in our country. He gave me an example. He was on a plane coming home from Vietnam because his daughter had been born with a birth defect. A well-known singer was on the plane and actually called Steve a baby killer. "A flight attendant overheard the guy, had enough compassion for me to switch my seat, put me in first class, and handed me a glass of champagne." I was sick inside when he shared this with me.

At one point in our conversation, Steve mentioned that he was telling me stories that, prior to this, he hadn't told a soul. While I could hear him crying, on the other end I was doing the same. The strong emotions he evoked reminded me of how poorly we treated our Vietnam vets who were only doing their jobs. My Uncle Melvin, who also served in Vietnam, had told me how awful it was to watch his troops as they came home to protestors who shouted and threw things at them. It was a painful time in our country.

I asked Steve if he has nightmares about the war, and he responded that he doesn't. Instead as he explained, "I have it all stuffed down and, aside from today's conversation, it never comes up – not even when I'm sleeping." He did say that when he first got home, no one dared to touch him when he was asleep. He carried a switch blade tied to his leg for *many years. Those are the kinds of things war does to young boys.*

I hope that my chapter reflects the respect I have for those who serve in our armed forces. They risk everything for the rest of us.

Tonight, we went to dinner with my friends Marsha and Jeff and her brother Larry and her sister-in-law Peggy. I announced that I had finished part of my book and that I need a title for it. While I had always thought the book would be named <u>Hollywood Beach Hotel</u>, none of them thought that was intriguing enough. We sat around the table, and everyone suggested titles for the book. Peggy came up with <u>Changing Tides</u>, which we all loved. Bingo! My book has a title.

Wednesday, February 22, 2012

I checked on the Internet, and there is already a book on Amazon called <u>Changing Tides</u>. There's also a song by that name, but the band is heavy metal, and I couldn't even listen to the whole thing. I am disappointed because I liked the idea of the changing tides, which seemed like it would have fit perfectly.

Back and forth I went with title suggestions and ideas. Finally, I decided that I am going to go with <u>Room 732</u>. It works for me because that is where it all happens. In fact, I rather like it.

Later on, my friend Joel asked me about the number and suggested I might think in terms of Kabbalah. He asked if 732 had any significance for me, and I told him it did. He then quickly figured out that the numbers add up to twelve and asked me if twelve is an important number in my life.

I told him I was born on December 12ᵗʰ, and that it was the reason I chose a room number that added up to twelve.

My days keep getting better and better. Today I spoke to Pat from Florida Bible College for one-and-a-half hours. I was absolutely fascinated by what she revealed and how she ended up going to school at the bible college. I already have a great idea for one of the characters in the chapter as a result of our conversation.

Pat explained how she found her bliss in being a Christian and went on to tell me what life was like at FBC. We talked a bit about certain beliefs she has, but I need to process them before I am clear enough to write anything that makes sense.

Thursday, February 23, 2012

Already Pat has sent me the names of others who said they would be happy to describe their experiences at FBC. I'm learning that they don't refer to it as Florida Bible College much and never <u>the</u> Florida Bible College.

Today when I walked, I decided to give each chapter a title name. That way, I can use "Changing Tides."

I had lunch with my friend Carol Safran today. After talking about my book and telling her the name I had decided on, she went home, did some research, and sent me something called Angel Number 732. It explains the compilation of the vibrations of the numbers 7, 3, and 2 and in some strange way, seems to be guiding me. I'm blown away by it.

"Angel Number 732 is a message to pay special attention to your dreams, daydreams, visions, recurring thoughts, and feelings. The angels, Archangels (messengers of God), and Ascended Masters (spiritually enlightened beings who were ordinary humans in past incarnations but who have undergone a process of spiritual transformation) are sending you

Divine guidance regarding your life path and purpose and ask that you act according to direction.

"The repeating number 732 suggests that you take time out to meditate, connect and communicate with the angelic and spiritual realms in order to find direction, balance, and clarity in your life.

"Trust that all is going to Divine plan in all ways."

Friday, February 24, 2012

I can't sleep. My book is coming alive for me. Pat sent me the email addresses of three additional women from FBC who seem excited and more than ready to talk to me: Suzette, Shelley, and Susan.

I called the hotel and found out that Room 732 is a condo – privately owned – and so I need to talk to the owner about renting it. The last week in April will work since, at the rate I'm going, I should be finished writing the first draft of the rest of the book by then.

Somehow this book has a life of its own. I have no idea where it will take me from one day or one page to the next.

Monday, February 27, 2012

I've spoken to the three women from FBC. Shelley and Suzette offered to send me yearbooks from when they were at FBC. Suzette confirmed that the girls slept on the sixth and seventh floors, which is absolutely perfect. She even described the rooms to me.

What strikes me the most about all these women is how open and eager to share each has been. We've had some intense conversations, every one of them being enlightening and eye-opening.

I am starting to get a better idea of their religious beliefs. What I'm most happy about is that none of them are imposing their views on me. I had hoped they wouldn't, but I wasn't sure what would happen in any of these conversations. Before working on this chapter, I had a lot of misconceptions which are slowly evaporating, thank goodness. It's a great reminder that until I am certain of the facts, I shouldn't be judging.

Friday, March 2, 2012

I'm up to five people from the bible college whom I've spoken to now. Within the past few days, I talked to Mary and Laura. Pat keeps giving me names, and it's impossible to turn any away, since each one offers me another slice of life at FBC. They have all been incredibly patient with my endless questions.

I also talked to Uri, the manager of Room 732, and am getting the room from April 22 – May 1. It's exciting that I have a date and know that this is actually going to happen.

Sunday, March 4, 2012

I was having an awful time beginning chapter four. At some point yesterday morning, I figured out that my issue was that I was trying to put myself into the characters. This cannot in any way be my story (not that any of the others could be either, but this one definitely will not be). Once I realized that one of the characters has to tell the story and that I must step far back, something shifted. I'm not sure why it was different from any other chapter I've written.

This weekend I spoke to two men who were at the college -- Stan, a former dean of the school, and Paul, who was a musical pastor. I finally feel like I have a handle on what went on at the school.

Wednesday, March 14, 2012

I sent my completed bible college chapter to a few FBC people. Of all the chapters, this is the only one that still has individuals who were at the hotel (albeit college then), and I want to make sure that what I've written is completely accurate. So far, they've helped me edit the various religious terms – like capitalizing word in Word of God – all things Christian-related, of which I am clueless.

Wednesday, March 21, 2012

I'm pleased with the reactions of those from Florida Bible College. One said she felt like I was at her wedding. Another told me it reads as if I went to school with them. I am most amazed that they all feel as though I got the religious piece right. Above all, that was the hardest part of writing that chapter.

When I sent an email to my friend Aileen describing my book in more detail and telling her about the U. S. Navy and bible college interviews, her response to my description was: "What a paradox – the same place – a "container" for relationships, socialization, fraternization and then a "container" to instill a relationship with an institution, an ideal. "I give my life for the good of country" or "I give my life in service to Jesus Christ."

Friday, March 23, 2012

I went to the Hollywood Historical Society and was able to get more specific information about the naval training center. I will be able to add more accurate and historical information to chapter two. I get excited when pieces like this come together.

Sunday, March 25, 2012

I have been writing non-stop and finished chapter six today. One of my favorite things about this chapter is that I wrote letters from a grandmother to her granddaughters. I took the first two letters to both Miriam and Esther right out of the journals I'm keeping for Sophia and Isabella (my granddaughters). I went to the first day each was born and used what I wrote to them and put that into letter form with pretty much the content being the same – just the names and places are changed and a little added to make it all work.

Now I've decided that in chapter seven, I am going to include part of the piece, On Being a Woman, which also comes from my journals. After all these years of keeping journals and all the times I questioned why I was recording my life day after day in hundreds of volumes, I now see how some of what I wrote can be used in different ways.

Friday, March 27, 2012

I wrote to Patrick Overton, a poet, to ask if I could have his permission to use his poem about faith in chapter six. He answered me yesterday saying I could use it with formatting stipulations, including no period at the end of the poem. I asked him why, and he explained that he literally "likes to leave it hanging," which implies that the sentence is not finished. To quote him, "Poetry is almost always about bad grammar put in eloquent form to justify breaking the rules!"

Thursday, March 29, 2012

When I was at the Hollywood Historical Society last week, I met Bill, who has an extensive postcard collection of Hollywood. We have been in touch with each other ever since, and today I received this from him.

From: Bill Schaaf
Date: March 29, 2012 10:17:36 AM EDT
To: Merle Saferstein
Subject: Re: Postcards

Dear Merle,

My collection pretty much covers the entire life of the hotel. I have cards from every angle of viewing and some are titled Florida Bible College, others are Naval Training School. Many show the beautiful gardens that were present before they built the 'new' boulevard bridge and took away most of the front of the hotel grounds.

Let me know the time frame you are looking at, and I will collect any cards you need. I will be happy to send them to you for use in your book.

Bill

And I ask myself: What could be more perfect than using postcards in a book about a hotel? I feel like I struck gold.

Thursday, April 5, 2012

I have now completed the first seven chapters of the book. I realize that I am a serious writer and certainly haven't chosen to write about anything that's light-hearted. Instead, I have included issues like losing a loved one, going to war, embracing Jesus, passing along one's legacy, experiencing the challenges of marriage, and fighting for women's rights.

From a psychological aspect, I have included thoughts on the importance of saying something out loud to someone and being heard, caring about others, verbalizing the truth, appreciating one another, learning to forgive, sharing life's journey, passing along wisdom, and setting and accomplishing goals.

In each chapter I have incorporated various aspects of motherhood: wanting to be a mother, having to give up a child, being loved by a supportive mother, understanding a mother's influence on us, and so much more. Writing about all of this for me has been a significant part of my dealing with the loss of my mother.

༄

5:45 p.m. Yesterday I felt so filled with joy sitting here looking out my window at the magnificent and vast sea. I began to wonder how the students at FBC were ever able to concentrate on their studies with the ocean in constant view. I decided to write to them and ask, plus I wanted to tell them a little about my experience here. I found these responses in keeping with how they originally depicted their lives at the college.

Re: Chapter 8 is happening....somehow...
From: Pat Wesolowski
To: Merle Saferstein
Tuesday, April 24, 2012 8:12 AM

When I was at Florida Bible College, the newness of studying the scriptures was so exciting and rich that I barely noticed the beach.

I did appreciate the beauty of the ocean, but it wasn't a distraction. It was the first place I lived without noticeable season changes, and I missed that.

Glad this is becoming what you had hoped for and more!

Pat

❦

Re: Chapter 8 is happening....somehow...
From: Carol Hoehn
To: Merle Saferstein
Tuesday, April 24, 2012 11:38 AM

To answer your question, as briefly as I can: How could I concentrate on my studies while living on the beach? The beach/ocean reminded me of why I was there. This motivated me even more to study. Plus, I loved what I was learning. It wasn't work for me. I was building a personal relationship with God and that was easy.

I put myself through college so I had to go to classes, then go to work, and after all day at work, I would come back to the dorm and study. Mostly, I had to memorize an average of seven Bible verses a day. My first and second year I had as much as three jobs at a time, especially during the breaks.

I did enjoy and appreciate when I had a room on the ocean side. Hearing the waves and constantly watching their dramatic changes, loud and soft, day and night – the memory has stayed with me over the years. You do fall in love with the ocean. I then began to understand why sailors fall in love with the sea and compare it to a woman.

∽

6:30 p.m. This morning I met with Clive Taylor, who is interested in old architecture and whom Bill, my postcard friend, suggested I contact. When I first spoke with Clive, we talked about the ghosts that I had heard about. He thought his friend Carol, who had attended FBC, might have more information about that, but it turned out that she didn't. Instead, she told me about these two big black lacquer boxes which sat on the second floor and looked like coffins. No one else has any memory of those.

Clive brought some postcards of the hotel in its original state and a magnifying glass for us to check out all the minute details on the cards. Once we did that, we went searching for them on the inside and outside of the building. We found a few remnants left over from when the Hollywood Beach Hotel was originally built. It brought things even more alive for me.

∽

DAY FOUR

Wednesday, April 25, 2012 10:25 a.m.

Daryl came here last night, and I took him on a tour of the hotel. After dinner, we went back upstairs, which gave him the chance to experience Room 732, my home during these ten days.

On our way back here, I decided that I was going to read him chapter one. I took a deep breath and went for it. I figured that I was ready to do this – that the time finally had come to share my baby.

While I had read each chapter aloud when I was editing, somehow reading it to someone else was even more helpful. As Daryl listened, I wondered whether he noticed the amount of research I had done for the book. Was he aware of the way I wove the story using intricate details? How did it sound to him?

Since he responded well, I also read him the second chapter. He was surprised at how different that chapter was from the first and how I portrayed the naval experience here at the hotel. I can't wait to read him more. This definitely is happening for me! My baby no longer belongs only to me. It is slowly crawling out into the world.

This morning on my walk, I talked to Paul, a man whose path I have crossed on the Broadwalk at least every other day for as long as I can remember. When I told him I was writing a book about the hotel, the first words out of his mouth were, "I spent a lot of time at the Hollywood Beach Hotel when I was growing up." He went on to tell me a little about it and related the following, "When I was about ten years old, I used to entertain myself out front among the trees, plants, and flowers all the time. My friends and I invented a baseball game of sorts that we would play in the gardens. The way to score a home run would be to hit the ball over the beautiful, tall statue in the fountain."

Paul also told me a little about the cabanas and how Mr. Lippe, a guard, would make sure not to let anyone in who didn't belong. Each summer, Paul's parents paid about three hundred dollars to rent one of the cabanas. This allowed Paul and his friends to cool off from the summer's heat in the hotel's pool.

I have a feeling that the more I begin to tell people about my book, the more I will hear all kinds of stories about this place. So far when I mention that I am writing this book, most respond with, "Oh, you mean the old bible school?"

DAY FIVE

Thursday, April 26, 2012 11:45 a.m.

Throughout the night, I had dreams about my book. All I can recall as I sit here writing is bits and pieces about the Navy, something about Elizabeth and her baby, and Christy and Cathleen praying.

My characters are a part of me. They feel like familiar family and friends as we share our sacred space.

When I think about it, for all this time I have kept these characters and their stories to myself. I will soon begin to expose the book, taking it out from where it has been tucked into my heart and soul. I have only given tiny bits and pieces away – not willing to expose much. By venturing out and sharing Room 732, I realize that my life may never be the same.

Mostly what I hope for is that my book will resonate with others in some way and that people might see the world a bit differently after reading it. Above all else, I am hopeful that Room 732 will continue to be a connector for me. Since I began writing the book, I have met some remarkable individuals through my research – people who already feel like friends.

My goal is that I will one day be out in the world speaking and teaching about those things that matter most to me. Then I will know that my vision for my life has completely come true.

As much as I might think I am in control, I am often reminded that it isn't necessarily so. I felt fairly sure that my walk this morning would be much the same as in the past – maybe a choppier sea or more seaweed on the shore and fewer shells than yesterday – but the rest predictable. Not so!

Instead I saw a few City of Hollywood trucks and a policeman on the Broadwalk. A man and his young son pulled up in a Public Works truck and walked right onto the sand. I looked east and, sure enough, there was something large that apparently had come onto the shore during the night.

Being the curious person that I am, I walked right over to where a crowd was gathering. There rested a handmade boat – most likely one that brought Cubans or Haitians, desperate for freedom. It reminded me of the summer of 1994 when I stayed at the beach and wrote _A Necklace of Pearls_. During those three months, I saw at least ten of these kinds of boats/rafts that had been put together with duct tape and rubber tubes. The people on the rafts had come to our shores filled with hope for a better tomorrow. Why else would anyone risk their lives like this?

This particular boat was sturdier than most I'd seen in the past. It was waterproofed with a thick plastic wrapping covering the bottom and sides. When I spoke to the police-woman, who was guarding the boat, her comment was, "Based on how this one looks, I feel pretty sure they made it safely on land. It is big enough to fit in a lot of people. Where they are now is anyone's guess."

The teacher in me couldn't resist talking to the young boy who was with his father. I don't talk to children whom I don't know unless their parents are with them. Since the two of them stood together, I knew it would be okay to strike up a conversation. I walked over to the boy and asked if he understood why this boat had landed on our shore. I also asked him whom he thought might have been on the boat. We ended up having a meaningful discussion. I wanted him to understand the price one often pays for freedom – a lesson a third grader will hopefully remember. We are the lucky ones here in the United States, and I try never to lose sight of that. All of this reminded me of chapter two and how my patriotic juices were stirred as I researched, learned, and then wrote about the Navy.

Later as I was walking back south toward the hotel, I passed a man who sat on the sand staring out at sea. When I walked by him, he looked up at me and out of nowhere said, "The universe unfolds as it should." I smiled and kept on walking. How right he is!

I never have to go far from home to have an adventure, to learn something, to experience life to its fullest. Right here at Hollywood Beach, the world comes to me.

DAY SIX

Friday, April 27, 2012 2:00 p.m.

Long ago after I had written one of my books, Ruth Gold, a survivor, told me that I will need to wrap myself in steel armor in order to tolerate what comes when one puts her writing out there. I have never forgotten it. I am sure that I will need it as I move along on this journey.

DAY SEVEN

Saturday, April 28, 2012 12:15 p.m.

I'm sitting on the sand today, although it is a gray day with storm clouds moving in. The winds are fairly strong, *but it feels wonderful to be out here enjoying the ocean in this way.*

I have been posting a picture on Facebook each day. It serves as a mini photo diary of my stay here as I complete Room 732. Today I wrote, Room 732 in the making: A stormy, solitary day at sea makes for wonderful writing weather.

DAY EIGHT

Sunday, April 29, 2012   10:40 p.m.

It occurred to me tonight that what I need to do is have total solitude to read my entire book from cover to cover before I leave here. I sent a few emails to tell those who might try to contact me that I would be out of touch for the next thirty-six hours. Then I turned off my phone, put away my iPad, and decided that I will not turn them on again until after I have completed what I set out to do. This may be a challenge, but I am ready for it.

DAY NINE

Monday, April 30, 2012   7:30 a.m.

Today is yet another stormy day at sea. I thought I would go for a walk in a little while, but I can tell from the raindrops on my window that I won't be going outside any time soon. The sea is raging. The wild waves start far out and rapidly make their way rushing onto the shore. Red and purple flags, signaling riptides and man-o-war, will be out today for sure.

Instead of leaving my haven by the sea, I will begin my day of silence by doing a little writing and then will get busy reading. I'm not sure I can read Room 732 in one day and night, but I am certainly going to try. This is going to be one of those rare and wonderfully secluded days made just for the writer in me.

Before I went to bed last night, I thought about each chapter in my book and more specifically about each character. I took the time to picture every one of them in this room – how they looked – what they were feeling while they were here. It was almost as if I was communing with them in a spiritual way. Who would ever understand?

3:20 p.m. In between the raindrops earlier, I took a walk. While meandering along the shore, I was reflecting on the past twenty-eight years that I have been writing about wanting to be a published author.

During the last six or seven years as I have culled through my journals and have read those particular passages, I found myself wondering what planet I was living on. Knee-deep in my work at the Center, any chance of soaring out into the heavens and actually fulfilling my dream seemed about as remote as my being chosen to go for a ride on a space ship.

Even though I had always known that in order to achieve my goals I needed to have a vision, still it was beginning to feel as if my thoughts were unrealistic. At some point in all of this, I tucked away my wish and accepted the fact that it was most likely never going to happen.

Instead, I worked diligently on taking excerpts from my journals in the hopes of one day completing the reading of each one of them and unburying any pearls that might be cloistered within the pages of these many volumes. Ultimately, because of the teacher in me, my plan was that someday I would find a way to combine my writing and my teaching and put myself out in public to do both. My journals seemed my only ticket to that goal.

What I understand now is that while it took time, all the hope that I have stored up within me to write this book is finally becoming my reality - similar to the way the sun comes out at the end of a storm and a rainbow appears. Room 732 is my rainbow.

Through this experience of staying here at the Hollywood Beach Hotel, I have had the opportunity to reflect in solitude, to walk back along the path I have traveled to arrive here, and, with great hope in my heart, to look at what lies ahead.

CHECKING OUT
DAY TEN

Tuesday, May 1, 2012   11:55 a.m.

After living at the Hollywood Beach Resort for the last nine-and-a-half days, I feel a strong connection to this place. There is a part of me that wishes that somehow, someone will refurbish the building back to its old, beautiful charm. While the effort is being made to update it, this imposing structure is still a gem on Hollywood Beach. My desire is that it will once again become a noted tourist destination as it was in years past.

As I close the door of Room 732 behind me, I feel confident that I will be opening another new and exciting door – one that will allow me to realize my dream of not only writing but also of sharing with others the many life lessons I have learned along the way. Room 732 will, in fact, become the ship that will take me to lands still unknown as I continue on this journey through my life.

ACKNOWLEDGMENTS

With loving gratitude and heartfelt appreciation to my patient and talented nephew Steve Rothenberg for designing and laying out the cover, editing the postcard and photo images, taking the author photograph, and creating my website.

Many thanks to Maxine Cohn, my friend of many years, for helping me choose the cover photo from those I took during my stay in Room 732 and for photographing the images that line the walls of the hotel and which appear in this book.

I am grateful to my daughter-in-law Sara Saferstein for designing the photo layout and to Rose Leopold for her help with the graphic designs.

A special thank you to my new friend Bill Schaaf for generously allowing me to use his historic postcard collection of the Hollywood Beach Hotel. Many thanks to the following artists, photographers, and publishers of these vintage postcards which provide images of how the Hollywood Beach Hotel looked in its earlier days: The Albertype Co., M.E. Berry, Color Picture Publishers, C-T Art Colortone, Dick Deutsch, EKKP, and Lake County Discovery Museum/Curt Teich Postcard Archives.

Thanks also to Silverio Lantigua, general manager, for granting permission to use photographs from the Hollywood Beach Resort Cruise Port.

Many thanks to Patrick Overton for giving me permission to use his poem and for the inspiration that poem has brought me through the years.

I used the following books and newspapers to obtain the history of the hotel: *A Guide to Historic Hollywood* by Dr. Joan Mickelson and *A History of Hollywood Florida* by Virginia Elliott TenEich, *The Miami Herald, Sun-Sentinel*, and *Hollywood Sun-Tattler.*

In the mid-80s, Barbara Gompers, Myrtle Gray, Jeff Newsome, and Al Theodore were helpful to me in obtaining information on the hotel. Thanks to Dr. Joan Mickelson of the Hollywood Historical Society for sharing her extensive knowledge as well as articles and photographs about the hotel and its many owners. Thanks also to Marion Fording who worked at the naval training center as a teenager and provided me with a few wonderful tidbits from that time in the hotel's history.

I began to understand the true sacrifice of war through talking to two Vietnam Vets, ETN2 Steven Ohlrogge who had been an electronics technician in the Navy, and SPC/4 Larry Medoff who was in Army intelligence and operations and who helped me by doing research at the National Archives in Washington, D.C. Thanks also to Captain Joe Fuchek, a retired Navy Seal, and Yeoman Second Class Joel Stieglitz. I am grateful to my uncle, Dave Rothenberg, who not only told me about his experiences during World War II as a Merchant Marine but who also has encouraged my writing in the way that my father would have if he were still living.

My gratitude to Susan Glaser who shared with me from the deepest corner of her heart and soul in order for me to better understand what it means to lose a child at birth.

I am deeply appreciative to those from Florida Bible College who devoted their time talking to me and sharing their wonderful college memories. I walked into a world unknown to me and walked out having made some special friends. My heartfelt thanks and blessings in alphabetical order to: Paul Benevides, Shelley Taeger Blackmarr, Susan Burdett, Carol Hoehn, Mary Englund Murphy, Stanley R. Ponz, D. Min., Laura Ann Sullins-Rajavuori, Lea Sword, Suzette Martinez Wallace, and Pat DeCosmo Wesolowski.

My thanks to Ron and Eileen Abraham, Dr. Paul George, Herb Gindy, Ruth Gordon, and Dr. Priscilla D. Jones for identifying individuals or websites that might be of help to me in the writing of this book.

Brandon and Jordan Weinstein served as the perfect resource when I was exploring what it is like to be a twin. Thanks, guys!

A special thank you to Deborah Berkowitz for her professional advice and expertise and to Lisa North for her validation on the paranormal issues I discovered while writing this book.

With deep appreciation to Steven Weinstein who provided legal advice and copies of my book for editing purposes and who promises to be the best book promoter in South Florida.

I am especially grateful and indebted to my dear friends and family who spent countless hours poring over *Room 732* in its various stages of development and whose excellent edits, careful critiquing, insight, and attention to detail transformed the book: Carolyn Kottler, Marsha Levine, Carolyn Lodish, Adele Sandberg, Lois Sklar, Rochelle Weinstein, and JoEllen Zalaznick - and to those who read parts or all of the book and offered endless encouragement: Margaret Ballanoff, Carol Bernstein, Carol Goldman, Laura Grushcow, Eva Grudin, Susan Hurwitz, Dr. Josse Lee, Elysha Rothenberg, Michelle Rothenberg, Dr. Daryl Saferstein, Rebecca Saferstein, Margery Sanford, Dr. Joel Sandberg, Linda Schlein, Aemi Tucker, Donna White, and Aileen Zarin. I am also thankful to Gerry Bell, Carol Berman, Michele Goodwin, Linda and Stan Green, Jane Blatt Guberman, Drs. Toni and Gary Kaplan, Lynn Kleinman, Shirley and Bill Lehman, Leslie Peiken, Leslye and Bill Rodgers, Steve Schlein, Bev and Mike Swatt, and Lynn Weisman as well as many other friends and relatives who have shown an interest in my writing throughout the last thirty years. I hope you know how much I appreciate all of you.

With heartfelt gratitude and respect to the Holocaust Survivors in my life for inspiring and encouraging me to follow my dreams. I promise to continue passing on your Legacy of Remembrance.

Collectively, the wisdom and love of my women's group has been a guiding force in my writing. Dr. Stephanie Layton has expanded my horizon and has shown me the true value and joy of research and adventure. Dr. Maya Bat-Ami has imparted her invaluable, skillful knowledge and has been a faithful and loving sounding board for my thoughts, feelings, and ideas. Marsha

Levine, my kindred spirit, has taken me to the depths of my innermost essence as she has shared hers with me and, for almost four decades, has faithfully and lovingly been there for me when I have needed to be heard. Adele Sandberg, my soul sister and "mirror," has shown her unwavering support for me as a writer, has devoted her energy and skills while encouraging me to maximize my potential, and has been at my side for the past thirty-six years sharing our lives together day-by-day.

Lois Sklar has accompanied me on many walks at various beaches for over forty years and has shown me how a close and loving friendship can be sustained regardless of the distance separating us.

Many thanks to Carolyn Lodish, my dear friend since seventh grade, who has graciously answered every grammar question, has given me writing tips I never learned in school, and has shared in life's joys and sorrows along the way.

Rochelle Weinstein has enriched my writing process with her understanding of what it means to be a writer, has paved the way for what is to come, and has accompanied me as I have taken each step along this sacred journey. We are only just beginning!

As I embarked on the quest of spiritual understanding, W. Thomas Osborne's wisdom and inspiration have guided me, while his profound influence, love, and knowledge of the bigger picture have led me to search and embrace those things that matter most.

I have been blessed with many wonderful cousins – among them, Carol Bernstein and Linda Schlein, who are like sisters to me, and Donna White and Carolyn Kottler, as well as my brother-in-law Arnie Saferstein, all of whom have shown me love and understanding during my darkest days and have encouraged me to follow my dream and become a full-time writer.

I wrote *Grandma's Loving Legacy* for the following with love and hope for a bright tomorrow and a more peaceful and just world in which to live: My cherished children Rebecca, Michael, and Sara Saferstein; my beloved granddaughters Sophia and Isabella Saferstein; my loving nieces and nephews Steve and Michelle Rothenberg, Aemi and Steve Tucker, Judi Rothenberg, Drs. Josse and Geoff Lee, Tara Madden, Sean and Laura Brewer; my special great-nieces and great-nephews Elysha and Michael Rothenberg, Jake and Halle Tucker, Holden Lee, Chloie Madden, Justin, Kyle, and Blake Brewer; my loving Florida "family" Sheryl Sandberg, Dr. David Sandberg, and Dr. Michelle Sandberg, David Goldberg, Dr. Amy Schefler, Marc Bodnick, and their beautiful families; and my dear cousins Laurie Schlein, Tim, Ashlee, Skylar, and Carlie Sokal, and Rabbi Stacy Schlein, Jeremy, Eliana, Aliza, and Benjamin Sosin.

A special note of appreciation and love to my son and daughter-in-law, Michael and Sara Saferstein, for your support and interest in *Room 732*. It is through your beautiful family that I have come to learn the true meaning of one's legacy. A special thanks to my granddaughter Sophia who, from the first day I described my book to her, has shown great enthusiasm and to my granddaughter Isabella who helped me identify all the pictures for the book, and to both of them who have been waiting with great anticipation for me to finish *Room 732*.

Thank you to my daughter Rebecca Saferstein who has helped me to know what is possible in a loving mother-daughter relationship and who has enthusiastically welcomed the details of my writing. While she still can remember the clicking of the keys on my typewriter when I wrote my novel many years ago, she now delights in the joy of my life as a writer.

To my devoted husband Daryl, thank you for listening to the endless stories about my interviews with others, for sharing in my happiness and excitement on a daily basis, and for being the first one to listen to the book with your critical ear and steadfast support. I love you!

And finally to my beloved parents Ruth and Bennie Rothenberg, of blessed memory, who believed in me from the start. They challenged me to do my best and taught me what it means to live a full and productive life. Most importantly, they showed me the significance and value of love and connection to others. I am eternally grateful to them for all that they gave to me.

Merle R. Saferstein is available for book signings, book clubs, and other speaking engagements. To inquire about a possible appearance, please contact her at www.MerleRSaferstein, Facebook.com/Room732, or MerleRSaferstein@yahoo.com.

Tristan how U lived yr life
w/ pleasure + i recommend
that 4 others -

Demonstrates— Real
Teacher

what doan it work 4 how u
mile have chosen differently

How did O treat his mother?
raw note

2.6 Daryl - Bay

Made in the USA
San Bernardino, CA
23 December 2012